KIDNAPPED BY THE KRAMPUS

EMILY SHORE

A Holiday Monster Romantasy

COVER by D Arte Oriel
INTERIOR DESIGN by Kate Seger
DECORATED EDGES by Painted Wings Publishing

Contents

8.
9.
10.
11.
12.
13.
14.
15.
16.
17.
18.
19.
20.
21.
22.
23.
24.
25.
26.
27.
28.
29.

Other Works By Emily Shore

POST 2020 AUTHOR JOURNEY:

Death and Destruction Series

Courting Death and Destruction – Book One (Kindle Vella Bestseller – Now on KU)

Her Monstrous Boys Series

The Sacrifice (Kindle Vella Bestseller/Trending on KU Kindle Top 100 New Release/Dragons)

The Surrender (Kindle Vella Bestseller/Trending on KU/Kindle Top 100 New Release/Dragons)

Hell's Angel Series

Bride of Lucifer: Hell on Earth – Book One (Kindle Vella Bestseller – Now on KU)

Bride of Lucifer: The Bride Trials – Book Two (Kindle Vella Bestseller – Now on KU)

Bride of Lucifer: Mate of Destruction – Book Three (Kindle Vella Bestseller – Now on KU)

Kindle Vella Original Works

Bride of the Corpse King – Book One (Kindle Vella Bestseller – Now on KU)

Bride of the Shifter King – (Kindle Vella Bestseller)

The Grymm Beauty (Kindle Vella Bestseller)

Find all of Emily's Kindle Vella works where she rebranded after finding her voice* * *

PRE 2020 AUTHOR JOURNEY:

The Uncaged Series* – *temporarily unavailable (Will return in 2024)

The Aviary – Book One, *The Garden* – Book Two, *The Temple* – Book Three, *The Temple Twins* – Book Four, *The Aquarium* – Book Five

The Roseblood Series

Roseblood – Book One, *Silhouette* – Book Two

Requiem – Book Three

Sanctuary – Book Four
Roseborn – Book Five (WIP)

To all my lovely monster-fudgers who have been very naughty this year.
I wish I could give you Krampus for Christmas, but let this story be a light for you this holiday season…as it became for me in beautiful and unexpected ways.

Author's Note

Krampus is more of a dark but cozy romance. Things get intense and spicy for sure. I kinked for Krampus hard. It's going to give you all those happy "spirit of the season" feels! And you might just fall for the monster. Oh, and I'm not responsible for any *extreme* emotions that should arise. I suggest you keep a partner or *toy* nearby. Maybe you will get an early Christmas/Solstice present. There are plenty of monster-themed dildos on the market now.

Happy Holidays!

Want the UNCENSORED version? See details below!

SUPPORT ON KINDLE VELLA *KICKSTARTER*:

After writing clean YA for years, I rebranded on Kindle Vella in 2021 where I became a bestselling author on the platform. I am very grateful to reach the Top 25 every month and still reigning in my "Dark Fantasy" category.

What is it? Amazon's serialized fiction platform.

Why? It kept our family afloat through 2021 and 2022 with my husband's cancer and all my chronic health issues. It also funds my road to paperback.

How? Please consider voting for any of my books on Kindle Vella and supporting me as an author. The minimum to vote aka **Top Fave** is less than $2.00 a month via tokens. Consider it like a Kickstarter since it enables me to bring my books to paperback!

PERKS: ALL my Vella supporters get exclusive super fan group perks like ***UNCENSORED NSFW art (above)***, voting rights, spicy bonus scenes, and even advanced chapters! If you Top Fave, connect with me on social media to get the perks.

PROs: NO signup. NO subscription. NO app download. It's an honors' based system.

CONs: Only for USA. (It's ok! Radish or Ream supporters still get the perks!)

Learn more at *"Emily's Vella Verse"* on Facebook: a public group where I share fun memes, teasers, games, and giveaways.

Please follow my TikTok: @authoremilybshore and my IG: @emilybshore.

PLAYLIST

"Melancholy Christmas" – Amy Grant
"Carol of the Bells" – Lindsey Sterling
"Carol of the Bells" – Pentatonix
"Miss You Most" – Mariah Carey
"Where are you, Christmas" – Pentatonix Version
"One of Us" – Glee Version
"Can't Help Falling in Love" – Dark Version by Tommee Profitt
"Monsters" – All Time Low feat. Demi Lovato
"Evermore" – Jonathan Young Version
"All You Wanted" – Michelle Branch
"Christmas Without You" – Ava Max
"Monster" – Dia and Meg
"Wrapped in Red" – Kelly Clarkson
"Believe" – Josh Groban – The Polar Express
"Believe" – Peter Hollens Version feat. One Voice Children's Choir
"Happy Xmas (War is Over)" – John Lennon
"I'll Be Home" – Meghan Trainor
"Everyday is Christmas" – Sia
"Welcome to Our World" – Chris Rice (This is actually my *favorite* Christmas song. I'd love for you to share yours with me.)

1

You've been reading way too much monster smut, Twyla.

TWYLA

I am so making the naughty list for this.

This is confirmed the moment the security guard stamps my forged VIP pass with the Krampus-themed seal and welcomes me inside the gates of Krampus World. He licks his lips, revealing rows of sharp, pointed teeth—along with faux blood and brown stains mirroring the makeup upon his wrinkly facial prosthetics. His lascivious eyes roam down my figure, and I almost regret *not* wearing something more revealing.

Angels are not uncommon at these celebrations.

Not that I'm here for the celebration. Unfortunately.

As I follow the long line of partygoers and tourists through the gates, I tap the flex phone on my left wrist, cueing up the holo-feed, which is linked with my contacts. Anyone else will see the Krampus Cat game that's trending for the holidays. But for me, it's the schematics of the Krampus World Penthouse—or more specifically, the VIP floor right below it.

I'll have only a couple of minutes to get in, get what I need, and get out. And the world will finally know if the urban legend is true or false. Is Krampus real?

Once I get beyond the gates, I soon realize the typical angels here range from mass-market angels with their store-bought wire-mesh wings, which will likely be thrown away and never used again,—or a wide variety of Victoria's Secret angels. Nothing wrong with either, especially when I'm a blend between them. But I guess I'll get *docked* points for creativity.

While every other costume and pair of wings are pure and white as the fallen snow, mine are tattered and gray like the color of slush following the tread of heavy winter boots. Too many eyes follow me, most curious, others admiring, and some confused. Not that I blame them.

It's probably uncommon for a *fallen* angel to show up at Krampus World.

Or for anyone to spend weeks handcrafting and hand-stitching her one-of-a-kind costume. The tattered wings of isolon and feathers—no two alike—are my favorite. The lace-up corset bodice and sweetheart neckline show just enough cleavage so I can *fly* under the radar. I spent two weeks alone sewing the skirt out of the same isolon to make ragged swaths—all different lengths. None fall below my knee.

I stop in my tracks as a group of gangly children scampers past me, growling and roaring beneath their Krampus masks. Their dad, I assume, chases after them with a larger mask while the mom shakes her head and takes a holo-snap with her flex phone—all the rage now.

The scent of cinnamon sticks, cloves, and gingerbread fills the air. Off to my left is a bakery: *Krampus Kookies and Kakes*. My mouth waters at the intricate Krampus-themed cakes and pastries on multi-tiered stands decorate the front windows.

If I weren't here for official business, I'd stop in for one of those cupcakes with molded chocolate horns.

Damn you, Colton! I curse my editor's name. This was supposed to be *my* holiday. Indignation rises inside me as I pick up my pace. My curls are as wild as my fuming temper when I think of my boss cornering me in the copy room two nights ago, the same copy room where I'd accidentally walked in on him with his secretary.

At first, he'd denied it, claiming I was making up a wild story to get attention. Right, just my imagination that the copy machine still had blurry black-and-white images of

Celia's tits barely covered by the $500 bra he'd bought her. Then, he claimed it was a "mistake". I'm still not sure how it's a mistake for his pants and her skirt to be shoved down to the ankles and his dick to magically pop into her pussy from behind.

And now, I am here…working during *my* holiday. All because Colton Dixon can't fuck his secretary in his own office like normal CEOs of Fortune 500 broadcasting companies. And because I'm an intern. And because he has a reputation with his secretaries and interns, specifically a reputation for firing ones who don't do what he wants. Since I prefer to do the basics like eating half-decent food, pissing in a toilet—even when it's cracked and yellow—, and living in a crappy studio apartment vs. the street, I'll do what I must.

After passing a few Krampus-themed gift shops selling ornaments, trinkets, toys, and masks, the crowds thicken. Normally, I love crowds. The hustle and bustle of this season—if I didn't have to hustle my bustle, of course. After all, I'm a single girl living on her own, dining on pizza rolls and TV dinners every night and drinking with friends at the pub down the street.

Absorbing the joy and wonder of the season reflected in the children's eyes around me is always special. Sacred in a way, I consider as some kids point up at the stage where a theater troupe performs a skit about Santa and Krampus. Laughter erupts when Santa bops Krampus on the head right before Krampus bops Santa.

I can't help but smile. Krampus World is more like the Christmas version of Halloween. Later, after the head-dancing sugar plum children are all tucked in their beds, the wild events will happen. And I'm going to miss everything!

A cold ache gnaws on my insides, not the festive warmth I'd wanted from this Christmas "break".

"I'm sure we can come to some sort of arrangement," Colton had cooed with suggestive brows bouncing while

hemming me in at the copier. "You're a pretty girl, after all, Twyla,"

Girl. Yes, I guess to a 55-year-old geezer, a fresh and hungry young woman of 26, I am just a *girl.* I still have some self-respect. Not much, but I'd rather risk a B&E on my record than let Colton Dixon's wrinkly dick get anywhere near my orifices.

When the theater troupe calls for all the children to gather on the stage, an invisible fist punches through my chest. My breath withers in my lungs.

Remembering what my pro-bono therapist taught me, I imagine my present self hugging my little past six-year-old self on Christmas Eve. A Christmas Eve like all the others that would define her. Dark and cold with no warmth, no light, no joy.

After mentally hugging that little girl, who stayed up all night waiting for a Santa who never came, I make my way past Krampus-themed art exhibitions with kids designing projects in the shops, Krampus-themed restaurants, the Krampus haunted house and escape room next to it, and the Night Market.

My chest squeezes because I'd rather head down the cobblestone road to that German-inspired vintage market with its eerie crafts and gifts of dark folklore.

If I get wrinkly-dick Dixon's "story of the century" or at least the "man behind the curtain", I'm demanding a raise and a big fat stocking stuffer of a Christmas bonus. If I don't get caught and make it out of here, I'm coming back and buying a two-for-one package with Christmas World—complete with the Christmas Eve Silver Bells Ball.

I cross the Devil's Keep Main Street, where the candlelit parade will be tonight. More of an opportunity for people to get drunk and get the stuffing scared right out of them when the Krampus-masked players roam freely in the streets. It will be a night of drunkenness, debauchery, and walloping birch whips.

There go my evening plans. Livid heat ignites my blood when I fantasize about how I would lure one of the Krampus-masked men toward an obliging alley. He wouldn't need to take off his mask. Just as long as he had the muscles to rut me against the wall. The Krampus Ball would be the big bow on the night. Maybe a smooth-talking stranger would offer to take me back to his place. He could be a handsome and rich tourist and take me back to his VIP-level suite in the Krampus Palace—what they call the Krampus's hotel home. He would give me a drink before showing me his birch whip.

I shake my head from the heady thoughts, chalking it up to how long it's been since I've had a good whipping. Nothing's in store for me tonight except the scoop my editor wants. With my luck, Mr. Krampus won't even be there. With my luck, he'll probably be a withered old man in his sixties because sexy, reclusive billionaires don't exist in real life.

This isn't *Fifty Shades*, Twyla, I roll my eyes as I hurry toward the Palace. Not that there were any decent whipping scenes in that saga.

A fleeting thought races through my brain. But I'm as cuckoo as Colton for even entertaining the thought that the urban legend could be true. Christian Grey is far more likely than some hot-as-hell monster demon with horns and huge muscles—with one particular bulbous muscle I should not be daydreaming about.

You've been reading way too much monster smut, Twyla.

If I come up empty, I'll go and blow my pithy paycheck on a new vibrator and a bottle of cheap rum and drink hard eggnog while watching horror flicks all night. I've had worse Christmases. Much worse.

After passing more shops, including artisan workshops where people can learn mask-making or woodcarving, Krampus-themed photo booths, and the grand train that circumnavigates Krampus World, I finally arrive in the hotel district.

The Krampus Palace is located in the center square where all the other hotels surround it. It puts the bell in jingle bells. Or any type of bell since the opulent pinnacle has all the bells and whistles with its architectural grandeur and regal mysticism.

It doesn't disappoint on the inside.

I spin all around, senses overwhelmed by the design of dark extravagance. Every pillar in the lobby is intricately carved wood, depicting Krampus-themed scenes. The life-sized bronze statue is not a surprising centerpiece, but I also didn't expect golden chandeliers, dimly lit, casting a warm and intimate glow.

On one pillar, signs direct viewers to the "Chains of Tranquility" spa, the Shadow Lounge with its adjoining restaurant "Devil's Delights," and the Shadow Lair—an immersive experience mostly for families with little kids who want to run through the haunted maze to find the Krampus's infamous cave.

The lobby is more deserted than usual, thanks to everyone preparing for the parade and enjoying all the attractions until nightfall.

I'd stomp my little foot to show my agitation, but I spent months making these hand-stitched lacy slippers. I mentally take a note to shake my fist up at the sky later and scream Colton Dixon's name to the heavens.

Or perhaps I could find an obliging witch or witchy pagan to help cast a curse on him. It wouldn't have to be too horrible—like making his Viagra give him itchy warts all over his ass and ass-face. Or maybe a delayed response, so it starts tenting in the middle of his meeting before his stockholders.

"Season's Greetings, little angel traveling in the shadows," says a voice like hot apple cider.

I turn to the hotel desk to find an elderly gentleman with balding hair staring at me from behind the desk. His skin is crinkly, and his graying white beard is coarse, but his eyes are warm and friendly. Despite all the other employees I've seen thus far of Krampus World, he is pretty tame with his pinstriped suit and easygoing manner. Except for the pair of horns spiraling from his head. Impressive at that since they seem so lifelike!

"You've arrived at the portal to a realm where the supernatural meets dark luxury and lavish indulgence…" he gestures to me before folding his hands behind his back. "How may I help you on this delightfully eerie day?"

I practically flit over to the desk and smile at the grandfatherly gentleman. Now, this is a Santa if I've ever seen one. Not that I've seen any with horns, but they make him more unique. His name tag reads: Mephisto. So fitting.

Reaching into my little cloth pouch I stitched onto my bodice, I take out my VIP pass and hand it to him. I say a prayer to Hel—since Hel is mythologically Krampus's mother—that it will make it through this hotel system. Shoulders tense, I watch as Mephisto taps the hotel flex-screen, keying in the numbers and swiping the pass.

"Hmm…Miss. Phoebe Dixon, we weren't expecting you and your family until tomorrow."

My blood practically burns at the realization that Dixon gave me one of his own damn passes and listed me as his *cousin*. Not daughter. Not granddaughter. His cousin. Oh, good grief! No wonder he wants me to finish this job in one night. By the time his whole family flies in tomorrow, he'll need it back.

Unless I "accidentally" lose it. Dozens of images of what I could enjoy with that pass parade themselves like a regalia of blinking, colorful Christmas lights.

At last, Mephisto finally smiles and hands me back the pass. I reach for it, only for the ol' devil to pull it back suddenly and wag his finger with a shrewd smile. "Now, now, dearie, care to make a deal with a demon in exchange for the pass?"

A soft laugh escapes my throat. He's joking. A chill shivers up my spine when I note his stoic expression. When his eyes blink, flashing with slitted, scarlet-red pupils, I nearly jump, but I discount it as a trick of the light or special contact lenses. What a character…

"What sort of deal did you have in mind?" I wink, playing along.

"Would you care to have a drink with a stranger, Miss. *Twyla Eyres*?"

I freeze. The chandeliers seem to grow dimmer. My blood fills with ice, and all the hairs on my body prickle. All my hopes shatter. My heart plunges to my stomach. No, make that the floor. It's having a bipolar pity party on the floor.

Only moments ago, I imagined myself in that spa getting a professional hot stone massage and drinking mulled wine. I imagined sneaking into the Krampus's Lair after closing with a handsome stranger he alluded to before skinny dipping in the outdoor pool. I imagined sleeping in a warm bed with fleecy blankets and cool sheets that don't smell like week-old hot pockets and cheap wine coolers. And someone with big muscles and hair on his chest, maybe a well-groomed beard but messy longish waves, would sleep behind me—arms wrapped around my belly as we swapped naked body heat.

I imagined that for one night, just one night, I could pretend to be someone different. Someone worthy of celebrating Christmas in the most beautiful ways possible.

Now, I'm wondering what I'll look like in orange. The handcuffs would be fine and kinky, but with my curly blonde hair and chocolate brown eyes, I'd look like burnt marmalade in one of those jumpsuits.

My throat starts to swell up from the big lump that feels like chalky coal until Mephisto summons me, "Well…Miss. Eyres?"

What?

I flick my eyes to him, brows lifting, voice cracking as I say, "I'm so sorry. This wasn't my idea, but I'll accept whatever punishment you see fit."

He tilts his head to one side, brows furrowing as he observes me. I lower my chin and shoulders, defeated.

"Your honesty and humility serve you well tonight, Miss. Eyres. But you still haven't given me an answer."

Answer to what? I part my lips, awed when I realize he was being serious. "Well…" I shrug before hugging my arms to myself. "You know my name, and I know yours. So, we're not exactly strangers anymore, are we?"

He postures. Oh, shit. I ridicule myself for letting my sassy ass free during such a serious moment. But if you can't find the silver lining in the darkest times, how will you ever find it when the clouds are gone?

"A drink with a stranger, Miss. Eyres. If I had meant myself, I would have said my name," he clarifies, voice insistent while he twiddles that pass in the air—almost like he's toying with my future.

I swallow the coal and focus on his words. He didn't say "handsome" stranger. He didn't say "rich" stranger. But he also said just a drink. Of course, he didn't say he wouldn't report me after said drink.

"A-are you going to contact the police?"

His lips part into a smile, revealing rows of sharp teeth, tops, and bottoms, ones I swear were not there just a few moments ago. "You may have been naughty tonight, Miss. Eyres, but you are not the naughtiest. I believe you are quite nice indeed. Nice enough to have a drink with a stranger."

Yeah, or desperate enough.

"Where would this drink happen?" I rub the goosebumps on my arms. Why am I bothering to ask? He's giving me an out, isn't he? Why look a gift horse in the mouth? Especially when it's a gift tied up in fancy wrapping paper and a big fat bow that doesn't have an attached jail sentence.

"That would spoil the surprise, Miss. Eyres. Now...do you wish to keep asking me questions I will not answer and try my patience? Or do we have a deal?" He extends his other hand to me, the one not holding the pass.

Desperate enough. Or crazy enough.

Oh, well...you only live once. "I'll deck the halls with your deal."

I close my palm in his, and the second I do, I swear something sparks. Like static electricity.

As soon as he hands me the pass, I scamper away—only to turn on my heel, scamper back, and stand on my tiptoes to kiss him on the cheek. He flinches, startled, but I shrug and say, "You definitely made the nice list."

I hustle as fast as I can to the elevator with his jolly chuckles ringing in my ears. I breathe a sigh of relief once I'm in the elevator and swipe my pass.

Oh! This is one of those glass elevators where I can see everything! I gush, swaying my body to the lively holiday tune sparkling from some speaker. Now, the bronze Krampus statue looks more like a children's toy. The dark folklore and shadowy opulence themes into every level, but when I sense a ray of golden warmth bathing me, I glance up. And almost melt.

It's not just one chandelier in the great domed ceiling beyond the elevator. It's like a maze of chandeliers all twisted together and showering sunlight-splintered prisms all over the area. They remind me of bouncing stars. But since the extravagant pieces don't move, I imagine it's some sort of high-tech.

I'm so preoccupied with fogging up the glass with my sighs, I don't notice the elevator's stopped until I hear the ding.

Twirling around with my golden curls and angel skirt swathes flicking the air, I stop in my tracks because it's not a VIP level lit up on the side. It's the giant, flashing P that glows. P for the penthouse. P for Palace. P for the best Christmas present that could ever happen to me.

A sense of warm giddiness bubbles up inside me. This is either a stroke of truly good fortune, or maybe it was Mephisto. Either way, I can tour the penthouse and get enough information for Dixon...or I may get to meet the man behind the curtain, Mr. Krampus, himself!

Threading my eager fingers together, I count an eternity of seconds before the elevator doors open. And a great, monstrous shadow devours my body.

Adrenaline pulses thrills and chills up my spine, exploding all my nerve endings and lighting up the reward center of my mind.

That is the sickest costume I've ever seen!

2

Might as well be naughty. Time to unwrap this pretty present.

KRAMPUS

She may be naughty but nice, but I am the naughtiest.

"Mephisto, you're the best friend a demon could have," I tell him after he's sealed the deal.

He huffs. "I'm your only friend, you damn devil. I have a good feeling about this one. She kissed me!"

I guffaw into my earpiece before feeling the heat flushing my very fur. I'll have a kiss and more, I determine while observing the girl in the elevator but ultimately concur with the demon. Well…half demon.

"Don't fuck this up, Krampus. You don't have much time left. And if you fuck this up, if you lose—"

I turn off the earpiece, growling low under my breath. I don't need him to remind me of all that will be lost. Not just for me but for the empire I've built, the one Mephisto and I have built together since he handles board meetings and public events as my representative while I appear as the silhouetted monster behind Krampus World. My favorite part is when I go on my own Krampus runs and scare the tourists.

The irony of how the world seeks me, and I hide in plain sight all the time.

Tapping my flex-tat, the prototype of the up-and-coming tech that works far better than the phone, I pull up my list. Because Klaus isn't the only one who gets to make lists and check them twice. Or a thousand times, in my case.

Don't show them your tongue.

Don't growl.

Don't open your mouth too much to show your teeth.

Don't urge them to check your body for some nonexistent zipper.

Don't wag your tail.

Don't offer them a ride on your horns.

Don't show them how well you can dance on hooves.

Don't tell them how nice they'd look with a big bow and nothing else. Or tied up naked with Christmas lights. Or bent over your knee while you show them naughty from nice with your birch whips.

I grunt at the last three that Mephisto added. Always spoiling my fun. But he's right. I'm running out of time.

And the pretty little angel in the elevator with her fallen theme is rising higher second by second to meet me. I'll show her how much lower she will fall—only so I may pick her back up again. Compared to me, she's a pure and innocent snow angel. Not too innocent, I hope.

Min engel. *My angel.* No, it's not quite right.

With her back turned to me as she gazes up at the gold and crystal sculptures in the ceiling, I can't help but enhance the camera feed, closing in on her plump little bottom. Too much covers it from her skirt to the edges of her wings.

I will make a new list. All the things I like about her.

As long as it's not covered in warts, her cute little rumpa will be at the top.

I love how she bounces to the music. But I hope she's not one of those girls who worships everything about Christmas and can't appreciate the darker parts of it.

Looks like I'll find out soon.

I turn off the flex-tat and advance to the Penthouse lobby, where the elevator has arrived. All it takes is one sweeping motion of my clawed dark hand to bid it open.

Her eyes nearly shoot out of her skull. Every nerve in my body tightens, every muscle tensing as she scans me from horn to hoof tips. I am easily three times her size. At first, she says nothing as her wide doe eyes roam all over me. I love their color. Dark and deep amber pools I will lose myself in every night…as long as she passes the test.

"Well…" she finally shakes her head out, blinking a few times to right herself. "I must say, I'm very impressed."

Don't wag your tail, you damn dolt.

I thread my thick brows low as she dares to waltz right up to get a closer look. Her angel curls catch the light of the lobby chandelier, brighter than shimmery stars. Stars, hmm.

"The level of detail on this is just incredible!" she gushes while leaning over, giving me a closer look at that ripe little bottom. She narrows her eyes on my fur. "The hooves alone must be authentic. And those horns are a thing of beauty."

Fuck…don't you dare growl, Krampus.

No engel at all. More of a frekke drittunge. *Cheeky brat.*

"Whoever did your custom work, I need their name." She says from behind me, and my fur prickles in agitation. "Even this harness…!" I stiffen when she dares to set a hand on my leather straps. "Or I could follow them on Crafts and Cosplayers. Even your tail looks like it has real muscl—"

As soon as she stretches her fingers toward my tail, I swing around and seize her wrist, careful not to dig into her flesh with my claws. Oh, I will give her plenty of marks later, but not now.

She startles at my grip, then throws her hands up in defense. "Right, right, sorry. Number one rule: always ask before you can touch."

Not in my world, søt ting. Sweet thing. My eyes practically gleam, and it takes all my effort not to unleash my tongue and coil it all the way around her lovely throat.

"I'm guessing it took forever to do those prosthetic muscles," she mentions while circling back around.

All real, jentebaby. Baby girl.

Don't flex them, Klaus-dammit! Something else I'll need to add to my list.

"So, are you like a butler or just a highly paid staff member? I mean that getup probably weighs a hundred pounds, if not more!"

Though I keep them closed, I spread my lips into an amused smile. Then cock my head to one side, trusting she is smart enough to read between the lines. I'll admire hers in the meantime. And her dainty curves. Her legs are lithe and blemish-free to her upper knee. If she passes my test, I'll need to check her for any infection or disease.

I cannot allow any potential threats to my realm.

When she parts her lips, the rosy cheeks paling, I know the realization has washed over her.

She steps back, her fingers flying to her mouth. "Oh, I'm so sorry. I didn't realize. Fucking fruitcakes!"

I lift a brow, enjoying her flustered state and the blush returning to her cheeks more than my curiosity over her Christmas-themed cursing. I may be a kinky bastard, but I have not once in all my centuries fucked a fruitcake. Why would anyone want to? She would make a far better Christmas treat in any case.

"Wait, are-are you the stranger I'm supposed to have a drink with?" She wags her finger. "He didn't tell me…Mephisto, I didn't know he was sending me to the Penthouse. If you want me gone, just say the word. I'll go. I'll do whatever you want." She lowers her chin, and my cock jerks in its pouch at her humble submissiveness.

She used those words far too carelessly. Oh, all the things I want to do to her. It's been too long since I used my chains on such worthy skin as hers.

When I tuck my claw beneath her chin, she flinches, not expecting the gesture as I tip her face. Tears glisten in her eyes. Like little snowflakes blotting her lashes. Fuck, all I want to do is snatch her up by her hips and cuddle her in my arms, recognizing the little girl inside her. While I may have been freed of the Krampus curse for a century, I have still maintained my power and essence. Somewhere inside her soul is a little wounded girl. Punished too much for things that were not her fault. The darkness in her soul pulls to me. It may be cold and deep, but she's clawing to get out and seeking the light.

I take a step toward her, but she does not cower at my towering shadow. Fuck, this girl has too many other demons haunting her to care about the one in front of her. And Klaus-dammit all, I almost don't give a fuck if she's a gift-wrapped Trojan horse sent by him.

I will see this star shine again…if it's the last thing I do. *Stjerne*, yes. Star. *Min stjerne.* My star.

"Krampus," I say, lifting my voice an octave so it doesn't defy the limitations of human vocal cords. To her, it must still resonate like a thundering bass. Confirmed when she shivers. Oh, I'll make her shiver much more.

A soft smile practically lights up her face. "I'm Twyla."

Pretty name. That bright smile like the twilight.

I gesture her down the hall and take a few steps forward, my hooves still making a clopping sound despite the grand rug covering the marble floor. After a moment or two of dazed bewilderment, she shakes out her curls and tears off to join me.

And fucking steps right on my tail!

It's only a splinter of pain. Enough to make me wince, but I hold it in, hold it back. Otherwise, I'll go caterwauling like a mad cat.

When her angel swathes brush up against my fur, all my nerve endings ignite. Fuck, she smells like cinnamon and roasted chestnuts. Hints of warm apple cider. No doubt, she stopped for a quick bite somewhere along the way. How I'd love to sink my teeth into her.

For now, I direct her to sit at my bar so I may make her a drink. Instead, she wanders about the main portion of the Penthouse. I roll my eyes as she stares at the enormous snow globe in the center of the room. One glowing with red and green hues, with a sugar plum fairy dancer atop a lake of ice. Perhaps I'll show her what else that fairy can do later.

Her eyes widen the more she takes in the surroundings from all the masks of intricately carved wood all over the place, the Christmas trees with their Krampus-themed ornaments—ones from art contests in times past—, and the various festive elements like icicle lights and frosted sculptures.

I slap the counter to get her attention, smirking at how she jumps and scurries to the bar. *Flink pike.* Good girl.

"So, do you ever talk?" she wonders, her fingers caressing the frosted glass of her cocktail.

I touch my chest again. "Krampus."

A fresh blush tethers her cheeks, and she tilts her chin, her curls falling over one shoulder. "Okay. So, you're mysterious. Everyone knows that. But maybe a little…eccentric?" When I lift a brow, she's quick to flutter her hands and add, "Nothing wrong with that, of course. An eccentric, enigmatic billionaire. Do you dress like this all the time?"

At least there's no scorn in her question. Just a timid curiosity. Her voice reminds me of the soft hush of a snowfall.

I nod.

"All year long?"

I nod again.

Her brow scrunches. "Huh…" she muses, but I catch a stray glimpse of her wandering eyes. And how they descend to where the counter blocks her sight of my pelvis. Not that she would see much between my black fur and pouch.

Just as I lift my hot, buttered rum glass, she pulls out her flex-phone to take a snap of me at the bar. An unwitting growl ripples up my throat, and I seize the phone, crushing it in a blink. She nearly falls out of her chair, gasping, her eyes darting up and down from the crushed tech to my eyes.

"I'm sorry, that was truly rude of me." She bows her head again in sweet submission. "But…could you do that again?"

Huh? I furrow my brows and eye the phone smithereens in my big palm.

She laughs, the sound like glitter. "No, not the phone. I mean…what you just did with your throat."

She wants me to…growl again? Oh, hell, she leans over the bar, propping her chin in her cupped hands and giving me the puppy dog eyes. "Pretty please?" Double hell, I sense the adrenaline thrilling her senses, warming her blood, and…bursting her pheromones to perfume the air.

Blood surges to my cock, and the damn thing with a mind of its own prods uncomfortably at my pouch. If it had its way, we'd have her bent over this bar, hitching up that angel skirt and plowing into her from behind. She's perfect for the dom inside my monster.

So, I deadpan. And let the growl rise—slower and deeper than before. A visible shiver shudders her little body. More of those pheromones pepper the air. That's when the first hint of wetness drips from her pussy…and tickles my nostrils. I growl again. My mouth waters, tongue aching to stretch all the way over the counter to tuck under those pithy skirt swathes to lick at that delectable cunny.

"It's probably a good thing that you keep to yourself." Twyla sits back down with a sweet press of her lips and her cheeks reddening more than ever. "Because if the greater population of women with their hidden monster-fudging fetishes heard that…!" She fans herself, imitating a swoon. Before I can react to such a gesture that has never before been used in association with me, she lifts a hand to me. "I honestly expected some old guy in a wheelchair or crotchety curmudgeon waving his cane at me."

I'll wave my cane at you, liten jente. Little girl. *And bring it down on your ripe rumpa.*

Instead of staring at her with my predator's eyes, I tip back the rest of my rum, allowing her to continue.

"Sure, you don't talk much, but you're like this big daddy monster guy. And you seriously work it. That crushing phone thing was right in character!" Her words trip over one another as she rambles. "But you're also super polite. I mean, Mephisto knew exactly who I was, and he sent me up here, and I'm guessing you two were in cahoots, so you let it happen. You could have kicked me out. I didn't exactly come with the best intentions, but I didn't want to be here tonight."

When I curve my claws onto the bar counter, she waves her hands. "Not that I don't want to be here now because I do! I just meant it wasn't my idea to try and break into your Penthouse, to find you. It was my editor's. And well, let's say he's nowhere near as *nice* as you."

I circle the bar toward her, my veins throbbing, muscles steeling. No one has ever described me as *nice*. Not even Mephisto. Because I'm not nice. Nor do I aspire to be. I'll never gravitate above the level of a kinky, selfish bastard of a billionaire.

Judging by how nervous and flustered she is, I'd wager more is at stake if she doesn't get something out of this night. Some form of evidence. She is untrained for this, and the asshole who set her up didn't want to risk taking the fall himself. Part of me wants to punish the bloke. The other wants to thank him for sending her my way.

"But I guess I'm glad you found me instead. I'm sorry. I stammer a lot when I'm nervous." She trembles as I approach, casting my long shadow over her.

All I need are two words, little Twyla. Two simple words and two syllables. And then…*you're mine.* According to the laws bound by the old magic of the world, she must offer it up freely. Or I have no claim to her, no power over her. But if she speaks those two words, I will take everything.

Her eyes glisten with those silvery tears again as she arches her neck, gazing up at me, at my eyes. Is she lost within my depthless dark pools as I am within her deep amber ones?

"You didn't contact the authorities. You welcomed me up here. You didn't get mad at me when I touched your costume. Or when I tried to take a picture of you. Well…not too much. And you offered me a drink." She glances over at her untouched glass, where her fingers have left an imprint within the fog. Lifting it toward me, she says, "And I didn't even have the courtesy to drink with you. I'll understand if you want to contact the authorities and send me away. But…this evening was more than I could have hoped for. *Thank you.*"

Hel be fucking praised as Christmas punch!

I surge my magic into her drink, smiling as she tips it back and drinks it whole. My smile grows, mirroring the swell of blood to my cock. Her eyes swirl. Her body grows heavy and languid and…warm.

"I feel funny." She scrunches her brow.

Her vision swirls. She dizzies. And the moment she tries to stand, Twyla falls into my arms.

"No, kjaere." *Sweetheart.* "I won't send you away. I'm taking you away." I lower my mouth to her brow, resisting the urge to stroke my tongue along her soft skin. If I so much as flick the organ that is as hypersensitive as my cock, I will lose control.

Instead, I carry my sweet gift to the second floor, where I bring her to my suite and place her on the bed. In the dim light of the candles, she reminds me of a slumbering angel—an angel with golden curls and fallen wings with the swathes of her skirt bunched up around her thighs.

Hmm, I know I shouldn't, but I'm a damn demon with no scruples who could never make it onto the nice list. Might as well be naughty. Time to unwrap this pretty present.

First, I claw at her bodice, easily tearing the strings with my claws. Such a flimsy, delicate thing. An ill-fitting lace bra covers her tits. Also easily discarded. Creamy white skin like the perfect shade of buttercream frosting I'd like to lick. Her throat is slender and elegant—perfect for my teeth, but when

I wrap my paw around it, I grin at the tight little throat—perfect for my cock.

Pretty tits, too. I indulge myself, lowering my hand and scooping them up, testing their weight. Not overly large and heavy like others, but they are an average size. They hold good shape. And hmm…I grin, feeling my horns harden because her nipples pebble beneath my paws. I take my claw and draw tiny circles around the buds with their healthy rouge pink like a blushing rose. I intend to turn them as red as holly berries.

I give each cute pink nipple a little pinch. Fuck! Her pheromones tickle at my nose, and I mentally catalog the discovery: nipples are quite sensitive and grow erect to touch. Pheromones released.

Oh, all the naughty things I could do to these sweet breasts. I picture gold clamps with dangling jingle bells. I picture rubbing sugar dust all over those tits and licking them clean.

Next, I move my paws along her petite body with her soft belly. Flat but with a hint of plumpness between her curvy hips.

I slash through the skirt, peeling it off her to gaze at the vestibule of her pleasure center that smells sweeter than a mince pie. No, I lean down to take a deep breath…sugar cookies. Her cunny is sweeter smelling than Christmas cookies. And the thin panties she wears are already wet. I tease one claw beneath the thin panty line and pluck at it like a thread.

Ahhh…fuck me, holy cunt of Klaus-damn mercies! She's as naked as a little cherub. Must have waxed for coming into my world. At some point, I would like to see the nest of gold curls that will surely grow.

But first, I spread her legs, pushing open her thick, ripe thighs while sinking my fingers into all that glorious flesh. My groin tightens as I retract my claw, open her nether lips, and inspect her for any impurities. The scent of her cream reminds me of white chocolate. But her folds are as lusciously pink as her rosy cheeks and hard little nipples. I rub my nose along her labia, my lips a fine hair from touching, from my tongue tasting. But if I unleash my tongue, I may not be able to stop.

Instead, I find that plump little nub at the top of her cunny and I work it back and forth like it's a fleshy bell. Her pheromones practically burst while more cream spills from her slit. Her nipples grow harder. So responsive. So sweet, even in her sleep. Is she dreaming of this monster?

I test her slit with one finger, knowing she will need toys to stretch her first so she may take my cock. Lifting her carefully, I inspect my favorite place on the body. Oh, she has such a sweet bottom. How I long to use my birch whips even now on such a ripe little ass of alabaster flesh. I imagine the wondrous shades of red she could bloom for me under my master monster hand.

I prod her back hole, testing her tiny pink ring. No hint of disease or infection. I turn her over again, chuckling, but a hungry growl follows. More pheromones. More cream. She's practically soaked.

I poke out the tip of my tongue, but I'm not about to unleash it yet. She's a bright, twinkling treasure. My very own Christmas star.

But I am curious if I may make her glow just a little first. So, I rub the large pads of my thumbs on her nipples, wondering if she can feel my silky dark hair tickling her belly. I pinch the pointed hard tips and knead her breasts before returning to her lovely cunny.

I collect some of the cream and rub it on her clit, which swells for me, responding to my touch.

"That's it, min lille stjerne." *My little star.* "You feel this in your erotic dream. Now, give me more like a good girl. Oh, yes, so dirty!" I rumble low when her pheromones erupt. "Flink pike." *Good girl.*

I peel the hood back, pinch her little clit, and rub it with two thick fingers, rub her slippery wet folds with my other two. Goosebumps break out on her skin. Her inner muscles clench up.

"That's my sweet, filthy girl." I slide one finger inside her, groaning at all that soaked heat that sucks me in harder. Hot as Christmas pudding. "Look at you. So tight for me. That's it, my star. Glow for me." Whatever sexual fantasy blazes inside her mind, the muscles inside her start to flutter. I pump my finger in and out while rubbing that sweet treat of a tiny bundle.

My cock is desperate to escape its fleshy pouch, slamming against the wall of skin, but I won't let it.

"Glow for me. Come for me, Twyla." Her inner muscles squeeze, then spasm. "Fuck, yes!" I growl as her scent explodes, practically flooding the entire Penthouse. She gushes a little stream of cream that oozes down her thighs.

I gather her little body into my arms, three times smaller than mine. My precious little golden treasure who said she liked the monster.

I must get her back to the palace. Yes, I will bring her home. I will keep her there. She will stay, yes, she will. She has to. Because she's my last chance.

Twyla will obey me, or she will be punished. And I shall love punishing my little star.

3

Time for some self-help. And maybe some therapy. Or a CAT scan.

TWYLA

Warm tingles shower every inch of my skin like stardust. I don't open my eyes yet, too attached to the sensations of the dream. A dream I don't want to end.

Because I have never been touched like that.

I remember a voice seducing me, commanding me, so deep and dark, it must have come from the land of the dead. He called me little girl and other words I've never heard before, but I recognized the accent…somehow.

Taking a deep breath, I hold onto that memory, to the sensation as long as I can. Of warm and strong hands massaging my breasts and rough, thick fingers teasing my nipples. A whimper escapes my throat as I remember the feeling of those same fingers fucking my cunt and rubbing my clit like it was a nugget of gold he wanted to shine. All while speaking the loveliest dirty talk in that deathly deep voice.

I feel liquid heat between my legs, and it sends an irritating tickle around my slit. The second I shift my legs, I freeze. A gasp catches in my throat. Because…these are absolutely *not* my sheets. Or blankets.

Without opening my eyes, too frozen with fear, I ever so slightly curve my fingertips and rub my arms on those sheets. Mine are scratchy and smell faintly of TV dinners and cheap body wash and shampoo. Nowhere near this soft and lush. The sheets and blankets all around me smell like cloves and balsam fir.

Oh, bloody elves, am I still dreaming?!

And why did I spend more time wondering about the nature of the sheets and not why I am fucking naked as a plucked goose? My nipples are still puckered, and they harden even more at the thought of someone taking off my angel costume.

Wait...not all of it, I register when I wiggle my hips and realize the wings are still bound to my back. Why on earth...? What in all bloody, red-nosed Rudolph is going on?

When I finally work up the courage to open my eyes, I tilt my head and narrow them at the canopy above my head. That is definitely not my ceiling. And my cheap mattress and box springs don't have a canopy. And it would never have one like that.

My pulse quickens with the telltale hum of adrenaline in my blood as I take in my surroundings.

Twinkling fairy lights weave with care and beauty into the lush fabric, a deep red like poinsettias in full fresh bloom. Sheer red curtains surround the bed, cocooning me. And while the sheets are black, the blankets are fleece—pure wintry white fleece! The tasseled ends of a soft wool throw, red to match the canopy.

Slowly, I rise, forgetting that I'm naked as a plucked goose until a low growl resonates from the opposite side of the room.

"Holy Santa Clause jingle shit balls!" Gasping shrill and fast, I scramble with the blankets, wrestling them around my breasts before narrowing my eyes to the dark figure in the corner of the room. The noise I make doesn't cover up the sound of his low chuckle.

His silhouette is a dead giveaway.

I barely hear my voice above the blood thrashing in my ears when I squeak out, "Mr. *Krampus*?"

Another low growl before he rises. My heartbeat pounds more at the way his shadow captures me in its eclipse due to his size, even before he advances to the bed. He's still dressed in the same costume! Hooves and tail and everything. I'll give him points for dedication.

He stops a foot away from me. While my frazzled breaths thunder in my mind, it can't drown out the sound of his heavy ones. All that separates us is that thin, gauzy red canopy veil. A split-second thought of horror washes over me, but I dismiss it, knowing it's not true. Given how long it's been since I was ridden, I'd have immediately felt it if he'd fucked me in my sleep.

Not that I mind the other things that happened in my dream…if it was a dream. *You're losing it, Twyla.*

I make a mental note to get a self-help book at the library next time instead of my normal smutty ones. Give the elderly librarian at the counter a break from the washboard abs of whatever man or monster graces the cover.

"*Krampus*," he corrects in a voice like a Christmas drumbeat.

I jump when he sweeps away the curtain with his claws and steps closer. But my very cell matter freezes as he drapes his large knuckles along my cheek.

"Twyla…" he adds.

"Okay, big guy, I've met some very committed cosplayers. I'd be one myself if I didn't have the attention span of a gnat on crack. This? This is a little extreme, don't you think? But I guess extreme pairs well with eccentric…" I trail off, doing that nerves-induced speed-talking that always gets me into trouble.

His knuckles don't stray from my cheek, but he does smile, a smile that seemingly spreads flawlessly with whatever perfect facial prosthetics he uses. Hell, he's an eccentric billionaire. He has the best that money can buy for custom-made costumes and professional makeup artists.

Remembering I'm naked, I whip my head around, searching the room for my fallen angel skirt and bodice. "Wait! Where are my clothes?" My curls flick against his arm as his knuckles drop. When he scrunches his brows, I stick one hand out while clutching the sheet securely to my front. "I was wearing the angel costume. Please tell me it's here somewhere."

He shakes his head.

I snap. Heat rises inside me, and I shout through my burning tears, "Do you know how long it took me to make that? How long it took me to plan? How long it took me to save up the money to buy the material?" I practically screech the last part.

I know there's something wrong with me because I should be way more concerned about the fact that I woke up buck naked in a different bed with some Christian Grey-themed Krampus watching me from the shadows.

"Did you…did I pass out?" I wonder, flicking my head up at him.

He shakes his head again. No words.

"Did you…drug me?"

He shifts his hand back and forth in a "kind of" gesture.

A chill rushes up my spine, tingling my skin in all the right places—unfortunately. I mean…at least he was honest. But I am absolutely blaming the warm flutter between my thighs on all those books. Time for some self-help. And maybe some therapy. Or a CAT scan.

When my throat burns, I realize it's from my breaths. Ragged, quick, panicky. Oh, shit, not now…I double over, struggling for breath and breaking down and crying. I wish I could say the emotion was more from the situation and not from my missing costume. But…it was mine. I saved for months and ate Spaghettios out of the can every night and blew off my friends and gave up liquor—all so I could spend night after night hand-stitching every fucking detail.

And then, this crazy, self-superior, entitled billionaire just throws it away? *And stripped you.* I force myself to acknowledge all the other things. *And drugged you—kind of. And put you in the most beautiful bed in existence. And naked. Don't forget, naked.*

All the heat and rage ignite, blazing an inferno through my veins. I snap. And he's too close.

I throw my fist, aiming for his groin, but all I meet with are packed muscled layers on his abdomen. Muscles that make every guy on those romance covers look like limp-noodled, tiny Popeyes.

Rolling off the other side of the bed, I make a beeline for the door, still holding onto the sheets for dear life.

I barely make it three steps.

And I get a first-hand experience of what it feels like to be a doll.

"What are you doing? Let go!" I thrash and kick, careless of how I might damage his costume. But nothing disturbs the huge arms with their giant biceps as he hauls me back to the bed.

At first, I expect him to just throw me back on the bed so we can talk through this like civilized people.

"Slem pike."

What-what did he say?

And when he sits down with a heavy grunt, when he grips my wrists in one hand and brings me down over his lap with my feet dangling helplessly in the air on account of how big he is, my whole being shudders. Then stills. A fleeting image of Krampus spanking a naughty child rushes through my thoughts.

Molten liquid gushes to my center even before his hand strikes my buttocks. Hard.

A cry leaves my mouth. My hips writhe without my meaning to. Because this is not the sort of spanking one gives to a child. Not at all. I struggle to contain my cries as his large, muscled palm comes down again—a strike like heated thunder to my skin. Powerful. Hard. Intimate. *Monstrous*.

He steals all my breath and sets my blood on fire.

One strong slap after another, burning my flesh. I've never been more vulnerable at any time in my life. My ass swells and inflames to his steadfast strikes that seem to come with no end. He overpowers me.

Hot tears spill down my cheeks onto the red throw beneath my face. But my shrill cry melts into a moan because the spanking turns into something else. Pain and pleasure mingle, intertwining with no end and no beginning. My breasts turn heavy, aching, nipples itchy and hard.

He renders my ass to a heated red as if he's baking a Christmas treat. Out of the corner of my eye, through my ravaging blonde curls, I catch a glimpse of him. The eyes and expression that he wears split my seams, unraveling my heart in a single beat. His neck is slightly tilted, gaze stroking and caressing my bottom, my thighs, my back, everything with tenderness, contrasting with the fire of his hand.

His unbroken attention arouses me. As if he doesn't see an ornery girl who punched him but a princess. More than a princess. Like a queen. A queen inside of a big, beautiful Christmas box wrapped in shiny gold paper and tied up with a big bow.

My body melts against him—all struggle surrendered.

I hardly know what's happening when I start to rock against him. Hips rising and falling. I'm squirming. All I know is the hunger and need trembling through me. This liquid fire flowing to my center. Trickling from my slit. Womb tightening. Muscles fluttering. So close. Hips rocking, I grind against him because if I get just one rub of my clit, I'll come. It might be just the best orgasm I'll ever have.

Oh, but he stops. I whimper. Until a solitary fingertip touches the nape of my neck and follows the curvature of my spine—all the way to my smoldering bottom, where he teases the crack. That single finger sweep sends shivers all over my body.

"Skitten jente."

That voice! It's deep, deeper than a chasm, deeper than the womb of the earth. Holy mistletoe!—not a dream, not a dream, not a dream. Unless I'm hallucinating. No, if I was hallucinating, my ass would not be scalded like a well-cooked ham…one sauced in its own juices.

“Perfekt rumpa.”

Did he just say I had a perfect…ass?

Before I can ponder more, much less ask, Krampus lifts me by my hips, gathering me into his lap until I’m curled in his arms, shaking and shuddering. But his fur is thick and silky against my sore buttocks, soothing the reddened flesh as he holds me. Masculine heat surrounds me.

I know I should say something. Something rational like ‘Who do you think you are?’. Or ‘you took this role way too extreme, all boundaries obliterated.’ Or ‘let me go right now, or I’ll call the fucking police, you chuckle-hooved, overgrown grinch!’

Instead, I cling to the dark fur on his chest that I swear wasn’t there before, inhaling the scent of fresh-cut pine trees and holiday spices. Instead, what comes out is, “I-I’m s-s-sorry.”—*for the punch I threw*, I hope he knows it’s implied. And… “Th-thank you.”

Something hums deep and warm from his chest. A gentle, rhythmic vibration, soothing and spreading a warm rush of tingles through my body. Is he…purring?

“Flink pike.” What?

Less than a second, he has me on my back, my head on the pillow, and his enormous shape drowning me in his shadow. My breath hitches in my throat, my heartbeat stuttering from how close he is, how the heat of his body tangles with mine as he hovers an inch above me. As he gazes into my eyes and gently brushes his knuckles across my cheek, I can’t think about my searing bottom—not compared to my inner muscles pulsing creamy flames in my center.

“Bli min,” he says in that deep, velvety timbre. I have no idea what the words mean, but they spike my adrenaline and send icy fear and hot fire deep into me.

Then, he lowers himself. Hooooly mistletoe, is he—he spreads my legs wide—oh he is! I cover my mouth with one hand, stifling the sound of my panting, gasping breaths as he parts my wet folds, breathes in the scent of my pussy, and drags his tongue in one slow lick along my clit.

My head snaps back, eyes shooting wide open—the reward center of my brain lighting up brighter than the fucking Krampus World Square's Christmas Tree.

Not even a soundproof chamber could drown out the sound of my screams.

4

There is more to Twyla's essence than meets the eye.

KRAMPUS

"Bli min." *Make you mine.*

I swore not to use my tongue, but she's made it impossible. Where I simply intended to teach my lille stjerne a lesson not to fuck with Krampus, she enjoyed it on a deeper level than I could have imagined. Endorphins raging through her, her blood heating, her pheromones damn-near flooding the air were all expected. And her sweet cunny cream.

But what struck me like hot iron in my chest was how much she clung to me. Sweet golden treasure trembling in my arms, torturing me with her tears and spearing me with her tender apology and gratitude. She may not understand the significance of the small gift, but she will feel it. Now.

I smirk at how she covers her mouth while I part her legs, my fingers crawling up her ripe thighs—the extra plumpness there, like vanilla fondant. Her pretty folds are soaked in her fluids, and it will take all my power not to extend my tongue—at least not with her noticing.

One slow lick. Fuck! I don't know why she's screaming. Not when her pussy is giving me a Klaus-damn tongue orgasm! I guess I can't blame my Twyla, given how my tongue's saliva and the thousands of microscopic nodules along it are all designed for maximum *pleasure*. But it works both ways.

And she tastes like a devilish molten lava cake. Richer and creamier than sugar cookies—and a tangy hint like a sweet cherry compote. There is more to Twyla's essence than meets the eye. I will never stop wanting to learn. Just as I will never stop wanting to lick her pink and silky wet heat.

I must grip her flailing wrists and pin them to her belly while holding down her bucking hips. It seems to turn her on more since she squeals, and more juice spills from her slit. With my other hand, I keep her spread, hood peeled back, and tongue licking at the plump little nub. I could stay here forever—mouth sealed to all this delicious heat.

When her limbs rattle and shake, and she rises with the climax, I purr against her pussy, intensifying her climax. I love to see her back arch and body rise for me. I love to see those firm little nipples turning to bits of hard, pink stone.

She comes down. Too soon. Barely a few seconds of tasting her. I want more!

"What are you? Oh, holy holly berries, pleaseohpleaseohplease!"

Her begging has my cock beating down the fleshy walls of my pouch, determined to break free and plunge into her soaked center. She grinds those hips, her shrieks and cries chiming off the walls as I gorge on her. Dipping and dragging my tongue into every line and crease of every fold, lapping and drinking her molten honey.

"Skitten jente," I praise my dirty girl, who's positively dripping all over my face.

All her limbs shudder with another impending orgasm. So responsive to my tongue. I can't resist her wet slit, slowly entering my tongue into the spongy heaven of her inner flesh. She squelches, and I chuckle, then purr, sending that vibration through her chamber and into her womb itself.

Ahh! Screaming again, she squeezes her muscles in climax, strangling my tongue, and it's too much.

I switch places, using my finger to fuck her instead and suck her ripe little clit. She lets out a raw moan. A glistening sheen of sweat coats her body, and the twinkly fairy lights of the canopy glow upon her body like stars.

I imagine taking her like this. Her hands—bound by red ribbon that I'd twirl around her body, highlighting her curves and luscious breasts. Ravenous hunger consumes my cock, but I don't stop torturing myself…or her. Those dainty hands clench so hard, they're digging nail prints into my hands. I kiss every part of the soaked valley between her legs, from lashing her sensitive tip to sinking into her folds and dragging my tongue all the way to her pink ring.

She screams her release two more times, begging and pleading for me to stop in a hoarse voice. Her high, round breasts heave with ragged gasps. Flushed skin, sweet flesh, lovely subtle curves. I reach up to cup her breast, thumbing her nipple, then plucking at the pebbled bud. More raw moans, each like a musical cadence. I could swirl my tongue around both nipples, but she's not ready for that. Or for my tongue to pleasure her clit and inner walls at the same time.

A string of whispered curses leaves her mouth as her thighs shudder. Sensing another orgasm coming, I latch onto that sweet, swollen nub and suckle while curling my tongue along one tiny spot on the left side. Her entire body softens, and her thighs twitch.

Fuck, my very horns harden for her.

Yes, kjaere, my sweet dirty girl. Come for me. I flick my eyes to hers, finding heavy lids and lashes blotted with starry tears as those eyes plead to me, praying for her release and relief. As beautiful as the twinkling lights dancing on her skin and the rosy glow casting her flesh. Her inner muscles pulse and throb with need as I thrust my finger in and out, fucking her with it.

My last little trick is circling her clit with my very tongue, squeezing and sucking the nub with my hypersensitive organ while flicking her tip at the time. Her body rises. Those inner muscles contract stronger than ever around my pumping finger. Squelching and sucking and strangling.

And my naughty, filthy Christmas star arches her back off the bed, screams her climax in a high, wailing soprano with all those muscles convulsing, and squirts her cream all over my face.

My hips jerk. All control snapped until my cock bursts. I grit my teeth around my growl from my hidden release, but it's going to be a pain in the pouch to clean that up later.

For now, I drink every last drop, lapping at her slit, licking the juice off her inner thighs and between the tight crack of her delectable bottom. Only to register she's stopped moving. Rising up, I chuckle darkly at the sight of her passed out. Golden curls cling to her sweat-soaked skin, fracturing her face. I wipe them away and lean down to rub my lips across her cheek, purring my vibration deep into her ear.

When she wakes, I will bathe her. Until then, I have no qualms about taking my little Twyla, my twilight stjerne, to bed. Her little body curled up to mine as I hold her from behind. Because while I love to look upon her face, so lovely and tranquil in her orgasm-drunken, passed-out state, I want to fall asleep with the scent of her hair filling my nostrils and those curls tickling my face.

I bind one strong arm around her frame, tiny compared to mine. And keep the other draped around her head so I may comb my fingers through her hair. Something I've never done to any woman.

Every time one learned my secret, Mephisto covered my tracks. All deals included a forgetting clause. Because Klaus isn't the only one who has them.

I never got this far.

Drunk on my Twyla, I press my lips to her hair, sigh heavily, and use every Christmas wish I've ever had on the hopes and dreams, and most of all, belief—that *she* is the *one.*

5

I'm naked in the shower with this crazy Fifty Shades of Krampus...

TWYLA

I stir from sleep. Not naturally but due to large and thick fingers playing with my hair. I always dreamed of waking up next to someone who watched me while I slept and stroked my hair. Then again, I've dreamed of *other* ways of waking up, too.

Not one dream involved the Krampus World CEO holding me in a spooning position with one hand caressing my curls and the other...oh, damn. I hiss, arching as those dastardly fingers dip into my pussy. It's still puffy and wet from earlier, so I know it was not a dream. With how swollen and sensitive my clit still is, it doesn't take much rubbing from his finger to send me over the edge. He chuckles above me, sifting my curls while circling my clit as I moan from another orgasm ripping through me.

When I come down from the orgasm, it takes me a few seconds to center myself, to breathe through this all, hoping he doesn't start the process all over again. One shift against him has me gasping from the hot flesh of my backside. Now, I remember how he spanked me, how he looked at me, how he worshiped me with his eyes before pleasuring me with his tongue. And gave me the most earth-shattering orgasms I'd ever had.

No sooner do I wince from the pain of my bottom than the Krampus CEO plucks me from the bed. "What are you—" I start to shout, but he hauls me over one shoulder and gives my ass a light slap. "Skitten jente."

I groan because I've given up trying to understand. But it doesn't take much to figure out what's happening when he carries me to the adjoining bathroom. The biggest and most beautiful bathroom I've ever seen. Once he sets me down before the humongous walk-in shower, he closes the door behind us. And locks it.

Center tightening, I cross my arms over my breasts, holding my shoulders while backing up against the shower wall. When he turns and approaches with clear intent in his predatory eyes, my body wavers between lunging for that door…and creaming itself.

"Kjaere…" he says in that deep voice I first heard in my dream and reaches for my trembling hands, wrenching them away from my chest.

My vulnerability washes over me because it's different in a well-lit bathroom where I'm standing naked before him vs. a dark bedroom with twinkle lights. But he still looks at me the same way. And cups the side of my face, thumbing away my tears.

"Kjaere," he says again and presses one massive hand to my chest…right above my racing heart.

I shudder beneath that hand, knitting my brows in confusion. He makes me feel like a child in his shadow, but I suppose he could make anyone feel like that with how huge he is. And hairy. Not that I mind all the fur covering him from hips and pelvis and downward. The reddish hue of the dark skin of his slabbed torso, chest, and arms takes some getting used to, but it's nowhere near the brightness of Santa costumes. More fur gathers between his pectorals before leading to a well-groomed ruff of fur and a trim beard.

Some parts of him remind me of a Minotaur but without the muzzle, of course. He does not look like livestock at all.

I swear that tail swinging behind him must be equipped with some sort of high-tech sensor, considering how it flicks in a variety of movements that shouldn't be possible.

I can't conceive where the costume ends and where he begins. Is he truly that tall? Is he a giant? Whatever the case, I feel even more vulnerable when I'm completely naked, and he's…the opposite.

When a muscle bounces in his jaw, I flick my eyes to his, parting my lips. Heat pools to my belly because he still hasn't removed his hand. And his eyes deepen upon mine. Before, I thought they were gray, but in the sharper light of the bathroom, I make out how effervescent they are—like silver snow globe orbs.

Sweeping my gaze down to where his hand presses harder to my chest, the base nearly falling on my nipple, I wonder, "Kjaere…heart?" I look up. He nods but gestures for me to continue, indicating I'm close. "Um…"

I look around, almost as if something in the bathroom will pop up in neon lights to send me a hint. That's when he points to the flower centerpiece on the table against the opposite wall. Deep red Christmas roses in full bloom.

Scrunching my brows, I turn back to him and ask, "Sweet…" Another nod, and he taps my chest again. "Heart. Oh…" Butterflies don't just flutter. They practically do a Christmas jig in my stomach. And warm pressure throbs in my center as I confirm, "Kjaere…sweetheart."

He plucks me from the floor so quickly, it steals the breath from my lungs. The next thing I know, he's turned on multiple streams of hot water. The kind that jolts my nerves at first but doesn't burn. Until it lands on my bottom, and I jump with a yelp at the scalding sensation on the inflamed skin of my ass. The shower falls upon my head, soaking my long curls to my breasts, but my aroused nipples still poke through the strands.

"Wait, your costume, won't it get damaged?" I pant as he closes the shower door. But he rolls his eyes and tips his head back under the highest spout, careless of the water raining down on him. I guess with all his money, he can afford the highest tier of waterproof ones—or countless replacements.

My lips press into a tight seam with the reminder of my ruined costume. The irony. I'm naked in the shower with this crazy Fifty Shades of Krampus, and I'm more preoccupied with my costume than the fact that he's kidnapped me, spanked me, licked me, and now...he's showering with me.

Not one part of his hooves changes from the shower. It's unfathomable how well this costume holds together. A deep grunt escapes his throat, and I work up the nerve to lift my eyes—but slowly. I take in the sight of the strength of his calves, rippled with muscle, muscle that only grows beneath the sodden black fur of his legs. The seething brawn of his thighs could be as hard as iron for all I know.

My breath hitches when something twitches behind all the fur between those thighs. Water streams over his massive chest, and I'd swear it moves slower than mine—as if the shower is in no hurry while it worships his form like one of those warrior god statues sculpted over decades by a master artist.

A fever burns inside me. My breasts ache. And I'm consciously aware of the tension taking over inside my pussy. Part of my brain tries to respond with reason. For all I know, he could be some old pervert beneath that powerful costume.

But when I roam my eyes along the muscled column of his neck, over the monstrous rugged jaw, and finally arrive at his eyes, something in them tells me to throw all sense of reason out the window. They are heavy-lidded with a black sweep of thick lashes that cast feathery shadows on his cheeks. Lust and desire flood those molten silver eyes, turning every part of my body hot at how he looks at me. Not even my ears are spared.

Why would I plead to reason? Why would I want to go back to my previous existence? The thought of him getting rid of me, because I'm too stubborn or scared, sends ice stabbing deep into me. Surely, any sense of limited freedom or loss of control—even vulnerability—can't compare to the opportunity of living out your fantasies dredged from a million romance novels.

Besides, if he wears the costume *all* the time, why would I care about who he is underneath? If he wants to take on this entire persona and keep me, pleasure me, even discipline me, I'd have to be nutcrackers to stop him.

So, I don't.

Krampus smiles down at me, captures my waist, and tugs me to him. But he doesn't embrace me. Instead, he turns me around, and I hear a squirt right before—oh, sleighs and stockings! I moan from him burying his fingers in my hair, massaging my scalp. The scent of festive cedar, oranges, and spices perfumes the shower, and my mouth nearly waters.

He alternates between hard presses of the pads of his thumbs to a soft raking of his claws. Every part of me is ready to melt, but instead, I lean back against him. A deep and heavy sigh leaves my mouth, followed by a whimper. He takes such care and attention as he washes my curls.

My head barely passes his upper stomach, where his muscles and body heat seem to warm me more than the shower.

I close my eyes as he rinses the shampoo from my hair. Another squirt is my only warning before his hands cover my neck and scrub a frothy soap into my skin. This one smells more like vanilla bean and oranges. It's not just bubbly but oily and softens my pores, liquefies my flesh, and sheens my skin in a golden glow.

My nipples grow harder beneath his palms as he washes my breasts. And I find myself arching, thrusting them into his hands more.

"Hmm..." he makes a low sound, halfway between a huff and a growl. His hot breath drifts across my head, competing with the shower steam.

Despite my arousal, he takes no prisoners, moving from my tits to wash my belly. At the first touch of his finger to my belly button, I lurch and giggle. He tugs me back by the hips and wiggles the finger again, and I let out a little yelp. It's more than the tickling sensation. Some invisible thread tightens the tension in my pussy.

With a deep growling chuckle, he reaches for the body wash and fills his wet palms with the froth before lowering his hands to my ass.

"Oh, god!" I shoot my head back from the stinging, burning sensation.

Krampus swings an arm around my body to keep me stable as he washes my backside. I groan, blinking back tears from the pain until his other hand caresses my breast and plays with my nipple. Desire rushes down my spine from how he tweaks and flicks the sensitive bud back and forth before moving to the other.

And then, I realize his other hand has moved to my front. Fingers sinking into my still-tender folds. My pulse skyrockets as he washes me there. I shudder.

Before I can barely blink, he has my back up against the opposite wall, my legs over his boulder-like shoulders, and his face buried in my pussy. Heated honey pools from my center, creaming my folds—folds he kisses, treasuring them with his lips as I gaze down at him through my vision, fractured due to the hot stream. Goosebumps attack my flesh as he drives his nose in deeper, parting my folds, breathing me in.

Then, his tongue…that hot, wet, wondrous organ licks my clit, sending wave after wave of liquid heat rolling through me. When I moan, he flicks his gaze to mine. The intensity in those silver orbs contrasts with the tenderness of his touch, of his tongue flicking my nub back and forth. While supporting my ass with one hand, he reaches up to cup my breast with his other. And squeezes.

"Mmm…!" I clench my thighs as the pressure coils tighter, and I approach the precipice.

Once he brushes his thumb across my nipple and tongues my clit in a staccato rhythm, my climax crushes through me, devastating me in storming waves of pleasure. I screech my release through clenched teeth.

Krampus lowers my legs from his shoulders to his waist, scooping me up and pressing me to his hard muscles and silky wet fur. My body is so opposite. Not only in size but in the light of the shower with the sheen of the oily soap glistening me in gold.

"Stjerne," he says and traces a finger down the side of my face.

I shake my head, confused, my body still twitching in the aftermath. "I don't know what you're saying."

He offers me a soft smile before reaching for the shower nob, turning off one.

"Wait..." I grab his arm. It doesn't startle him, but he flinches and regards me with brows screwed low.

I bite my lower lip, unsure if I could be more flushed. But he's...he's been so kind to me. Even the spanking, however intense, was attentive and meaningful. And while some part of me says this is simply a desperate attempt to make sure I stay in his good graces because I don't want to go—at least not yet—, I listen to the other part. The other part comes from my aching fingers, my orgasm-laced emotions, and the outpouring of my heart.

I don't let myself wonder if he can feel it beneath all...that. I simply gesture to the wash on the marble shelf and ask, "Can I...wash you?"

6

I find my home inside her smile.

KRAMPUS

Shit, shit, shit on that bearded behemoth bitch! What in all fucking festiveness am I supposed to do?

A thrill surges through me at the sight of my glowing star looking up at me, her eyes so earnest and pleading. Warm as amber in this light. Her dainty palms are open with the soap ready for me to give my consent. She's sweet, so sweet. My kjaere.

Dark hunger pulses through me, and my cock nearly breaks free of the pouch at the mere thought of her fingertips descending upon me.

If I let her wash my back or my front, will she learn what I am? And when she does, will she run like all the others have—only for Mephisto to work his forgetting magic and send them home? But if I don't give this to her, if I reject her advances—this opportunity—, I may not get another chance. Despite how I made her come, her little nipples are still stiff from arousal. Her flesh still pebbled with goosebumps. I scent those pheromones like a heady steam curling in the air.

She…wants. I can't say she wants me. But she wants *this*.

All I know is she cannot touch my tail. Or any part of my fur. Or my horns, for Klaus-damn sake! The throbbing desire in my groin is already painful. But she's so small, and I can't risk her touching any of those places. I won't risk breaking my lille stjerne in my craze. If she gets one glimpse of the beast, she will run. And I'll have no choice but to chase, to hunt.

My breath turns heavy as I capture her wrist, thumbing it gently before positioning her fingers at my abdomen, where I draw a secure boundary line, showing her exactly where she may touch.

Surprise flashes in her eyes before she smiles, a thrill in her gaze. Oh, if only I could capture that smile and place it in a dream jar—something I would open on dark nights when the demons stalk me. It would be the guiding light to pierce through the darkness and lead me home.

I find my home inside her smile.

Stop acting like a lovesick teddy bear, Krampus, I almost hear Mephisto's voice in my ear. Some things he says are helpful. The list of no-nos seems to have served me well with Twyla. But I can also acknowledge how much more devastating it would be if she left.

Devastating, I groan and growl at the first touch of her palms on my abdomen, Fucking torture! All my muscles harden. My fur prickles with agitation from how much I want those hands to stroke down and not fucking up. Her eyes are focused, exploring. As are her hands. They trace every firm ridge and linger along the shadows.

I don't know what to make of this. It's easier to watch her body twitch and writhe and shiver from my hands on her. When I command her pleasure and taste the rich, sweet cream of her arousal, it does not give me the pain that her touch does now. Her fingers glide along my lower chest. Soft and pale as starlight. Everything about her is soft and silver and gold. Radiance on a dark winter's night.

Fuck, I love the way she curls her fingers into my fur. Would she want to do the same when it covers my whole form? Would she want to stroke me the way she is now?

Her heat and scent surround me, and I breathe her in deeper, knowing nothing else in the world could smell as good as she does right now.

When she reaches around my body to gather more soapy wash, I hold my breath. Her hands stroke my pectoral muscles, her fingers curving closer and closer to—

"Ahh!" A rushed huff of want leaves my mouth at the touch of her fingers on my nipple. I twitch. But when she tilts her hips, her body brushes the fur and gently nudges the firm skin of my pouch. My length grows. More pain as it throbs and pushes.

She pauses. "I didn't hurt y—"

"Nei!" I press her hand, moving it in slow circles.

"Okay, okay..." she laughs, but it's a soft, airy laugh. Like a handful of fresh powdery snow tossed in the air to shower snowflakes for tongues to catch. I wish to bottle that up, too.

"Can you...feel this? Can you feel my touch?" she lilts.

My lips compress as I nod. I hadn't believed her cheeks could grow redder than they already were.

Then, her hands ascend, fingers roaming along my neck where my veins throb and sinew tightens. I heave gasping huffs through my nostrils because she doesn't fucking stop. Her fingers rub the slight amount of soap upon the fur of my jaw. And that's when I notice the rapid flutter of her pulse. A moment later, her body is flush against mine. Hard pink nipples rasping along my fur.

Fuck my jingly balls, she stands on her tiptoes! Her fingers strain to touch my hair. So, I lower my head, dipping my chin.

"It's long and soft," she says, combing her fingers down the strands to where they linger at my shoulders. She tugs at the ends. "Is it your real hair?"

I debate on whether to tell her. Would she see right through her presumptions about the costume? Regardless, I find myself nodding.

"It's so soft, softer than mine. And so straight. I'd love to braid it sometime."

She would? I'm so distracted, I almost don't notice her hand straying toward my horn. I seize her wrist before it can land.

“No horns. Okay.” She nods through flustered breaths. “Back, then.”

Every last vein and muscle bulges because after she’s squirted more wash into her hands, she winds her arms around me from the front before I can turn. I inhale a sharp gust of breath from her firm body and soft skin pressing against my front. Her nails rake gently along my back, the muscles tensing wherever her fingers travel.

What is more astonishing than this is how her chin lifts while her eyes capture mine. She gazes at me as she strokes my back. No woman has ever stared at me for so long. It may not be my true beast form, but the face of a demon is not exactly one that belongs to a handsome Prince Charming. But her eyes glisten, lashes fluttering as she stares at me. I feel her heartbeat thrumming harder against my lower chest.

She strokes down, following the curve of my spine until she reaches the line of my hips. It takes everything in me to pluck her up by her hips, preventing her from roaming those fingers to my clenching buttocks hidden beneath my fur.

I turn off the water. With her trembling in my arms, I grab multiple towels and carry her into the bedroom, where I lay her upon one. She does not protest as I dry every part of her body. More incredible is how she does not protest when I take the after-oil, which will seal in the healing soap I used in the shower. And add a layer of protection for warmth in the icy winter of my realm.

Her body rises, back arching as I massage the oil into her flesh, kneading and caressing her breasts, plucking at the nipples and tweaking them until she shifts her hips from side to side. The sweet cunny desperate for friction. So, I give it to her. Her skin glitters with the golden sheen of the oil as I sweep my slick hands down until I arrive between her legs.

“Oh, merry jingles,” she squeaks when I rub the oil into her folds and along her slit, then stroke her plump little nub with my thumb. Not long before she clenches the towels.

I work the sensitive clit with my fingers and my tongue, bringing her multiple back-to-back climaxes until she finally passes out.

She looks so beautiful spread for me in her sleep, her pussy all wet and puffy and deeply pink from the pleasure. I love how her damp curls are even wilder than her dry ones.

Despite how much I long to extend my tongue and slick it along every part of her skin, I leave my Twyla to sleep. A star in the center of my bed.

Smiling to myself, I move to the wardrobe, selecting one of the gowns I had prepared in advance for her arrival. She may not forgive me for ruining her other dress, but hopefully, this will make up for the loss. Before I drape it across the chair before the bed, I make a few adjustments to the color and add my own personal touch. Sometimes, being a demon god has its advantages.

When she wakes, she will be hungry. Time to prepare her a Christmas feast. Once she wakes, I will invite her to dinner as my honored guest.

7

I am the shiny tree Krampus is trimming.

TWYLA

I wake up alone. Or at least I believe I'm alone. No monstrous heat unraveling all around me. No deep, grunting breaths. No Krampus-shaped figure lingering in the shadows, watching my naked body. The soft, silky sheets tumble to my waist as I rise and eye my breasts. My nipples, more erect and rosy than usual, betray the evidence of what happened earlier.

I've never passed out from multiple orgasms.

Despite how my hair is damp from the shower, and the rich and luxurious Christmas-themed room is evidence, it's still surreal. Like something out of a dark fairytale.

When I catch the glittery vision on my right, that dark fairytale comes true. I practically scramble out of bed to gush at the gown draped over the chair. At first, I shift my gaze from side to side because this can't possibly be for me. But a little envelope sealed with a crimson red wax bearing the Krampus logo is pinned to the strap. An envelope with my name in bright, gold-embossed calligraphic letters.

I break the seal and open the letter without hesitation. A silly smile tugs at one corner of my mouth because it's not a letter. It's a simplistic illustration of my name and an arrow pointing directly at a hand-drawn gown—just like the one on the chair.

Once I try it on and approach the mirror, the silly smile grows into a warm and glowing awe. Tears glisten in my eyes from the emotion welling up inside me. I imagine the butterflies in me are blushing or humming or fanning themselves. Despite all my cosplays over the years, from elves to fairies to angels, it's the most exquisite gown I've ever worn.

A form-fitting bodice with a sweetheart neckline hugs my proportions to perfection while the short sleeves, like a simple drapery of fabric, rest just below my shoulders. I'm hard-pressed to remember when my cleavage and collarbones were so tantalizingly exposed—but soft and angelic. I attribute that partially to the glowing oil he used on me in the shower. The gown, as a whole, has a silhouette designed to capture my subtle curves and emphasize them in a captivating but not overly seductive way.

At my waist, the gold-laced embroidery stops, spilling in a silvery white cascade of luxurious chiffon. I trace my fingers across the gold-threaded patterns dancing all over the gown. Like starlight shimmering on a moonlit lake. The threads catch the twinkle lights, radiant and lovely.

When I take a step, I must lift some of the fabric, careful not to step on it. Silver and gold embroidery complete the hem of the gown, and the delicate train swirls behind me like an enchanting trail of stardust.

My long golden curls look so natural with the dress, I don't bother to try and pin them up.

I glance around the room, almost expecting him to suddenly appear from the shadows, but there's no one. Does he mean for me to wait for him here?

When I lower my chin to the floor, I cover my mouth's surprised reaction. More envelopes with the Krampus seal riddle the floor—all with arrows that practically beg me to follow them.

I'm more surprised when the last arrow in the room directs me beyond the closed door. At least any prisoner shut-in assumptions are gone. So, I turn the door handle and open into a narrow but ornate hallway of red runner-carpeting over hardwood floors and stone walls decorated with holiday elements from real evergreen garland and holly berries to sconces with glimmering candles that cast flickering shadows.

My breath catches in my chest at the thought of fulfilling this lifelong fantasy. It can't be real, can it? Am I truly wearing the most beautiful gown and following mysterious envelopes through a labyrinth of richly adorned passages to some surprise location?

At one point, the arrows split, offering me the opportunity to pause at the hollowed-out alcove on my right side. One with a floor-to-ceiling arched window. So, I take the moment to wander into the alcove and take in the landscape.

My chest strangles my gasp before it can rise. This isn't just a large house or even a manor. I'm standing in a whole damn castle. One that rests above a frozen lake that seems to span for miles. A symphony of serene winter beauty with soft, muted hues of night unfolds before me. Ice crystallizes the patches of winter forest around the castle as if Jack Frost himself wove his artistry of intricate latticework upon them.

On each side of me in the distance, the castle rises to high watchtower pinnacles with turrets like snow-covered crowns. Stars cluster without end or beginning within the backdrop of the deep indigo sky. The wintry wonderland of a dark fairytale.

I take a moment to catch my breath. And to let the tears fall. Because…this can't last, can it? Sooner or later, I'll wake up. Krampus will remove his mask and costume, and I'll learn it was an act. Or this is simply a game to him. He has all the money in the world to kidnap a young woman with trespassing intentions and whisk her away for a romantic rendezvous at his winter castle, where he treats her like a princess.

But I'm no princess.

I'm just a girl who lives on Canal Street—bordering the Warehouse District—with a car that is mostly four wheels and a rust bucket. And I own more second-hand clothes than fancy dresses. And the closest thing I have to a crown is my artificial two front teeth after a lamentable accident involving a chew toy and a game of tug-of-war with the dog. As in the dog won, because the chew toy should have been in my hand…not my mouth.

In the end, he'll get tired of me. This will be a holiday fling, and I'll be forced to sign an NDA and return to washed-out yellowing walls, box springs poking through my mattress, and cheap smut novels.

Things like this, dreams like this…they don't last forever. And fairytales aren't real. At some point, the game will end.

I try not to let the heaviness of that expectation ruin the moment for me. Squaring my shoulders and touching the gown to center myself, I forsake the alcove and follow the envelopes again.

Around the next corner, I bump into a familiar face.

"Oh!" I gasp, clutching my throat at how he startled me. "Mephisto."

"Good evening, Miss. Twyla," he greets me, still dressed in the same pinstriped suit and impressive spiraling horns. And his eyes are as warm and cordial as ever. "I see you've found the notes. Krampus is quite fond of games."

Yes, a game. That's all this is. But I muster a warm smile and nod. "Would you like to come?" I gesture to the envelopes.

"I'm afraid I have some castle duties to attend to. You might say I am Krampus' right hand. I take care of all the details so he can focus on what is most important." His eyes narrow and sparkle upon me while his lips twitch into a smile. "For now, *you* are what is most important."

Yes. For now.

When I say nothing in the pause, Mephisto directs me back to the envelopes. "Just another corner at the end of the hall, and they will lead you down the grand staircase and into the supper hall. He is waiting for you."

"He is?"

"Indeed. He is quite eager to sup with you."

I part my lips, brows threading in surprise. When Mephisto simply chuffs a laugh, I throw a puzzled look his way. "What is it?"

He waves a hand. "Forgive me, Miss. Twyla."

"Just Twyla," I tell him. "Or Twy. Or Lady Twyla," I tease, given the surroundings.

"Oh, of course, Lady Twyla, please forgive my lack of manners and address of our royal princess." He makes an elaborate sweeping flutter of his hand, lowering his head so his horns parallel the floor. "I simply found it…curious how you seemed far more surprised by the knowledge of my master waiting to dine with you vs. the rush of questions you must have over your surroundings and *unprecedented* situation."

My turn to laugh. "Well, it's not like he stuffed me in a sack kicking and screaming the whole way here." My cheeks redden from the knowledge of what happened when I did kick and scream the first time.

"And you have no questions?"

"I have a million, of course. But I don't want to risk asking." I rub my left arm, squeezing my insecure shoulders.

"Why not?"

"I'm afraid one question might poke a hole in the situation. I don't want to poke holes. Or pinch myself." I blush more and look at the floor.

"And you are not disturbed by his appearance?"

I chew on my lower lip, aware of the flush gravitating to my breasts. "It might take some getting used to, but it's his choice. And maybe I like the games, too. Besides, monster smut is all the rage these days." I clamp my hand over my mouth, turning every shade of red. Did I seriously just say that?

Mephisto blinks, then tips his head back and roars a deep, bellowing laugh.

Cringing and backing away toward the other end of the hall, I say, "I think I'm going to rush outside and bury my head in the snow for a while. If you could, please just don't tell him I said that!"

Deadpanning with me, Mephisto gives me a devilish grin and winks. "No promises, Lady Twyla."

Shit.

I take the steps two at a time, almost tripping over some envelopes, and follow their trail into the supper hall. "Holy holly berries!" I exclaim.

It's not just a small supper hall. It's more like the Grand Hall. Everywhere I turn, there are tapestries, draperies, and vaulted ceilings. The towering arched entrance above my head has been decorated with garland and twinkle lights and yes…mistletoe. Festive scents like fresh-cut pine, apples, and cinnamon fill the air.

On the one side of the hall, a grand hearth with a crackling fire casts a warm and merry glow. More yuletide elements line the mantle while a tapestry depicts a snowy, picturesque landscape.

Smaller pine trees line the archways on each side of the hall, but it's the enormous Christmas tree in the center of the hall that enthralls me the most. I feel small—but in a sacred way. Like I'm breathing in the scent of times gone by and standing in the doorway to a realm of magic and mystery. The tree sparkles with a symphony of colors, featuring hand-blown glass ornaments, carved wooden figurines, delicate angels, and stars! Gold and silver stars catch the light of the chandeliers, and the torches cast prisms all over the room.

I barely notice the long wooden tables on each side of me as I move toward that Christmas tree. After years of saving for Christmas World tickets and never getting close to the cost of admission, all I had were the trees in the holiday stores. And well…apparently, there is such a thing as too much window shopping, considering how long I loved admiring all the displays.

This is unlike any commercialized display. It's a tree that belongs in a medieval fairy tale book—so beautiful, royals would come from far and wide to gather before it and sip Christmas punch and dance in its lights.

I don't realize I'm crying until a large, thick finger brushes the back of its knuckle across my cheek. So lost in the reverence of the moment, I barely flinch at Krampus's touch. Out of the corner of my eye, I can see where he's changed for the evening. A royal blue robe, adorned in gold and silver thread, complements his black fur and softens the intensity of his monstrous form. The collar's edges are trimmed in ermine fur, which I recognize from Norse tradition, one of many eras I've researched in my time for cosplay purposes.

A series of ornate silver and gold clasps and buttons hold the garment together. Motifs of vines and snowflakes curl in delicate patterns to decorate the robe. And I realize his snowflakes mirror the ones on my gown.

His breath grows heavy next to me, his eyes fixated on me, which brings a smile to my lips. He gestures to the tree, taps my cheek again, and scrunches his brow, the folds around his eyes creased in concern.

I lift my brows and open my mouth to correct his assumption, "Oh, no, no, Krampus. I'm not crying because…I-it's beautiful. It's so beautiful, and I could stare at it for hours. It's the most beautiful Christmas tree I've ever seen or ever will see. It deserves to be in a Christmas museum, but I understand why you keep it here."

All of me stills when he captures my chin and lifts it in a subtle tilt. He gestures for me to continue. "It wouldn't fit in at Krampus World or Christmas World," I tell him in the simplest way possible. "It's too precious. This castle hall is worthy of its presence. As amazing as Krampus and Christmas World are, they are still for play and entertainment. They aren't real. This…" I circle my finger to our surroundings and lower my voice to a whisper, "...is real."

And I am the fake figurehead who doesn't belong here.

Krampus leans in and presses his lips to my brow, brushing the silky black fur of his beard along my lower head. I'm astonished I don't dissolve into shimmery particles right after.

At the end of the meal, I am stuffed to the seams, wishing I hadn't eaten so much. And longing for some exercise.

While I was dubious of the roasted boar, I found it succulent, rich, and nutty. And I may have had one or two glasses of red wine too many. Fresh-baked bread and roasted root vegetables, seasoned with herbs and drizzled with honey, were also menu items I couldn't stop consuming. And I definitely shouldn't have eaten so many baked apples and plums since it barely left room for the star-shaped honey cakes and the berries with clotted cream.

Other than the staff or servants ushering in with various dishes for the meal—all bearing horns or similar Krampus-themed features—, it's been quiet and uneventful. I guess that happens when there's a language barrier. And when you don't want to ruin anything. No poking holes, Twyla.

Until now, Krampus has merely observed me between his eating with an appreciative smile. I'm only confused over one thing.

"Aren't you having dessert?" I wonder, gesturing to his dessert plate, empty of anything.

His smile grows into a grin. And while I want to dismiss it on the wine, it's that wicked grin and his eyes roaming to my breasts and lower that has the butterflies erupting and my womb tightening.

Once the servants clear the table, including the ornamental pieces of candelabras and garland with candles, it's just him and me alone again. And Krampus fishes into his abundant robe and retrieves a long length of silk rope. One jut of his finger to the table and the narrowing of his eyes are a command and warning.

A heated chill shivers up my spine as I flick my eyes to the table and back to him. "Are you saying you want *me* to be *your* dessert?"

His simple nod while holding up the rope and snapping it is my confirmation.

"You'll have to catch me first!" I turn tail and run like my tits depend on it.

I can practically feel his shit-eating grin burning a smolder into my back. I'm no prude, but the idea of him using ropes and whatever else he might have in store rushes fear down my spine. Sure, adrenaline, too. And heat charges into my blood. And maybe some wetness slicking my inner flesh. Okay, maybe a lot.

But I'll still make him work for it.

Thankfully, the glass doors leading out onto the terrace are open. After all, I said I wanted exercise, and it will be a good test of how far I may go and what my boundaries are inside and outside his castle. Besides, the fresh air will help with my molten lust burning me up on the inside.

I get as far as the gazebo in the center of the ice sculpture gardens before I finally need to pause. My breath thunders in my ears and sends ghostly puffs into the air. But maybe…I lost him? Some deep sense in me knows it's wishful thinking. And that I should just turn back and throw myself at his mercy.

The huge bicep slinging around me and the hand fisting in my curls are my first sign that it's too late. He rips the breath from my lungs as he hauls me into the gazebo thrashing and screaming. I kick at his legs, but I may as well be a butterfly attacking a castle wall. By the end of this, I know I'll end up with bruises.

Once he gets me into the center of the gazebo, Krampus growls and pushes the straps of my gown off my shoulders, ripping it off me. My pussy damn near gushes. And my nipples harden to erect points. The lacy panties are all that's left covering me. I shiver from the wintry breeze rippling over my naked body until he tugs me toward him, surrounding me with his body heat. I tremble against him. Heart pounding. Legs shaking.

"Slem pike," he rumbles the familiar phrase, not that I know what it means. "Du har vært slem." Or that.

No chance to respond. No chance to protest. No chance to beg. Faster than humanly possible, especially with his heavy costume, Krampus locks leather cuffs attached to chains around my wrists. A gasp tears from my throat as he swings the chains like a master to catch onto the hooks in the gazebo. Something he's no doubt done many times. Angry tears burn my throat, but I recognize the jealousy in them because I may not be the only one he's brought here. Or chased.

He's suspended me just high enough that it strains my arms and forces me onto my tiptoes. At least until he puts his hands between my legs and spreads me, attaching a long, metal rod to keep my ankles out, my legs open, my thighs spread. Oh! All of me flushes. More arousal wets my panties, and Krampus knows it because he pauses at the spreader bar. And sniffs the air between my legs.

I clench my eyes shut, battling tears of humiliation. Not from my body's responses, but I'm nearly naked in the middle of a public gazebo. And because of how stupid it was to run from him. And the horror-laced curiosity of what he will do next.

"Skitten jente," he says while stabbing his nose against my pussy clad only in those wet panties.

"Oh, god!" I squeak when he starts to slide them off at an agonizing pace, exposing my soaked folds to the biting wind. Goosebumps sprout all over my skin.

One dip of his finger is enough to make me buck. I almost go over the edge right here. But he chuckles and rises, towering over me, and capturing me in his shadow. His eyes gleam wickedly—full of mischief, and the seductive way he looks at me spreads a deeper blush to my cheeks and a surge of endorphins to stoke my blood.

My whole body tenses as he fishes into his robe and retrieves a set of jingle bell clamps. Wagging them with a knowing grin. A lump lodges in my throat, and I suck a deep inhale. Less than a second later, he clamps my left tit with one. It bites the nipple, pinching softly, hardening the bud. But it doesn't hurt like I imagined it would.

"Oh!" I moan when he applies the second clamp because they weigh down my breasts. Impossible not to feel them, for all my nerves to zone in on those two regions.

One simple shift of my body, and the bells jingle in a soft musical lilt. Heated mortification ripples through me until Krampus takes hold of my breast, squeezes, and then gently slaps the side—jingling the bells louder. A tremor pulses through me as he fixates on my breasts, thumbs the right nipple, heightening my arousal. This time, he slaps the swell of the right breast, mirroring a flawless jingle to the other.

When he reaches into his robe, I learn he's far from done. My eyes grow wider and wider with each object he pulls out—like his robe is some magical storehouse for glittering trinkets.

One by one, he places the objects onto various areas of my skin. Twisting snake bracelets of the purest gold. A snowflake crystal pendant he tucks onto my navel, securing it with some sort of adhesive. Angel wing earrings with ends that skirt along my neck.

Most of all…stars. Dazzling eight-pointed silver and gold stars with glittery gems that seem like diamonds. But…they couldn't be diamonds, could they? The more he applies the stars to my skin, the hotter I seem to grow—which should be impossible with the bitter cold of winter rifling through my hair.

My hair, he takes in his thick fingers. My center spasms at the feeling of those fingers braiding the strands. Now and then, he pauses to weave in thin strings of shimmery tinsel. Like he's…oh, holy mistletoe—he's *decorating* me.

I am the shiny tree Krampus is trimming.

Tears glisten in my eyes. Because as twisted as his kinky appetites are, I can't help the warmth stroking my insides. Or the welling of emotion. Because Krampus, CEO billionaire of Krampus World, sees me as something worthy of decorating. Not with cheap, store-bought baubles either. Even the jingle bell clamps are forged from silver. Judging by his expression as he admires his work while circling me, I am something he loves to decorate.

My nipples throb at his roaming gaze.

As he pats my right breast from the base to shake the bells, I bite my lower lip and blush redder than ever. Despite how beautiful I felt when I tried on the gown earlier, this feels *deeper* for some reason. I may be naked, strung up like an object, but Krampus has turned me into something precious, something he wants to show off in a way, something he…loves.

"Du er så vakker," he utters with reverence while gazing into my eyes and tracing his fingers along the stars patterning my skin.

Just when I believe he's finished, he produces a final decorative object connected to smaller ones. My breath hitches. It's a charm, a gold bell shaped like a star, dangling from a tiny three-ring chain connected to another clamp.

He lowers it to my pussy! I hiss from the touch of his skillful fingers as they clamp the top portion over the crest of my labia, spanning my clit. The sensitive bud constricts, growing plumper, seething with feeling. And the star bell rests like a cold kiss along my outer folds.

I clench my hands in the cuffs, gasping for breath because it's too much. Between the clamp and the weighted clamps on my nipples, I can't fathom how I will—

Something else sinks in deeper. His fingers are so gentle as they nudge something round, cold, and metallic into my center.

"Wh-what are you doing?" I whisper, my voice cracking. Fear and lust tangle in an extreme web as he grins up at me, flashing the little gold ball before fitting it into my pussy to knock against the other. "Oh!" They feel so strange, so awkward and cold…until my inner flesh warms around them. But I'm so wet and slippery down there. They'll just slip out.

But Krampus growls, cups my pussy, and pats the area just above my slit in a firm gesture of command. Of course, he wants me to keep them in, I huff but contract my inner muscles and suck in the balls. He kisses each side of my nether lips in a tender approval.

Something about that little appreciative gesture sends heat spiraling through me. The urge to please him, the idea of rising to this challenge is irresistible. The desire is so strong—not only because of the praise he may give me. But because he's put so much effort into decorating me so beautifully like his prized Christmas tree.

I want to show him I'm worthy of such effort and beauty. Worthy enough to take whatever he gives me.

Finally, he stands before me and removes his robe. One striking and familiar object rests in his strong grip. A corded whip of birch branches. Small and thin, but I can imagine the force he will wield with their punishing wood.

Endorphins roar through me. More cream spills to my center, but I clamp my eyes shut and squeeze my muscles harder around those balls, determined to hold them inside me through this punishment.

He's got me strung up. I'm not about to let him down.

8

Twyla was made for me.

KRAMPUS

The moment her eyes melted in recognition of what I was doing, she was never more beautiful. I wondered if she would understand. More than her believing this is a gift she is giving me—to see her suspended and decorated like a Christmas tree—I want her to know how much I adore giving her this gift.

Her pheromones practically exploded when I ripped off her clothes and suspended her with the spreader bar. But once the fear and humiliation in her eyes transformed into wide-eyed astonishment, overwhelming emotion, and heated determination, her pussy damn near squirted from her arousal.

By the time I'm done with her here, the endorphins, adrenaline, public thrill, and pain and pleasure, she will squirt for me. And I will savor each drop.

My first course of action is to touch her, pet her. If I desired to simply punish, her sweet little buttocks would already be welted from my birch whips. Instead, I admire how her breath hitches as I trace one long finger along her spine, memorizing the shape of her vertebrae. I trail my fingers down the hair I wove into a thick plait, adorned in tinsel. Her golden hair is like a star on top of the Christmas tree.

A dark chuckle breaks from my throat as she shifts from my touch, the nipple clamp jingle bells tingling from her movement. I love how the frigid wind combines with the clamps to swell and redden her little buds, stoking her arousal.

At the sight of her thigh muscles squeezing, I touch two fingers to her slick, hot cunny, a silent commendation for how hard she works to hold those balls inside her.

"Mmm..." she groans and tilts her head up, squeezing harder.

"Flink pike," I tell her while fingering her. Then cup her breast again, give it a gentle squeeze, followed by a few pats on each mound, listening to the bells ring the sweet lilting music of her tits.

Despite the fear still lacing her blood, it bows to her arousal and sweet desire for submission present in her flushed cheeks. Let us see how well she submits.

Switching the birch whips from one hand to the next, I remove my robe, stripping down to my harness fixed to my chest and fur. She releases a little gasp at the baubles on my harness, and I smirk at her. My bells will ring loudest when I discipline her, and hers will respond with their obedient tingles.

Tremors ripple along her body. My cock swells as I raise the branch whips and bring them down in a warm-up strike to her lovely buttocks. My bells ring. She seizes up, letting out a sexy little yelp. Her bells tingle from her bouncing tits. But she is so soft and warm. So responsive. And she works those inner muscles with such driven grace.

Each time I strike her, she clenches her hands in the cuffs, stretching herself but miraculously...still keeping those balls in. If she takes her punishment like a good girl, I will reward her. If she manages to hold in those balls, the present I will give her will make my time on the bed and in the shower with her seem like a distant dream.

When I whip her again with the branches, she arches her back and rocks her hips, receiving the hot blows. I memorize the sounds she makes between the soft bell chimes. A whimper here. An adorable squeak there. A steady moan.

Sweat beads on her brow. Her muscles have not stopped clenching through the entire beating. My cock throbs with need for her. Twyla was made for me. She was made for my punishment and dominance and care. Her body responds to my degradation and discipline, but her heart and soul respond most when I treat her as the treasure, the princess, the star she truly is.

Fuck, her pheromones shower the air all around me while her scent and body tantalize me. The endorphins, adrenaline, and emotions conspire to paint her in a breathtaking portrait. One I wish to capture forever.

This time, when I swing my branches, painting her ass in the fiery patterns, I kneel and stroke my tongue along the marks. She gasps. I smirk, sensing her muscles loosen. One silvery ball squeezes through her slit. Somehow, she finds her awareness, that drive and strength, and sucks the ball back in with her inner muscles. The fine hairs on her skin raise to attention, evidence of the altered state she's found herself in. I smile at the knowledge of the floaty sensation where she can't fathom where the pain ends and the pleasure begins.

So, I swing again. She seizes and shrieks, but I am quick to grant her my tongue, my lips, my feathery caresses, and kisses. I give her all my attention and respect, treasuring her with each strike of the fiery whips, each massage, each kiss until her eyes roll back in her head—lost in the heady trance and the stimulation of her nerve endings.

I build her up and break her down, bringing her closer and closer to the edge each time. And still, she does not release those vaginal muscles. But her body makes the most enchanting music due to all her shaking. Along with the long and deep cadence of her breaths.

Rising, I find her pulse quickening, her eyes glazed over. When I grip her hair in a sudden tug, demanding her eyes, a vibration overcomes her whole body, sending a rippling wave of lovely music from her clamped tits jiggling their little bells.

For the first time, I read between the lines as her lips part, and her eyes slowly lower to my mouth. So, she longs to kiss the Krampus, does she? All the fine tufts of fur do not give her a moment's pause. The desire in her eyes and the longing in her sensual lips are undeniable.

Best not to disappoint her.

For the first time, I kiss a woman who is not repulsed at the sight of me. I kiss a woman who desires me. I brush my lips over hers, softly, slowly, inviting her as much as I seduce her. And when I press harder, she responds, opening her supple pink mouth to me.

If I use my tongue, if I taste the inside of her mouth or so much as flick my tongue against hers, my cock will break free. It takes everything within my power to keep my tongue in check when she leans in. Instead, I tilt my neck and purr deeply into her mouth. Not for one second does she pull away. A groan vibrates in my chest. She shivers from the sound rumbling into her throat, those tiny bells ringing.

I kiss her. And touch her. Attacking her mouth, hungering for her, I throw my birches down and squeeze her breasts before slapping each one. Delighting in the playful shake and cascade of musical notes like crystalline giggles. Her delicious moan into my mouth confirms how much she loves my treatment. I roam my other hand to cup her sore bottom. I take her whimper deep into my throat and capture it in my lungs.

And finally, I lower my fingers to her pussy. Fucking soaked for me. She can't stop shaking, limbs rattling. Her muscles are worn and fatigued. So, I dip my fingers into her slit and pull out the balls she's drowned in her fluids. She lurches against me. If she were not bound and hung like my Christmas tree, I imagine she would double over.

At the same moment, she pokes her tongue along the seam of my lips, tracing the shape and curve of mine. Wrenching myself away before I lose control, I kneel before her instead, and slide my fingers into her wet pussy lips. Still clamped and weighted by the tiny dangling balls, her folds have turned swollen and puffy. Such a delirious shade of pinkish-red. Her delicious little kernel of pleasure is plump and throbbing, awaiting an expert tongue.

Now, she shall receive her reward.

9

I want to show him how I can give him a gift.

TWYLA

I almost came from him removing the balls.

My body trembles against his mouth. The little weights he's fixed to my clit and lips weigh them down, swinging back and forth, stimulating me all the more. He doesn't remove them, but he presses his supple lips to my labia and sucks upon them while sliding two huge fingers inside me. I buck, shaking the bells, their little jingles intertwining with the winter breeze, creating a melody together.

When his rough tongue sinks into my folds, my whole body hums. I squirm. And twist against the restraints. His fingers curl inside my wet and aching flesh while his tongue strokes its torture along my folds, only flicking my clit at random with long gaps between each touch. He's proving my pleasure is his to command. No matter how much I buck, arch, thrust, or thrash, I can't make his tongue stroke higher and claim my throbbing clit.

Time ceases to be. His tongue and fingers dance in this place, bringing me to the precipice so many times before hurling me back. By now, I've trickled streams down my thighs, my nipples are engorged and inflamed. He pumps his fingers deeper, harder, shoving them in and out of my soaked pussy.

My voice has turned hoarse from my begging and moaning through the cold air. But I'm still begging with everything my body can give. Sweat drowns my skin. Violent shudders attack my limbs. Fire and ice howl through my nerve endings.

"Please…" I whisper and close my eyes with a desperate thrust.

Instead, he rises, jerking out his fingers. More fluids trickle from the slit. The cold wind smites my center. I moan from the loss of his hot tongue, his skilled and full mouth caressing my center. He opens my mouth beneath his, and I can't help but lean toward him, savoring the rich, tangy taste of myself. Or hints of it since he still won't give me his tongue.

I stopped wondering why.

He pulls on the little chains attached to my nipples, and I seize up from how much they burn. My pussy flutters at the endorphins and impending climax.

And then, he spanks me—right between my legs. My vision spins. My pulse thunders in my veins. I shoot my head back and release a soundless scream. It's not from the pain. He's using just enough force to give me a hint of pain, but this discipline is denying me what I want most, making me more and more dependent on him and aware of his control.

More shaking jingles fill the air. His and mine. A wicked paradox.

He strikes my cunt again, hitting the clamp and the tender bud of nerves that seems to stick out like a throbbing fat holly berry. I manage a weak screech through my clenched teeth. When his other hand squeezes my breast and slaps it with tender control, followed by striking my pussy again, I find his admiring smile. Enjoying the one set of tingling notes on the cusp of the other one.

He spanks me over and over, hitting my clit each time until my body is practically swinging and dancing on the chain. And alternates with slapping the sides of my breasts or bouncing them from the base to shake the bells, then tugging on those chains until my nipples burn. Liquid fire assaults my pussy from the delirious torment of his hand and wreaks havoc on my muscles.

Blackness swirls my vision, but I can't possibly pass out from all the adrenaline and arousal. But one thing I'm certain of: I have nothing left to give. Sheer exhaustion plagues every part of me. No will left to struggle or strain for my release.

When his hand pauses from striking his flaming heat, I close my eyes and cry more, praying it's done. But at the same time, I beg for more, wanting to know how far he will take me, how much he will stretch my boundaries, and how rapturous my orgasm will be.

Through my blurry vision, I notice him reach for something attached to the harness at his back. He flashes it at me. I get barely a glance at the pointed tip, the soft rounded head, and the countless textured veins and puckered buds along the generous shaft—before he removes the pussy clamp, freeing me from the pressure and weights of the balls, and shoves the dildo deep into me. In one fell swoop.

Wave after spasming wave of pleasure convulses through my cunt and surges through me, igniting my blood and the reward center of my brain brighter than a million fucking Christmas lights! His mouth crashes against mine, and with one twist of the dildo, he prolongs my orgasm. Sparks burst a shower of heat through my nervous system, riding on more waves of adrenaline. The release roaring through me deafens and blinds me to all other senses except for the shattered pressure in my pussy. And just when I believe it's tapering off, Krampus tugs on the chains, freeing my nipples.

"En gang til, kjaere," he growls. Then pulls the dildo out before slamming it back inside my needy flesh. At the same time, he captures one erect nipple with his hot mouth and rubs my swollen clit throbbing a heartbeat between my legs.

It doesn't matter that I can't understand. My body responds. My soul itself responds. With strong suction on my nipple and him rubbing circles on my clit while pumping that dildo inside me, I scream my climax to echo all over the walls of the gazebo, ricocheting to the wind.

I can't tell where the orgasms stop and begin. They send rippling tremors of ecstasy through my blood, shimmering up my spine and splashing a shower of tingling constellations inside every pore of my face until something hot and carnal gushes out of me in torrential spurts.

Before I can blink, he yanks out the dildo, kneels between my legs, and captures each drop of my squirting fluids while licking his dastardly tongue in pressured twirls around my clit. Sending me over the edge again. Another white-hot wave shudders through me and floods his face with more pulsing squirts like feminine honey bursting from my center.

I come down from the torrential orgasms—my body feeling like one great shining star twinkling with millions of tingles all over the edges of my skin.

As he laps softly at the stream of juices pooling from my cunt, drinking heartily, I'm convinced I'm still floating somewhere above the clouds. Because he sent me to the heavens, and it'll take some time to find my way back to earth again.

I'm not sure if I ever want to.

Two Weeks Later

It's the first time I wake before he does.

My whole body stills because the last thing I want to do is wake him. Not with his big furry chest nestled against my back, and his soft growling purr vibrating into my spine, raising all the hairs on my arms.

I love how his heavy breath unravels my curls with its warmth. And how we fell asleep with one hand resting on my breast and his other hand over my naked pussy—one finger dangerously close to my clit.

I can't remember another time I slept so well.

Every day, he wakes me early as if he'll burst if he doesn't get to soak up every last drop of time with me. Soak is right. I hardly know what to make of it when I've woken to his mouth sealed to my heated cunt with his fingers buried inside me. On some special mornings, I've opened my eyes right before he penetrates me with a new dildo.

Each one seems to grow more and more unique in its shape and texture. Not to mention bigger.

After the morning workout, he is dutiful in aftercare, showering and scrubbing me—as if his fingers and palms wish to memorize every piece of my skin. Especially my nipples and my pussy and even my back hole, which seems to be his more recent play area. The first time I refused to accept the butt plug and tried to run, he bent me over a padded bench, beat the ever-loving fuck out of my ass, and I still wound up with it inside me.

We take every meal together. He even serves me at times. And after every supper, when I've finished my dessert, he spreads me on the table and binds me to it so he may have his. Once he's satisfied with my legs shuddering and my voice turning hoarse, he carries me to the bath for more aftercare. Normally, I fall asleep in the steamy water with him washing my hair.

I always wake completely naked next to him—spooning being our most common position.

Not once has he removed the costume. Not during showers. Not during baths. Not when he's given me a tour of the castle and the grounds with their ice sculpture gardens and gazebo, of course.

What baffles me more is how he has never asked or urged me toward something more. Something for…him. Despite all the dildos, which seem to be a training method, he has never shown me his cock.

This morning, I find myself more curious than ever. Fear pulses a thrill inside my veins as I slowly and carefully turn onto my other side until I'm facing him. He breathes a little heavier, but he doesn't stir. So, I take a moment to touch his long, silky hair, the fur stroking his jaw and around his mouth in a soft beard, and down to his chest.

They might be the finest prosthetics, perhaps even surgically enhanced, but he does seem to feel something beneath those huge, muscled ridges. My nipples pebble as I glide my fingers along the slabbed muscles, down, down, down toward his iron-packed abdomen and flawless Adonis Belt, where the thickest of fur begins. I have to believe his cock hides somewhere within all this fur.

Maybe it's more than curiosity. Maybe it's suspicion and fear of what I might find beneath the mask he wears. If I learn he's a wrinkled old man, who's just using me for his twisted holiday games, I need to know before it goes any further.

But if he's not, which is much easier to believe due to his stamina and how expertly and selflessly he wishes to pleasure me while never hinting at anything in return, I want to show him how I can please, too. I want to show him how I can give him a gift. And enjoy myself supremely in the process.

So, I skim my palm along the fur of his pelvis. My fingers begin to tremble as I sink my fingers into that fur. It's so thick and so soft, but I get the sense that he has just as much brawn beneath his fur as he does on his chest and arms.

Just as I press my fingers down, seeking that cock and rejoicing when I touch a bulge, Krampus seizes my wrist, dragging my hand away. It's the incensed expression on his face that steals my breath the most.

Turning multiple shades of red, I lift my other hand to touch his face. His beautiful monster face. "I want to, Krampus. Why won't you let me touch you? Why won't you let me *see* you?"

He huffs wind through his nostrils, but a muscle bounces in his jaw, betraying his desire. All his muscles are taut, the veins throbbing in his thick column of a neck.

"Skitten jente," he says while wagging his finger. At least Mephisto helped with some of the foreign phrases. 'Dirty girl', 'good girl', 'sweetheart', and 'star' are Krampus's favorite names to call me. He uses 'star' the most.

Before I know it, Krampus grips my hips, twisting my body down, so I'm lying with my stomach on the bed. Until the sharp strike cracks fire on my backside. I shriek and writhe into the blankets, but I take his belt as he deals his blows on my ass. My fingers claw at the sheets from the fire spreading all over my buttocks. Sometimes, he barely needs a reason to spank me. All I know is it seems to relieve his tension, and if he won't let me touch him…

By the time he's finished, my tender backside is aflame, the sensitive skin blazing an inferno from the belt. My legs quiver. The bed is damp beneath my thighs, betraying my arousal.

Quicker than lightning, Krampus wraps the belt around my wrists before gripping my hips and forcing me to kneel. He spreads my legs, chuckles darkly at the juices dripping from my pussy, and then, he jams a new dildo inside me. At the same time, his tongue lashes my clit, bringing me to orgasm in no time flat.

Rarely is he ever content just giving me one. So, without removing the dildo, Krampus turns me over, sucks my breasts, plucks my nipples, then he turns the dildo on, vibrating it at the strongest setting and forcing me into back-to-back orgasms.

Limp from pleasure, practically drooling, I slump over his chest while he absentmindedly caresses my back. Golden tingles soak my skin as my body twitches and shudders in the aftermath.

"Krampus, I know what you're doing..." I say and kiss his chest, making my way to his big dark nipples.

His fingers pause in their strokes while mine tiptoe along his chest to those rounded centers. I look up, finding his gaze centered on me, chin tilted, horns casting shadows upon me.

With a heavy sigh, I trace one finger around his nipples and progress in tight circles. "What do you want from me?" My voice is so weak from fear of the answer, it barely leaves my throat.

A grunt is my only response, followed by his fingers stroking my spine once again.

I part my lips, telling myself not to speak the words, but I dare to anyway. "Don't you...*want* me?" My voice cracks in a whimper.

A deep groan vibrates in his chest before he reaches for that dildo once more. I flinch at the thought of more when my pussy is already puffy and hot. Until he lowers it to his pelvis in a suggestive manner.

I blink at him, then scrunch my brows. "Yes, you have a cock, right?" I try to read between the lines.

He rolls his eyes with a growling huff before he gestures to the dildo. Shifting my body, he removes his arm from my back and uses it to make a motion. My eyes get bigger and bigger the more he extends his fingers longer and wider than the dildo.

"N-no," I stammer, shuddering a little at the implication. "That's not possible, right? Something that big...it could rearrange anyone's organs."

A firm nod is all he gives me.

So, I settle back down against his chest and kiss the prosthetic skin near his nipple before opting, "I could do other things, Krampus. I could use my mouth, my tongue, my hands. You could even use my breasts."

He groans, closing his eyes and flexing his muscles in obvious want. But in the end, he cups the side of my head, brings my cheek down upon his chest, and returns to caressing the tips of his fingers along my naked back.

One final time, he sends me spiraling into climax with me straddling his face, rocking my hips as he eats me out. I clutch the headboard so hard, a couple of my nails break.

Another shower. And breakfast. Rinse. Repeat. And no Krampus cock cake for me.

10

"What will she think of who you truly are underneath your costume?"

KRAMPUS

If I tell her the truth, if I *show* her the truth, she will…I can't take the risk. Not when I'm closer than I've been in a century.

Once I've ensured she's passed out for the night, I kiss my little stjerne on her cheek, drape the blanket over her, and slide out of the bed. In the soft glow of the twinkle lights, she is every inch my little star fallen from the night. Golden gossamer curls. Lissome body like a petite dancer. A piece of the heavens itself. In my bed.

She is the greatest Christmas gift I could ever desire.

Too good for the likes of me.

My chest hardens in that knowledge, and I cage my grunts as I don my harness, careful not to wake her while fixing my chains to the leather. Everything in me overheats when I turn to look at her. Violent hunger stalked every drop of my blood when she touched me, pleading to see me, asking if I wanted her—as if she could ever be un-wantable.

The urge to protect her from all threats, particularly my past, is my ironclad resolution. If I can grant her a gift of a single happy breath, I will damn myself to do it.

Two weeks, I've spent every waking moment with her. Each one is new. I'll stay up well past midnight to watch her sleep. And wake her up at the crack of dawn because I long to see the sunrise glittering in those brown eyes, gilding them to a sun-stroked amber.

In my past, I could not abide by naughty children, and I was quite effective at striking fear into their innermost beings. A solitary, ancient warning for them to behave. But when Twyla is restless and displays her playful feistiness, I wouldn't trade it for all the good behavior in the world. Especially when she seems to love my punishments as much as me.

As I shove myself into my robes, I smirk at the memory of the ones she's enjoyed the most. After she melted when I turned her into my pretty Christmas tree, I incorporated more into my repertoire.

While it couldn't rival suspending her in the gazebo, her eyes still lit up when I dressed her in the rich violet and soft pink tutu-like skirt of fondant-like ruffles and matching bodice adorned with gold thread. Her eyes grew as big as wreaths when I rolled the snowy white tights along her legs, added the ballet shoes, and arrayed her golden hair into a lavishly styled bun with an amethyst tiara topping it.

All the demons on my staff reveled in the sight of my sugar plum fairy as she blushed from their adoration. And mine. At some point, I fully intend to wrap her up in nothing more than a giant red bow, spread her upon a velvet Christmas tree skirt, and feast upon her in the glow of the candlelight.

She shifts on the bed, releasing a sexy little moan—whether gratification or longing, I can't tell. But if I don't leave this room soon and get a breath of fresh, cold air away from her raw scent of cinnamon and vanilla and her body heat, I'll go too far.

Before she may stir more, I muffle the sound of my hooves and depart from the room, closing the door quietly behind me. She will need her rest for what I have planned tomorrow. She's seen Krampus World. It's time to introduce her to my realm of Yuletide.

But first, I need to find some way of relieving this tension. Strung so fucking tight, hunting may be the only way. I remember how she scampered into the gardens like a frightened rabbit, inviting me to hunt her as prey. Perhaps she will again sometime. For now, I will summon Mephisto to look out for her until I return by dawn to rouse her.

Unfortunately, the first face to greet mine at the crest of the staircase just beyond my room is not my loyal subject and oldest friend. I gnash my teeth at the familiar and unwelcome figure in his carmine-colored clerical robes.

"What the hell are you doing here, Klaus?" I growl and shove past the immortal bishop, not wanting to give him any hint of Twyla. If he so much as breathes her air…no, I can't kill the devil in disguise, but I can damn well pluck out his beard strand by white strand.

"Why, Krampus, my old friend, you seem a little perturbed today. Would a present cheer you up?" he taunts me with his rueful smile creasing lines around his eyes. "Oh, that's right, we both know you are only interested in one gift. One you cannot see, hear, smell, taste, or touch."

I stiffen at the reference to my soul tether. My hand pauses on the railing of the staircase. Not that this is uncommon for Klaus. Mocking me is one of his favorite pastimes, along with thievery, long-winded speeches heralding his wonder and pious pity plays. He's simply increased the tension in my body. Every vein has turned to a live wire—ready to snap.

"From what I have heard from my dear elves…" Klaus approaches me, his voice growing louder and pitching to a lilt, "…you may have a new and pretty present."

With a growl, I turn my chin to the side and address him, "You know those subordinate clause leprechauns of yours will gossip about anything, Klaus. And I know how much you love to have your eyes and ears everywhere," I grunt.

He shrugs with a crooked grin. "He sees you when you're sleeping, Krampus. He knows when you're awake. And with whom you spend your time."

He reaches into his robes and produces the blasted spying snow globe that has become one of many banes of my existence. My chest throbs at the vision of Twyla appearing in the globe—on one of many nights she'd fallen asleep in my arms. A dusting of snow, and the vision changes to the time in the gazebo.

"She is quite lovely," he adds, narrowing his eyes upon her naked figure he has no fucking right to. "Her innocence, no doubt, caught your eye. Among other notifiable assets." Undeniable lust gleams in his eye.

Hot embers of blinding rage ignite inside me. Peeping fucking Klaus. I snap. Regardless of how the fucking ball will magically rebirth, I grab it from Klaus's hand and throw it down the staircase, shattering it to smithereens.

Klaus makes a show of sighing with even his beard hairs drooping. "Your temper is unchanged, I see."

Yes, that happens when someone steals your soul from the Underworld and holds it for ransom for centuries.

"Get the fuck out of my castle, Klaus."

"Hmm…has *she* seen your temper yet, Krampus? Have you shown the poor little dear what you are capable of?"

Fury tears through my veins. "Perhaps I should remind *you* what I am capable of."

"Poor Krampus." He clicks his tongue as he would do to a child. "You still hold to your vain belief that you are not some demonic monster."

"I know what I am," I growl, turning my back and gripping the railing so hard, it cracks. "I am what you made me, Klaus. When you stripped everything from me and turned me into the villain you could use while your Crusaders helped spread your consecrated cult far and wide to the world under the guise of festive charity."

"I've shown you charity for nearly one hundred years, Krampus." He approaches me, invading my space and casting the infuriating scent of incense and holy water. "I have given you chance after chance, and you continue to deny who you are. As long as you do, someone will always get hurt. And in far worse ways than a few marks from your birch branches."

"Shut the fuck up."

"If you truly cared for her, you would show her who you are beneath the mask. Show her the monster all know you are. She will run from you as all others have. Must she pay the price for your own selfishness? Do you seek to ruin her as you have all the other women who came before her? Your time is running out, my old comrade."

He goes so far as to touch my shoulder with his wizened fingers, which stokes furious heat in my blood. "Give the girl to me," he lowers his voice, "and I will grant you more time if you wish, Krampus. You may continue to run your little commercial empire and enjoy the wealth of your hard work.

"If you give me the girl, I will return her safely to her home before you have the chance to corrupt her or destroy her. She will only have happy memories and abundant gifts she could only ever dream of—ones that will more than provide her with the life she desires. A life without monsters haunting her every night."

I almost waver at first, forgetting what a masterful manipulator he is. And how he did this with a couple of others over the decades. He lived up to his promise, too. After the girls tasted Klaus's glittering generosity, they forgot all about the monster in the shadows.

"You know she would choose it in a heartbeat, Krampus. What will she think when she learns you denied her the choice? Once she discovers you have lied to her all this time, what will she think of who you truly are underneath your costume?"

"Get out, Klaus!" I turn and snarl, shoving his hand off me while balling mine into a fist.

That sick, sinister grin twisting his features is his way of celebrating. "I am only trying to help you, my friend."

“I am not your friend. And you sure as hell are not mine, Klaus.”

“You always choose to see the monster in me while denying your own,” he raises his voice, though it cracks in a superficial whimper. “Must this Twyla pay the price for your pride?”

I snap for the second time. Primal fury blinds me to all else but the cloud of hot, vaporous red smothering my eyes. He has no fucking right to say her name.

My fist flies before I register. I don’t stop after Klaus has hit the ground. Rearing back, I drive my fist again and again into his face, bruising and bloodying the flesh. More hits to his ribs. And his stomach, shredding the breath from his lungs.

My fucking pride? Klaus’s damned pride could fill ten thousand limitless sleighs. Pride that led him to deal with dark magic and enter the Underworld to steal what was not rightfully his.

Blood and broken bones. He begins to plead and cry, his words desperate, but I recognize the telltale smirk crooking one corner of his mouth. The bastard knows I can’t ultimately kill him. One cannot kill a fucking god. But I sure as hell will make it as painful as possible. I beat the fuck out of him, bring the wrath of hell down on him.

After a few moments of blow after blow, until Klaus can barely breathe, he grins with bloody and cracked teeth. And wheezes laughter. My blood itself freezes as he lifts a finger. Out of the corner of my eye, I catch the horrific sight in the snow globe suspended in midair.

“As usual, Krampus…” Klaus coughs and wheezes another laugh, “…you ruin everything. She is running from you like I said she would. You have shown her the monster you truly are. And she will pay the price for your selfishness and pride.”

Twyla. Twyla. Twyla.

All-consuming fear devours my depraved heart as she runs through the woods, stumbling through knee-high snow in the darkness—dressed in little more than a nightgown and coat. Does she even know she's running on the edge of a sheer slope? Does she know that one misstep will send her to certain fucking death? My fear turns to bone-crunching terror that thrashes my blood to roar in my ears when she stumbles, when her balance wavers. My heart slams against my chest as she crashes over the embankment's edge, falls through the wind and snow, and plunges right through the ice!

Her body sinks.

My heart sinks with her.

11

"Please, I need to know," I whimper...

TWYLA

The shock of the cold water hits me like a million icy bullets. By the time I'm able to form a struggle, some deep, primal fear understands it's too late. My skin stings like electrical currents have been jammed beneath it. My muscles tense, and my limbs curl in an act of desperation to protect myself. Countless bubbles escape my nostrils like a slow-motion ballet, disappearing like clear ephemeral pearls to the surface I cannot find.

Nothing but silhouettes, shadows, and a vague sense of moonlight around me. Any panic I just felt fades to a numb sense of weightlessness. Of surrender. Because the cold has clawed its way down to my bones.

As soon as my chest tightens and my mind acknowledges its need for breath, adrenaline charges into my veins. Fight-or-flight response kicked into overdrive. I thrash and flail, straining for the surface—reaching, reaching, reaching. But the water is a soul-chilling wall of resistance. My fingers knock against more frozen water. They hunt for air but discover more thick sheets of ice. I lose all feeling. Skin shutting down, I turn numb as a ghost lost to a watery abyss.

Time warps, stretching and bending until I can't determine if I've been here for seconds...or minutes.

Visions flash before my eyes. Memories of dark years growing up without so much as a candle burning on Christmas Eve. But the past couple of weeks burn like a firestorm in my mind as I remember what it felt like to have Krampus decorate me like a beautiful Christmas tree, to eat me out every night as a scrumptious dessert, to punish me like his prized possession, and to shower with me—scrubbing and massaging soap into my weary limbs until I smelled like vanilla and cinnamon. And how he tucked me into his bed every night, holding my naked body against his while I fell asleep to the sound of his purring.

Damn my fear and my paranoia. I shouldn't have run. Why should I care if he was using me? He would have kept the costume on the whole time. And I loved being used—in every single way. Even if he planned to take me back to the real world after the new year, I could have…I would have remembered it always.

An icy coffin is more than appropriate for me.

Darkness washes over me. A black, monstrous shadow. I imagine it's the hands of death reaching out to grip me. But I never imagined it would have fur.

When my body breaks free to the surface, and my burning lungs gasp for air, sucking breath after breath, I wonder if this is death carrying my spirit far away from the lake and abandoning my body to the icy grave.

So, why am I still so cold? Why do my teeth chatter? Why does my body seize while my heartbeat thunders in my chest? I'm still just as numb, but my mind registers a will to survive. It registers how someone or something very powerful is hauling my form over uneven terrain and deep snow.

As my heavy limbs and soaked clothes weigh me down, the air gnaws on my skin and sinks into my very pores. I can't move a muscle. They are too frozen to obey. My eyelashes can't even shake off the tiny crystals searing them to the skin below my eyes. Every tattered inhale splinters cold shards of pain down my throat.

Through my in and out consciousness and the chattering of teeth snapping in my skull, I hear the sound of a door slamming open. Maybe it's wishful thinking, but I swear a glow blossoms beyond my thin eyelids.

A warmth begins to thaw my marrow-chilled body. A wet ripping noise disrupts the warmth, and my body is jolted. Now, I register the crackling of a fireplace and my naked body glowing in its embrace like a shimmery pale orb. The crystals on my lashes melt enough for me to open my eyes.

Great log walls with high-vaulted ceilings surround us with an enormous, floor-to-ceiling window in the shape of a diamond to my right. A window that overlooks the frozen scape of the lake and mountains in the distance. Wreathes crafted from glistening holly berries and silver-flecked pine cones hang from every window, along with antique wooden snowflakes. Sumptuous curtains and tapestries adorn the windows and walls with twinkle lights woven into each one.

The grand hearth before me features old Christmas themes carved into the surrounding ornate wood. Birch and pine boughs and greenery rest on the mantle—quaint glimmering snow globes lining the greenery.

More beautiful than everything are the Christmas trees. Towering evergreens that reach to the ceiling, casting their fragrant pine needles and decorated with cascades of red and green silk ribbon, ornate gold baubles, and thousands of twinkle lights.

Out of the corner of my eye, I'm somewhat aware of the garland and holly berries coiling around the spiraling staircase railings and the mistletoe dangling along the arched doorways. But my eyes can't take in everything.

As soon as Krampus takes my hips, grunts, and tugs me back against his chest, the crystals of the chandeliers capture me, dancing prisms on my skin. He rubs his fur-covered hands along my arms, bringing heat back into my shivering flesh. I feel his heartbeat hammering against my spine as he holds me between his legs with my body facing the fire. His chest and fur might be damp from him pulling me from the ice, but they are still warm with masculine body heat. Too much heat. I tremble in that knowledge of how he pulled me from the water. Icy water that would have been too insurmountable with such a heavy costume.

My heart trips. It stumbles with the awareness of what has gone from curiosity to suspicion to the sheer gravity of belief. Belief in how the urban legends were correct all along.

For the first few minutes, we say nothing. He doesn't stop massaging my skin, applying pressure to my stiff muscles, and working at the knots in my back. In and out of an hour, perhaps, I give him the time he desires until my teeth stop chattering, my body stops shaking, and my heart rate returns to an even pace.

At one point, he growls out the words, "Jeg slår den fine rumpa snart."

I may not know what it means, but I can guess, judging from the word 'rumpa' and understanding how grievous my latest offense was. My ass will be a blistering, well-cooked set of cheeks before morning. The notion charges fresh adrenaline from the quivering fear, but any fear bows to the arousal stoking my blood and launching raw liquid heat to my pussy. My nipples pucker. And my breasts ache.

By the time he works his hands back to my chest and fills his palms with my breasts, I'm already a near-drooling, warm mess.

But I've had time to sort out my thoughts, too. Fitted the broken pieces together as best I can. How he never takes off the "costume". How he's never showed me his cock. How masterfully he punishes me and always seems to know what I need even if I don't want it at the time. The castle like a shining gold gem amongst the barren polar landscape. Mephisto and all the other demon-themed servants with their various horns. My interaction with Klaus.

So, I lift my hands to stop him from touching my nipples before I lose control and turn into a hot, wet puddle in his arms. "K-Krampus?" I whisper in a hoarser tone than I had anticipated. The water and cold air did a number on my vocal cords.

Regardless, he stops, pausing. His palms don't leave my breasts, but he dips his head, tickling his hot breath against my cheek and ear. I don't have the strength to look at him yet.

"Thank you," I say first because it's beyond warranted—because I know what it means to him. If my theory is true, and I'm pretty damn certain it is, it might place me in an eternal debt of servitude to him. But if my theory is true, then I will have no qualms about submitting to and serving Krampus with my whole being.

After he presses his full and warm lips to the barest corner of my jaw, right beneath my ear, I dare to curl my fingers into the thick fur on each side of his thighs. Muscles twitch beneath my hands—the hard-packed muscle that flexes right up against that fur. Nothing like a costume.

With a deep groan from the effect of my touch, he kneads my breasts, squeezing the mounds before lowering those hands to what seems to be his favorite part of me. My pussy is already warm and drippy. And on display thanks to my open legs.

Just as he slides his fingers down my belly, I grip a firm handful of fur on each thigh and pull as tight as possible. He snarls. He has me on the floor and below him in less than a second. Breath knocked out of me. Hands on the hardwood above my head. And all his primal, beastly heat hovering over me, straddling me.

"It's true, isn't it?" I ask him.

He blinks, but he doesn't release my wrists yet.

"Please, Krampus…" I plead with him, arching my neck toward his face until my lips are a thread of a breath from his. He deadpans with me, his pupils dilating, but not with a swollen black chasm. Instead, they swell with effervescent silver. Spectral orbs that were born in some deep underworld abyss.

"Please, I need to know," I whimper, shifting my hips under him as he gazes down at me with those eyes shining like frost on moonlight. "I know you don't owe me anything. And I promise, I *swear* I won't be upset, especially with everything else. How could I be after all you've done? For me. And it means Klaus was wrong. So fucking wrong! And I want him to be wrong. Because it means you are right, and you've never lied to me and haven't used me." I can't stop my desperate rambling. Maybe I don't want to—no matter how silly it makes me. "And-and-and I told you monster romance is trending, and I don't want it to be a costume because I might love—"

He crashes his mouth against mine. Oh, holy—no, *unholy* holly berries. Because they're poison. And so is his taste. So is his wondrous tongue. For the first time, it flicks against mine, sending my spirit into a tailspin. Slamming my eyes shut, I feel it stretch—his tongue literally *grows* inside my mouth. It extends far past my tongue until his tip breaks past my gag reflex and prods the back of my throat. A deep groan, edged by a growl, vibrates in his chest and purrs into mine. I answer with a moan as much as possible, considering his tongue is spearing my throat. He kisses me and touches me in ways I can't even fathom.

For the first time, he grips my leg and hooks it over his hip, grinding against me. Lust floods my pussy with a hot tidal wave, and my throat constricts around his tongue. I can't tell if it's from lack of air or the feeling of his humongous cock closer to his fur than ever.

But just as my vision whirls because I'm going to lose consciousness, he slides his tongue out of my throat. I suck down gasps of air. My chest heaves against his.

When I open my eyes, *he* grows.

Second by second, black fur grows to eclipse his bulging arms and swells to enrich the sides of his slabbed chest muscles. More grows along his iron column of a neck. And spreads along the sides of his face while leaving his features intact.

Not once does he release my wrists. Not once do his eyes stray from mine. They shine with that otherworldly luster as he gazes down at me. And finally, he opens his mouth and wags his tongue, which I'm convinced is the Eighth Wonder of the World. The moment he coils that impossible organ in a wet embrace all around my neck, tingles shiver along my spine, and desire overwhelms every last nerve-ending. His tongue shows its inconceivable strength when it squeezes my throat, shredding my breath once more.

I arch for him. Lift my hips and rock them against him to show my want, my need. And with every breath I can muster, I tell him in an exclaim of a whisper, "You are so fucking hot!"

He loosens his tongue, snaps it back into his mouth, and brings his body down on mine to say in the deep voice of a demon, "I. Am. Krampus."

12

"You can have me. Take whatever you want."

KRAMPUS

Everything fucking stops.

All that exists at this moment is her breath tangling with mine. Her petite body with her rounded hips, wet pussy, and hard, pink tits beneath mine. For the first time, I let her hands roam. A deep groan leaves my throat as she sinks her fingers beneath the fur of my pelvis, hunting for what she desires. I imprison her eyes the whole time—not once allowing her to escape my gaze.

Blood surges to my cock, thickening it more and more the closer her fingers get. I must force myself to breathe. The sweet determination in her eyes, the hungry glint warming them to a molten amber in the firelight, the way her wanton lips part…

Fuck punishment. There will be time for that soon enough. Tonight, I'll let her see and touch and smell and fucking better *taste* what she wants so much.

She's still not ready to take all of me. When I penetrate her tight, sexy pussy for the first time, it will break her. And I will remake her.

"Krampus…" her little whimper comes right on the cusp of when her fingers find their target.

A soft, deep growl leaves my throat at the same time. And my cock throbs to life.

"Oh, sweet Christmas cock!" she exclaims, her eyes hurling spread wide as a tree skirt as she presses harder on the pouch holding my dick. Not holding it well, considering it's this close to breaking down the damn door. "Mmm…please, Krampus," she begs in a moan.

The second her lips brush against mine, I come unhinged.

Rising, I sit up and lean against the sofa behind us, curving my thighs, and resting my cloven hooves. Giving her an unobstructed view. Heat tightens my groin at the sight of her threading her fingers. Like she's eagerly waiting for a special Christmas treat to be unveiled.

That's all it takes for the mere flap of skin on the pouch to loosen. My cock bursts free, and she lets out the most adorable squeal. What I love most is how her eyes don't leave mine, but she takes me in her hands. And lifts. I'm too heavy and hung to rise to the arrow of my desire.

My breaths struggle, laboring against hers as she touches every unholy part of me. Her lids grow heavy with hunger as I harden in her very hands. And swell.

"You're so...you absolutely weren't lying earlier," she refers to the comparison with the dildo.

I chuckle darkly and throb beneath her fingers, savoring her little gasp. "No, kjaere, I will never lie to you."

Her brows lift as if surprised by my string of words—the most I've used in her language despite my thick brogue. All of her flushes from mortification—no doubt from how much she has shared and mouthed off under the assumption of a language barrier.

Putting her at ease, I place one claw beneath her chin and tilt her face up, forcing her lovely eyes to mine. "Close your hands around me, lil stjerne, and fist me."

"It feels so different!" she whimpers, that sweet and sexy whimper I adore while obeying my instructions. "I love it. All these bumps and ridges." She gushes while exploring my demon dick.

All I want to do is grab a fistful of her hair and force her mouth to my cock and fuck that tight little throat of hers. I want to go deep, force her to swallow me, choke her with my cock, and leave bruises on her throat for days. I want to string her up in this cabin and keep her naked, wet, needy, and ready for me for days.

But she's so damn small. And I'm more than aware of my power and how easily I could snap her in two. I've spent centuries perfecting the art of punishment—and knowing just how much each of my victims can take. With her eagerness and sweet submission, Twyla can take more than usual. The way she bends before me, kneels for me, and the light kindling in her eyes whenever I show the value she holds through each punishment has wrecked me for all others.

"Would you like to know what else it can do, kjaere?" I tempt her with a pronounced grin.

Her eyes widen, but she shakes her head almost as readily. "You should know better than to spoil any surprises, Krampus."

Fuck, this girl! Hun vil være døden for meg. *She will be the death of me.*

Twyla arches her neck and rubs her mouth at the corner of mine, brushing them back and forth. A smile tugs at my lips. I recognize how she's using my fur, stroking her lips along the soft strands on my face.

"Bli min," I tell her in a husky voice as she increases the pace of her hands. Those dainty little fingers can barely surround me. "I will make you *mine*."

Her brows lift. Her lips part. And then, a soft smile like the unraveling of twilight appears on her face. "I am yours." Her voice is the chime of a million bells lighting the night with their song. "You can have me. Take whatever you want."

When I flick her stiff, little nipple, she groans and tightens her hold on me. I twitch and pulse, on the verge of losing it. But I am bound and determined to make this fucking last. It's taking everything not to spread her wide and pound my ferocity right into her like the demon beast I am.

"Please…tell me what you're thinking," she requests. And then, she lowers herself. Down, down, down past my stomach, past my pelvis until she arrives before my cock. My tail wags uncontrollably, smacking the floor on each side of us. She darts her eyes to the swinging appendage and beams.

"Ahhh…fuck, Twyla," I growl as she closes the distance between her mouth and my cock, sealing her lips over the crown in a light kiss. Klaus-dammit, I almost come from that wet, warm kiss of lips alone. I groan deep in my chest. Tremors erupt in my thighs.

"Has anyone ever done this for you?" she wonders. Then, she fucking licks the tip!

"Demoness hookers. No humans."

She blushes and moves her hands up and down while her tongue strokes along the ridges of my length. "Well…I'm not as experienced as a demoness—"

I pinch her nipple and give it a sharp twist, reveling in her little yelp. When she looks up, I meet her with the full force of my savage dominance. In my eyes, my muscles, my breath, and my bones.

"Take me in your mouth, little stjerne. And suck my fucking cock."

Her eyes glimmer. Her nipples harden to bits of stiff, pink stone. With a deep inhale, she lowers her head, and I hold my breath, imprisoning her eyes with mine as she captures my cock with her soft, warm lips. And slides down, down, down…sucking me to the very back of her throat.

Hel be fucking praised for all the sweetest sinful presents! Fuckfuckfuck!

She barely gets a couple of inches beyond the crown before she gags, and I dig my claws into the rug beneath us, snapping and shredding fibers. It does no good. Too fucking long since anyone sucked my dick apart from my own tongue—which is nothing like this.

My hips shoot forward until I'm thrusting deeper, plunging past her gag reflex. Tears glisten in her eyes as my skitten jente works to swallow me. Powerful suction. Her torturous tongue tangles around the veins and ridges and raised nubs covering my cock.

Grunting with my near loss of control, I work to get it back. So, I snap my tongue out. Quicker than a fire arrow. She lurches, shrieking and losing her balance from the sudden strike of my tongue lashing at her sweet pussy. Klaus-dammit, she's already wet—dripping all over my tongue. I give her a sample of how much I can do with my tongue by curling it around her plump little clit and plunging it through her folds and straight into her slit.

She clenches, her inner flesh sucking my tongue with equal fervor to how she sucks my cock.

I'm not going to last.

When her eyes roll to their ceilings, I pull back, granting her the gift of breath. But I'm a damn devil. Between the taste of her delicious cunny and the hot suction of her mouth, I give a deep groan, grip her hair around my fist, and thrust back into her mouth, forcing my way down into the chamber of her throat. As tight and hot as I'd predicted on the first night I met her.

More tears stream down her face while I rock my hips, pull her down, mashing her face against my shaft as far as she can go. I fuck her mouth, her throat, holding back as much as possible while I push deeper. Her throat constricts. Her hands struggle with my shaft, but they find their purchase on my damn balls—where she strokes me with tender fingers.

"Faen, du er vakker," I growl at her. *Fuck, you're beautiful.* "Ta meg, skitten jente." Take me, filthy girl. "Ta hele meg!" *Take all of me.*

Her mind may not understand, but her sexy little body responds. Those ripe, thick thighs flex. Her pussy clamps down on my tongue, strangling all the hypersensitive nerve endings. Fuck, I'm going to come!

Determined she will, too, I sink my tongue deeper and curl it up to strike at the secret little vessel with its firmer tissue. The moment she ignites, I pull out. Too eager to hear her scream. What she gives me is a shrill screech around clenched teeth from the intensity of her orgasm from her inner and outer pleasure roots.

Her scream. Her muscles clenching around my tongue. And those delirious fingers still caressing my balls through her climax.

Her fingers claw at my chest. I watch her unravel. Fire pulses through me at the sight of her surrender. And amid her orgasmic throes, she closes both hands around my cock and pulls me to her breasts. The sight of my huge cock sliding between the sweet valley of her tits undoes me.

With a great roar, I snap my hips and release hard, hot, and violent ropes of my seed all over her chest to soak her breasts. "Ahhh, kjaere! Så jævlig god!" *So fucking good!*

I come harder, hardest in all my centuries. Somehow, I manage to hold back on what I long to show her, but as she said, best not to spoil the surprise. I will save it for when I'm inside her the first time.

While I'm still twitching in the aftermath, Twyla's shuddering limbs give out. I catch her as she doubles over, her body flush against mine. Flush and fatigued from everything that's happened.

Before she can pass out, I crook my lips into a side smirk, rub my hand across those pretty breasts to collect my cum, and plunge three fingers into her mouth.

She jerks. Her eyes glow warmer and softer than candles as she sucks my fingers with a content little moan. And a whimper.

"Krampus!" she gasps and touches the wetness dripping down her breasts. "It tastes...you taste like eggnog!"

"Surprise." I bob my brows.

And my little sweetheart dives right back to devour my cock.

"Oh, faen I helvete, jà!" *Fucking hell, yes!*

13
I'm totally fucked for this big demon guy and his giant candy cane.
TWYLA

After I sucked his cock for the second time, I must have passed out. Because I wake up with my body draped over his—on the couch. At some point, he must have carried me there. The fire still crackles with a steady glow nearby, warming my skin in its glow. And while Krampus placed a light blanket over our lower halves, I hardly need one. Between his body heat, his fur, and big muscles, as well as the fire, I'm practically baking.

It might be a little uncomfortable to have his cum crusted all over my upper half, but I love how he didn't sheathe himself. I scoot to one side just enough to give me a glimpse at his cock. Even in its calm resting state, it's a work of wonder. A dark beast of ridges and bumps, shadows and veins lying between powerful thighs adorned in black silky fur. A demonic masterpiece sculpted by the gods. It's an honor to suck him off. With the surprise holiday taste—one of my favorites—it will be an honor and a temptation to take him in my mouth again.

I touch my throat, lowering my brows in confusion. It should be sore and inflamed. Maybe bruised. Or at least tender.

Krampus chuckles darkly, and I flinch, not realizing he was awake. His fingers, drawing circles on my back, settle me until I touch my cheek to his lower chest, lips pressing to the hard-packed muscle.

"I may give you bruises with my birch whips, my stjerne. Or I may heal them away. One of many benefits of being a god."

"A god?" I nudge my chin onto his chest, gazing up at his demon face. His muzzle has grown, and I wonder if it's because he's more at ease. Was he using glamour before?

"Mmm…" he continues tracing those circles. "More of a demigod, but nonetheless. My mother is the great Goddess, Hel."

"The Goddess of the Underworld…" I muse on some old Norse lore, though I don't know much.

"My grandfather and I may be close, too, but I assure you, I'm nowhere near as mischievous as the trickster, Loki." He snickers while sweeping a finger along my spine, prompting a shiver for more reasons than one.

"Oh, I think you could give him a run for his money," I murmur and touch my lips to his chest, then curl my fingers into the hearty fur on each side. "For the past two weeks, you've played some very naughty tricks on me."

He curves a claw beneath my chin before he tsks, clicking his tongue in a comical lecture. "You call them tricks. I call them gifts."

I blush as I give him a sheepish smile. "I…like your gifts."

"I am happy to give them…when you are naughty or nice, lil stjerne."

"Am I the only one you punish?" I wonder but can't bring myself to look into his eyes. Will he suspect where I'm going with this?

"What do you mean, Twyla?"

"Are…?" I swallow a lump of emotion in my throat when I consider the history of Krampus, the urban myths associated with him. "Are the stories true? About you? Do you…do you punish children, Krampus? Do you hurt them?"

I hold my breath for an eternity in the silence. I can't hear the crackling of the fire. I can't hear his deep breaths or his heartbeat pounding in my ear. All my being suspends in this place until he inhales, caresses the back of my head, and confesses, "Yes, kjaere."

A tear slides down my cheek as he adds, "I *did* do this. But not by choice."

I flick my head up, but my chest squeezes with the need to know more. "Why? Who could possibly force you to do something like that? Was it magic or some blood command? I just…I can't imagine it. Not you. Please…explain it to me."

He heaves a deep sigh and combs my curls. "Do you truly believe I would wish, much less choose, to beat a child for not knowing their prayers? Or the belief many traditions hold of other companions of Klaus like Zwarte Piet, Belsnickel, or Servant Rupert?"

"But some traditions aren't necessarily wrong. I like Krampus World. I like the Krampus runs. It's like the darker side of Christmas. Like Halloween but with a festive side."

"Jà," he grunts in his thick brogue. By now, I've learned he speaks common Norwegian for the most part, but now and then, he slips into a stray word or two of Old Norse. I shiver, cheeks turning red as he strokes the side swell of my breast while lowering his chin to rub his lips upon my head. "Em glad du likes my world. I loved watching you from the moment you stepped into my hotel palace, kjaere." He snickers and drags those lips to tickle his breath at my ear. "You may have tried to take a picture of me, but you were not like all those irriterende tourists flashing pictures as soon as you waltzed in the door. You smiled at my statue, admiring it. But you fawned over everything else. I'd never seen brighter stjernes in one's eyes than yours."

I hiss as he moves his hand to cup my breast and rub his thumb across my nipple. My center heats from the little bits of affection. "You made something special, Krampus."

"While you slept, I went through footage from the moment you passed through my gates. Such wonder, such emotions dancing on your face. So much, it could not be contained as you gazed upon my world. But it did my hjerte a deep wound when you lowered your eyes to the ground and held yourself together. Such tristhet did not belong with such lykke."

I may not know the words, but I read between the lines and shift until I've rolled onto my side—nestled into the crook of his arm with my back to the side of the couch. I want to see him better, for him to see me. "It wasn't because of your world. I love your world. I love the dark and the light, all of it.

"But…growing up, let's just say there was no light, only dark. And the darkness wasn't filled with sacred solstice traditions like decorating a Yule log with holly and the house with candles. Or giving back to nature. Or crafting with orange pomanders." I blink back tears and lower my head, hiding them behind my curls so he can't see. I try my best not to make my voice crack as I go on. "I would have loved that. My family would have done yoga together and drank hot cocoa on a nature walk."

"Your holiday darkness was not warm or cold, sweet Twyla. It was not full. It was empty and hollow. They taught you to be numb, but your hjerte felt too much and wanted more. You were the little girl who would sneak out of her room on Christmas Eve and wait by the fireplace." I break down little by little, shuddering in his arms as he reveals what he knows of my past. "Sometimes, you would tie a wool blanket around your throat and climb the trellis outside your window until it led you to your roof. Du ventet. *You waited.* You waited a very long time."

Tears fall freely, uncontrollably, as Krampus tucks his big hand beneath my chin and raises my eyes to his. I purse my lips as he breathes the fragrance of cinnamon and evergreen across my face. "You may have come to me, Twyla. But you were still waiting for something. You were waiting every moment of your time in my world, kjaere. I wasn't going to let you wait any longer."

He wipes away my tears as I manage a weak smile. But the last thing I want to do is relive any of my past. So, before I break down completely, I touch the back of his hand, squeeze his fingers, and ask, "Tell me about the Krampus runs."

I love how he plays with my curls, sweeping them away from my cheek. "Yes, I remember the footage of you staring at the Devil's Main Street. Like you were picturing my parade. What was running through your lovely mind, min lille stjerne?"

His knuckles pause at my cheek, and I feel my face heating even more when I remember my fantasy. At the determined press of his lips, I know I'm not about to get out of this without confessing. The contrast between his iridescent silver eyes, his knowing grin, and that wondrous tongue sliding out of his mouth, wagging to one side, all have me liquefying to a puddle of goo.

I'm totally fucked for this big demon guy and his giant candy cane.

So, I share my fantasy with him—about a Krampus-masked man rutting me against an alley wall without removing his mask. And how I imagined the stranger taking me to his hotel suite in the Krampus Palace, sharing a drink with me, and then showing me his birch whip.

At the end of my story, Krampus spreads those lips into a wide, cheeky grin. I bury my burning face in my hands at the same time that he tips his head back and laughs. Not a mocking laugh. It's a rich, warm tenor of merriment and joy.

Within a few seconds, he's prying my hands from my face—too strong to allow me any struggle. But he goes further, tugging my body until he's shifted on top of me. Holy mistletoe! A gasp catches in my throat from his body, at least three times my size, trapping my naked one against the couch. Close enough for my hard nipples to rasp against his chest, tangling with his fur. His cock bulges but is contained behind whatever fleshy pouch exists beyond his fur.

“Hel be praised for bringing me this gift as beautiful and sweet as a Christmas star,” he says before touching his tongue to my jaw and sweeping it up my cheek.

I giggle at the adorable lick and wipe at my cheek but jut my finger up in reminder. “Krampus run.”

Shaking his head with a roll of his eyes, he props his elbow up on the side of the sofa, keeping his weight off me to respond, “The Krampus runs are founded in the pagan spirits of my land. They occur between winter solstice and January 6th.”

He curves his fingertips onto my belly, tracing around my navel. “Your skin is soft as a snowfall.”

My turn to roll my eyes. “Focus, big guy.”

Snorting, he continues, though his fingers don’t stop. “My origins stem from the Winter Solstice, kjaere. I represented the balance of nature. Both strong and ugly. Dark and light. Much of my role was similar to those of the early Halloween period. I watched over humans. Protected them. I scared off the ghosts, the demons worse than I, and helped people. Especially children. I helped them overcome their fears of my monster kind. They never had to fear those of us who went bump in the night.

“There was far more to fear from those who boasted by day.” He pauses between my breasts.

I blink at him, my pulse quickening as I dare to say, “Like Klaus.”

Krampus nods and resumes his fingertip dancing along my skin. “And since they associated me with the devil, the Catholic and Christian churches united to banish me. But the Krampus tradition only grew. Not in the ways I desired.”

A soft smile tugs at my lips, and I lift my finger and draw it across his cheekbone which is much higher than I first believed. Even in his monster form.

“That’s why you made Krampus World, isn’t it? You wanted to show everyone the true meaning and traditions behind you.”

When he snaps his tongue to flick my nipple, I gasp, arching my back.

"Fuck, the way you stopped before the Night Market. So much longing in your eyes. You seemed ready to throw away whatever plans were in store so you could explore my shops." He twists his tongue all the way around one nipple until I'm raking my nails into the couch, moisture growing in my pussy.

"It was…mmm…what I looked forward to the most. And the Krampus run, of course."

"Soon, Twyla, I will show you something better than the Night Market. But tonight…" he positions himself on top of me again, sparking electricity in all my nerve endings, then lowers himself, kissing down the center of my body while finishing, "I will show you how much my tongue adores your sweet cunny."

For the first time, my fingers dig into his fur as he shows me the fullest, uninhibited, and unbelievable skill of that wondrous organ.

14

Twyla must love the monster. Every dark part of him.

KRAMPUS

"Holly?" Twyla asks, gesturing to the garlands of holly and mistletoe decorating the banisters and doorways.

I smile at my lille stjerne. She is quite unaware of a dollop of whipped cream coating her upper lip from the hot cocoa we just shared. "Our tradition. Holly was the symbol of the Pagan King of Winter, who battled the Oak King and won the right to a cold and dark season. Of vinter. But the Holly with its bright rød berries and greenery reminds one there is still liv in vinter. *Life in winter*."

As she flits off to the nearby windows, I fold my hands behind my back and enjoy the sight of her plump lille rumpa bouncing beneath the little red dress I gave her. Her eyes brightening when I took her upstairs to the cabin's main suite and retrieved it from the wardrobe were more than enough reward. I simply shook my head with a smirk as she hid in the closet until she'd finished trying it on. The delicate gold embroidery complements her cascade of rich, abundant curls. The fitted bodice with its corset-like lacing in the back adds a sensual element.

With her bare feet, as pale as cream, dancing against the hardwood floors and their red rugs, Twyla acts as carefree and at home in this trite cabin. Not once mentioning the castle glittering naught a half-mile away.

If she doesn't stop rushing about, unable to contain her zeal over every festive piece in this cabin, I may just grab the tulle and lace skirts, bunch them around her dainty round hips, and bend her over to spank that sweet rumpa. Fuck it all, I intend to do so regardless. She still requires a punishment for running off and endangering herself by falling through the ice.

"Wreaths?" she wonders while pointing to the window display.

"Ours," I say again and advance toward her from behind. Heat mounts within me because she's also quite unaware of my closing in as she admires the wreaths, which originated as ancient symbols of protection. "This is why we place them on doors and windows," I explain, along with the representation of the Wheel of Life.

Rising on the tips of her toes, she sways from side to side, her eyes taking in the silver snowflakes twinkling as if touched by starlight. Blessed by starlight with the gift of awe she gives them.

Just as I stretch my clawed hand toward that bouncing little bottom, she spins out of my reach and scurries to the doorway leading into the small rotund sitting room. Tempting fate, no—tempting my control, she stands beneath the mistletoe and points up at it while regarding me with a mischievous glint in her eyes. Oh, she's asking for my punishment.

"Ours," I cage a low growl and march toward her. "An ancient symbol of peace, reconciliation, and love. Norse warriors of old would lay down their arms under a bough of mistletoe. Druids brewed antidotes and fertility tonics from the plant. And no matter how much those persnickety Puritans tried, the practice of kissing under the mistletoe could not be outlawed."

Again, I reach for her. This time, she ducks under my arm with a giggle. No caging my growl now.

"Candles?" She motions to the ones on the mantle above the hearth.

"Ours," I snarl. Stalking her closer. My hooves echo on the floor. I hear her heartbeat thundering. And scent those pheromones practically showering the air. "Light in the darkness. Imitate the sun. Ward off evil."

“Hmm…” she muses and snatches one from the mantle, holding it up, wagging the flickering flame. “I might need one right now, judging by that look in your eye.”

“You’ll need much more than a candle if you run from me again, kjaere,” I warn her and prowl around the sofa, making a beeline for her.

The mischief in her eyes grows the closer I get. I raise a finger in warning, and as much as I want to smirk at her endearing defiance, I press my lips into a firm line. Baring my teeth, I set the full force of my predator gaze on her. Muscles bulging. Beast awoken. She shivers. And I love the sight of her cheeks reddening, the scent of her blood heating, and the light igniting in her eyes.

I cannot afford to show her mercy. Not if I wish to make her mine. To keep her for eternity, Twyla must love the monster. Every dark part of him.

At the very last second when my shadow falls over her, she chucks the candle into the fire and bolts in the opposite direction.

My heart burns. My blood boils as she scampers around the sofa, all blushing cheeks, swinging gold curls, and bare feet. With panting breaths, she charges up the stairs, stops at the top, and points to the crest of the Christmas tree that reaches the high vaulted ceiling.

“Christmas trees?”

I roll my eyes because I highly doubt this is one she does not know. I’d wager she knew others, too, but she wanted to hear it from my lips. Confirmation from the highest supreme authority of the festive season.

“If you know what’s good for you, lille skitten jente, you will drape yourself over that balcony railing, flip up your skirt, and take your punishment like a good girl.”

“I want to know!” she whines. Oh, that little mewl will cost her an extra round of spankings. As well as her hesitation.

Hooves nearly cracking the wooden steps, I ascend to her, locking her in my gaze. "Rooted in medieval plays. Back then, they were called 'paradise trees'. They related to greenery decorations, which warded off evil spirits. And the ancient tribes of Europe considered them symbols of life like wreaths—and tied offerings to their boughs. And if you do not present yourself like min lille offering…" I advise her as I arrive at the top of the staircase, approaching her from the side and giving her the opportunity to submit, "…you will be reminded of your punishment whenever you sit down clear until the Klaus-damn new year."

She does more than present herself. She flips my entire fucking world upside down with one simple but beautiful motion of her body—when she falls to her knees. The steady beat of her pulse, the tender bow of her chin, the sensual parting of her lips all stoke a fever through my veins. And swells blood to my cock.

Not in all my centuries, not once has a being ever kneeled before me…by choice.

Emotion constricts my chest. Burns my throat. The level of ease with how she takes this position…is deep and soulful. Two weeks. Within two weeks, I've kidnapped her, stolen her from a life she had, ruined her handcrafted costume, punished her the moment she woke in my bed, and exposed her to forms of degradation and punishment, adoration and praise I could only fantasize about for ages.

She became my muse. My masterpiece. My experiment in exploration. My hope.

But this is the moment. Right here, right now. Kneeling before me, heart in her throat, breath stalled, pulse thrashing in her veins, Twyla is far more than my hope.

She may have fallen to her knees. But I've fallen much harder for her.

Krampus, the demon monster of Christmas, has fallen in love. With every piece of my damned monstrous heart.

I ache to bury myself deep inside her. Lust is damn near uncontrollable in my system. She will have her reward later for this extreme act of sweet surrender. But the soon-to-be burn on her lovely lille rumpa will remind her not to run. And to accept the unleashing of my beast while trusting I will always protect her and care for her—even amid her punishment.

Because she is mine. And I protect what is mine. I love what is mine.

So, I do not hesitate to raise her up, kiss her brow, then slowly turn her toward the balcony until she faces the Christmas tree she adores. Sweeping her curls to one side, I move her into position, appreciating the willingness of her body as she obeys my guidance, curving herself at the hips over that balcony.

"Don't move," I whisper the low snarl in her ear before retrieving the grouping of birch branches from the nearby basket propped in the hall outside the bedroom door. Birch branches are one tool I stockpile in strategic places around my castle, my cabin, and any other location I deign. These are bundled together. Different than the flail I used upon her in the gazebo. These will leave a sharper mark and one that will last longer.

She is right to be trembling upon my return. Right to grip that railing with white-knuckled fingers.

I won't coddle her, but I won't give her punishment without acknowledging her strength and submission.

"Flink pike," I tell her. "Flink pike." And stroke my knuckles down her cheek, a smile longing to form from how she leans into my hand, desiring my affection.

This will be hard for her. So, I take it slowly. Lifting her skirt, so the soft ends brush against the backs of her thighs, I bunch it around her hips and set her midsection against the fabric, trapping it between her and the balcony. Nothing but thin lace panties covering her backside.

"Lovely lille rumpa," I praise her first, smirking at the damp slickness shadowing her panties.

This bundle is worthy of her pretty skin. A rustic red string binds the birches with a sprig of holly and two jingle bells snug within that string.

A soft tremor ripples in her legs as I take hold of those panties and slowly slide them down her bottom, her thighs, her legs. Inch by grueling inch, building her up, preparing her. I could simply rip them off, but as I give her my full and undivided attention, I demand hers in return.

"Birch branches are symbols of new beginnings, of growth, and rebirth. After revelations and renewal tonight, Twyla, let this be more than a punishment. Let this be a new beginning."

She responds, stepping out of the panties after I tap her ankles. A wicked thought burns in my mind, and I act on it, opening my pouch and tucking the panties around my throbbing hard cock. If I do come, the likelihood being quite high at present, I will enjoy soaking the damp lace all the more.

I can feel her skin heating as I study her ass. She shivers as I trail a single finger down her spine, then press upon her lower back, prompting her into a subtle arch. Good girl. My touch pulls goosebumps to the surface of her skin.

Outside the cabin walls, the blustery wind twirls flurries of snow in the moonlight like a glimmering dance of stardust vortexes. Inside, I have my own starlight bent before me. With the twinkling fairy lights casting an enchanting warm glow along her face, paired with the flickering light of the delicate candles, it feels like a spell. While I may hold great power as a god, this sweet, little mortal girl holds me like a thrall to her magic.

She is the light to my dark. The angel to my demon. The magic to my curse.

Respecting the intimacy of the moment, I take my stance. A precise position I have down to the nanometer. I breathe for a few heartbeats, permitting them to assail my ears.

My hand grows warm as I grip the bundled branches. The same branches forced into my hand by Klaus. The same branches bound to a selfish curse of pride.

This is the first time I will wield them selflessly. A desire to possess in my punishment…and to protect.

One little whimper escaping her throat is my signal. I let the branches fly.

I paint her ass over and over with the branches, lashing them in stinging kisses across her flesh. Wherever I strike, the bells jingle their melody I vary the strikes between light burns, flesh-bruising blows, and bone-hard strikes. Her body, her breath, and her voice all become a symphony, timed to my strokcs. Ragged gasps, the muscles clenching in her bottom and thighs, her fingers flexing. Her eyes catch fire, shimmering to all colors of rich, warm amber in the light of the Christmas tree. The sight of her lips moving in silence as if she's praying to my tree, or speaking soundless words of sacred reverence, rocks me to my core. And nearly shudders my hand.

I reinforce my strength, the technique I've mastered over centuries. I don't stop until she melts.

When, at last, her limbs soften, her muscles liquefy, and her breaths deepen, I throw down the branches. First, I breathe and take a few moments to admire her plump rumpa glowing with stripes as red as poinsettia leaves. Those lovely pink lips drip her fluids down her ripe thighs. A long, heavy sigh leaves her mouth, and I can almost imagine it taking shape like a six-pointed star of a breath. The candlelight captures her marvelous little ass, turning the skin even more radiant.

She sucks a sharp breath when I touch my thumb to a stripe on her rumpa.

Lowering my head, I press my lips to her hair and whisper, "What do you feel?"

Tears glisten in her eyes. She squeezes her shoulders, swallows hard, and confesses, "It hurts."

I applaud her internally for her honesty. But my attention burns for her words, her emotions. Fucking need more. "What else?" I take the laces of her corset bodice and claw them one by one to give her a hint.

"Mmm…m-my pussy…hurts, too."

Resisting the urge to chuckle, I slit a smooth line down the remaining laces, opening her bodice, letting it fall to the floor. Her breasts are heavy and flushed. Nipples pink and hard as mistletoe berries in need of a kiss…and more. Without the bodice, the lace and tulle skirts barely hold to her hips.

"What else…?" I palm her ass.

She hisses. "Oh! Um…I don't think I'll ever run from you again."

"Hmm, you don't *think*?"

I pinch her buttocks and smirk when she gasps and corrects herself, "I know! I know!"

"Are you prepared to express your gratitude for your punishment, min skitten jente?"

A few heavy pants. A whimper that might as well be a choir of Christmas carols to my ears. "Th-thank you for spanking me, Daddy Krampus."

I snicker. "Cute. Unnecessary but cute."

"Um…it might be strange, but I loved the first time you did it in the bedroom the most. Will you—spank me again? Like you did then? Just a little, but with your hand? Spank me again, Krampus? Please?"

Oh, I will do much more than that, min flinken pike, sweet Twyla.

15

That cheeky Krampus devil.

TWYLA

Ugh, I'd take that birch branch spanking ten times more over this!

After he'd spanked me a couple of times with his hand—light and warm strikes with his palm that only fueled my pleasure—, I couldn't have imagined what else was in store. Certainly not this.

If there is one being in the universe or any dimension of it who can offer the flawless balance between pain and pleasure, degradation and praise, humiliation and worship, it's Krampus. And mind-blowing arousal.

My limbs ache from where he's kept me bent across the table with my pelvis positioned right over the edge, so it's propped on the wood, keeping my ass in the air, and my legs dangling helplessly. The ropes bind me to the table, holding me steady. It was clear how much of an expert he was at wielding them, considering how little time it required for him to tie me up.

While I've wriggled and squirmed for the past hour with my skin tingling, my pussy soaking itself, and my fingers and toes turning numb, Krampus has remained in his chair the whole time. But it's not his relaxed state or demeanor that has frustrated me most while simultaneously arousing me. It's that he's turned my burning backside into his fucking plate!

It's the wee hours of the morning, but after he'd tied me to the table, Krampus returned with a bountiful board of sweets and treats. All of which he arranged on my blazing arse. Gingerbread cookies, marzipan treats, crisp waffle cookies filled with whipped cream for a Norwegian treat called krumkake, almond tarts with cloudberry cream, caramels, fudge, sandkaker shortbread cookies, and I finally lost track.

He warned me that if one treat fell to the floor due to me moving my ass, I would not get a single treat more. And he'd leave me tied to the table until morning.

That cheeky Krampus devil.

He leans back in his seat, propping his elbow on the chair and lifting his book again to read. Oh, holy holly berries, I'm going to fucking come without him even touching me this time! The buildup for the past hour has driven me crazy. And not just because of how regal and handsome he looks with spectacles perched on his nose while he reads a trashy romance novel to me. After all, I told him monster smut was trending. So, he knows how much this turns me on.

But it's his tongue.

At random times this past hour, the big damn devil snatches a treat from my ass with nothing more than the expert swing of his tongue. Nothing like a frog. He curls the tongue around a treat and slowly and sensually retracts it into his mouth. He repeats with a second treat but directs that tongue to me, only permitting me to open my mouth while he slides the sweet inside. My tastebuds stand up and sing a Klaus-damn Christmas carol every time!

I moan as he does it again, tasting the heavenly flavor of the cloudberry cream with a hint of vanilla, paired with the crisp almond tart.

"He kneaded her ass, careful not to dig in his claws as he tried to control himself," he reads aloud, his voice a velvety husk. "But she made it impossible with how she rubbed against him until he longed to flip her over, bury his raging hard beast of a cock inside her drenched cunt while his tentacles stroked her full, round tits and her swollen, ripe nub. He would show her how a monster could truly fuck."

He pauses to fetch another treat with his tongue, but that devilish bastard knows *exactly* what he's doing when he wags that tongue along the wet folds of my pussy and teases it in a tantalizing circle around my anus.

"Ohhhhh!" I moan, nearly bucking, but I remember his warning. And my pussy's been aching for fulfillment since I started running from him in the cabin while he taught me his pagan traditions.

"Steady, Twyla," he urges me, flicking my back hole a final time before curling his tongue around a shortbread cookie. This time, he gives it to me first.

"Is that even sanitary?" I wonder with a desperate gasp.

"Oh, I assure you, lille stjerne, my tongue is far filthier than your lovely rumpa."

"What a comfort," I drawl and accept the cookie, trying not to imagine him using that tongue on his anus. I moan from the sweet shortbread flavor and crumbly texture that somehow melts in my mouth. No sooner do I swallow than he swats me on my cheek with that wet tongue. "Hey!"

"Don't make me wash that mouth out, kjaere," he warns.

Shut up, Twyla. Don't you dare— "Will you wash it out with eggnog?"

He snorts and swats me on the opposite cheek. "Skitten jente."

I flush and grin, feeling something wet squeezing out of my slit, making it itch. Oh, fuck! I'm not going to make it. I almost want to focus on the grains of the wood table, but Krampus has insisted I spend most of my time focusing on him as he reads.

Using that lithe tongue to turn a page, Krampus continues in that voice I'm convinced he uses for the power of arousal. "She would ride him and scream his name for the whole realm to hear and know that the Wendigo King had fucked the untamable maiden of the mountain. His tribe and her people would know who owned her. Who possessed her. Who ruled over her. And the only monster who could ever fuck her to completion and fulfillment."

“Krampus!” I sob, on the verge of kicking my suspended feet. My pussy tightens, my core kindling with hellfire by now.

“Shh…almost to the end of the chapter.”

Did he seriously just shush me?

“The maiden of the mountain knew this with every fiber of her soul when the Wendigo King pushed into her soaking wet snatch inch by inch until he’d buried himself to the hilt.”

A silent gasp of awe catches in my chest at the sight of his fur shifting and his cock springing free. As huge and erect as the Wendigo King in the story. No, bigger, definitely bigger. With his free hand, he strokes that shaft absentmindedly without so much as an eye blink in my direction. Oh, that fucking fruitcake!

All my extremities turn numb, which I can’t fathom, considering my pussy is about to burst like a molten hot geyser. My inner muscles flutter with need as he describes in intricate detail the carnal nature of Wendigo on human woman fucking. Especially when he seamlessly slips into his Old Norse accent like a rugged echo of the ancient lore of mythic landscapes and heroic deeds. Words that remind me of a longship cutting through an icy fjord. A rhythm as natural as the wind howling through snow-laden pines.

I can almost see the runes rolling through the air like a white-capped wave—and imagine myself a part of his legend. The untamable maiden conquered by the Krampus beast. Well, not a maiden, but when I’ve had nothing but dildos and inferior dicks for the past five years since I moved away from home, my pussy is as close to maidenhood as it can get. Minus a hymen.

Everything around me blurs at the edges. But tingles shiver through my goosebumps and tickles my pores while more heat invades my pussy.

“You will not come until I tell you, Twyla,” Krampus deepens his voice with a low growl erupting in his throat.

"Remember, kjaere. Do not spoil the surprise when you know how much you love my gifts."

"Ugh!" I give a long groan and lightly bang my forehead on the table. A few sweets shift on my ass, seeming to slip, but I clench my glutes, holding them steady. Breathe a sigh of relief right after.

"Flink pike." After he compliments me, Krampus continues, "Rata munn létumk

rúms of fá ok um grjót gnaga;
yfir ok undir
stóðumk jötna vegir,
svá hætta ek höfði til…"

Shivers tremble up my spine with every word he speaks, giving me the English translation of the Old Norse poem about a good maiden who gave Odin a gift. And he returned her 'heroic heart' with 'her spirit troubled sore'. The beauty he enjoyed. And while I don't know the whole context, I do know Gunnloth signifies the sign of Virgo. A poem, a story that has my heart trembling, though I don't know why I should be surprised by him knowing I am a Virgo.

At the end of his recitation, the damn demon growls and lowers his tongue to my ass, sweeping from my back hole down to my labia. I slam my eyes shut as that tongue licks at my wet folds and…ohhhholymistletoe! It splits! That organ actually splits with one extension penetrating my slit while the other lashes at my swollen clit. I let out a high-pitched squeal, followed by a cry. My wrists chafe from how hard I'm clenching at the ropes.

My pussy overheats.

That miraculous tongue folds and curls all around my clit. Through my sweat-drenched hair clinging to my cheeks, I catch the sight of Krampus fisting himself out of the corner of my eye. It makes my nipples harden even more—makes my clit throb and hot liquid pool in my pussy.

A wet squelching sound ruptures from my center as Krampus circles that tongue all around, tasting my inner flesh—lapping and drinking.

I rub my tits against the table, desperate for friction. It's uncontrollable, and my body rises. Pressure mounts, ready to snap. I have no choice but to arch. His tongue is fucking scorching me, burning me from the inside out.

"Krampus, I'm-I'm not, I can't—please!" I sob and wiggle my toes, wanting nothing more than to kick my feet, clench my thighs, and let my whole body jolt.

"Come, Twyla."

All my inner muscles spasm. Convulse around his tongue so hard as hot, torrential waves of orgasmic bliss rip through me, exploding electrical tingles through every muscle and igniting my blood with a riptide of heat like a thousand candle flames. The shrill scream that leaves my throat is so otherworldly, I'm certain some primal creature has taken over my body while I float away on a high of euphoria. Something like hot pudding drowns my cunt. And my ass.

Gasping, panting, whimpering, I turn to see Krampus with a twisted smirk and eyes gleaming to give a whole new meaning to the words "merry and bright". That's when I notice the source of the hot pudding-like feeling on my ass. He charged his release all over my backside, drenching the remaining treats with his eggnog-flavored cum.

As I come down from my orgasm, Krampus retrieves his tongue, snapping it out of my pussy. I lurch but crane my neck with a goofy smile on my face. Because he wags that tongue with a knowing grin before he plucks a cum-soaked marzipan.

"Eat up, Twyla. Every last crumb and drop, kjaere."

This is one command I have no trouble obeying at all.

16
What sort of girl loves monsters…?
KRAMPUS

THE NIGHT BEFORE CHRISTMAS EVE

What is more beautiful than Twyla's grateful smile when I gifted her a new dress is how her eyes light up as I escort her on a tour of the castle town—the one for which the Night Market in Krampus World was modeled. Krampus Haven.

Tonight will be a true test. Perhaps it's why I've held off from bringing her here. Despite how she expressed her desire to visit the Night Market most, she will soon understand how Krampus Haven is different—on a far deeper level.

The cobblestone roadway sweeping down from the castle narrows to the gates of Krampus Haven. Gates formed of massive, gnarled trees twisted together to form a worthy framework. Decorated with carven ornaments, dried fruit, candles, and twinkle lights, the trees echo the dark folklore of my people while reminding us of the growth and light in the depths of winter. With the dense forest on the opposite side of the town, patterning random areas around it, Krampus Haven serves as a refuge for the unwelcome ones. And a sanctum between the realms of the living and the dead.

The lanterns suspended from the lower branches reflect in Twyla's eyes like guiding beacons. More than appropriate since she is my way home.

She sways, sending a rush of heat to my groin with her fine rumpa in the evergreen-colored ruffled skirt that swishes like a bell. Paired with the silver-embroidered white bodice reminiscent of frost on a winter morning and the snug leggings to keep her warm, the dress is perfect for this evening. Aside from the emerald-studded gold combs I insisted upon for one side of her hair—however her protests regarding the opulence—, she's kept her starry curls cascading down her chest.

I look forward to helping her out of the bodice and skirt later this evening.

One wave of my hand commands the trees to shift and twist their branches until the organic gates bid us entry.

Twyla gushes at how the moon's light illuminates the cobbled streets, their stones shimmering with a radiance like starlight. She takes a deep breath, and I know she scents the pine and roasted chestnuts perfuming the air.

"Ooooh!" she practically squeals, takes my hand, and rushes to the nearby vendor selling the chestnuts roasted with cinnamon, sugar, and other spices. Candles flicker upon each end of the wooden stall. The vendor herself wears a dark robe with a hood masking her features, lending to the air of mystery. Tis the season for tourists, after all. Not that we get many *human* ones.

"Two cones, please," I say to the vendor, smirking at the old demoness. "How is my favorite chestnut roaster this evening, Vesperys?"

Twyla tilts her head to one side, narrowing her eyes, scrutinizing the shadowed figure.

"Ack, Lord Krampus, I am the only chestnut roaster you know," she says in her wizened voice before removing her hood.

Twyla parts her lips in awe at the revelation of the creature with her fur, boar-like features, tusks, and breath that escapes in a random snort. Thankfully, Twyla doesn't gasp. Not that I expected her to, considering the weeks she's spent in my castle with similar demon staff like Mephisto. She will simply be treated to more of a variety here.

Just after she speaks, Vesperys turns to Twyla. And she is the one who gasps. Heat sparks within me as the crowds gather. It's not often that I make surprise visits, but this is a special occasion. How I hate spoiling the surprise. My people may consider this a sampler before the grand event tomorrow: the Krampus Eve Ball.

Tonight, I am not the subject of attention. My lille stjerne is.

Before she takes her paper cone housing the roasted treat, she is greeted by a group of Hollythorn sprites.

"Oh, my!" Twyla exclaims as they manipulate the soil around the human's velvet ankle boots, sprouting winter roses and poinsettias to grow in bunches. Curling higher and higher until one rose bloom is tall enough to arrive before Twyla's face.

The woodland fairies chitter to my kjaere in a language she cannot understand. One even I have trouble mastering at times. But their intent is obvious. So, I pluck the rose from its stem and watch Twyla's cheeks heat as I tuck the flower into her combs, securing it for the evening.

Twyla looks down at the sprites, these pale winter woodland creatures with their bodies, tiny and thin as little bones and hair as black as a river at midnight. "Tha—" I cover her small mouth with my large hand before she may finish.

She lifts her brows until I explain, "Those words are for me alone, kjaere. I prefer no others to hold power over you. Nor will you owe a favor to anyone—aside from me." I turn to face her, bearing the fullest force of my countenance upon her. My shadow itself consumes her, and I furrow my brows so she may acknowledge this vital rule of my realm. "Is that understood, Twyla?"

"Understood, Lord Krampus," she says, a little dazed, breathless even.

"Krampus always to you, min stjerne."

The sprites flitter away, off to grow more flowers despite how most will die by the night's end. A consequence of their ability to merely manipulate magic and not control it. Still, they will work tirelessly.

That's when I notice Twyla's eyes practically ricocheting between the dozens of others gathering to get a glimpse of her. Mostly lower demons like Vesperys or house imps and gloomroot gnomes, dwarves, gargoyles, and the rare vampire or two. She doesn't pale under their gazes. On the contrary, she seems to blush even more. The surrounding candlelight conspires to radiate those cheeks, casting a flushed glow upon her skin.

"Your chestnuts, min freyja..." Vesperys alerts Twyla, who spins around, eager for the distraction.

I smirk at how she clamps her lips, remembering my command from a moment ago. But then, she swings her eyes up to mine to ask, "Um...what should I say if I can't...?"

Chuckling darkly at her naivete—this girl who shines like an evening star in my realm—, I lift the backs of my knuckles to brush her cheek and say, "You may express your gratitude or pleasure for the treat. But do not ever use those other words."

Wide-eyed, she nods and turns back to Vesperys, smiles, and samples a chestnut. Her entire expression practically melts. Not one second later, Twyla grabs two more chestnuts and quickly gobbles them up, moaning through her full mouth.

Vesperys snorts her laughter. "That is more than enough gratitude. Have a wonderful evening in Krampus Haven," she adds to Twyla before offering my little sweetheart another cone.

Mouth full of chestnuts, Twyla widens her eyes but snatches up the cone while fluttering her hand in a farewell wave.

As the crowd approaches, I touch the small of her back and nod to the rimefang drakes nearby, clearing them to guard us. While I may be the most terrifying being in the land, the ice-breathing guardians serve as appropriate security. Similar to a half-dragon shifter but without the wings. If anything, their presence will assure Twyla of her protection.

"I like your scales," she chirps to one drake with his silvery-white scales shimmering like molten glass in the moonlight.

The drake regards her with a surprised curiosity. But he doesn't get the chance to do more than lift his brows before she's gasping at the next spectacle.

I crook a grin as she tugs on my wrist, motioning toward the chillspike specters performing in one of many squares scattered throughout Krampus Haven. The frozen apparitions spinning frost to form ice sculptures and patterns in midair mesmerize her.

"Lord Krampus…" the lead specter bows before offering to spin something for min freyja.

Brown eyes wide and eager, Twyla shoves the remaining chestnut cone against my chest and waltzes toward the ghost. A deep chuckle rumbles in my chest as she threads her eager fingers, their tips speckled with cinnamon and sugar.

I nod to the specter and mouth the simple word "stjerne". Then watch as my lady's eyes brighten, and her lips soften into wistful longing as the ghost spins a delicate and intricate crystalline star about the size of a baby's fist—six-pointed and multi-dimensional. Before he lowers it to her waiting palms, the specter casts a breath upon it. One that will spell the star with eternity frost. It will never melt or break.

"It's beautiful!" Twyla gushes while holding it to her heart and smiling at the ghostly figure before her. "I will treasure it always."

"My honor, min freyja."

My cock throbs and aches in my pouch, my need and longing for her spiraling out of control with every passing moment. They adore her. They fucking adore her. Most are content to simply follow and observe. Heat surges in my veins, and I flex my hand before returning it to the small of her back. So tempting to lower it to palm her plump bottom.

But it's probable she would lurch, considering the stripes I gave her earlier this morning are still fresh and raw.

Everywhere we turn, a new experience captures her attention. Luna wisps float about, offering an eerie glow like steady fireflies. The luminescent spirits purr and lilt in a beckoning call to Twyla to follow them deeper into the heart of Krampus Haven. Laughing and straying from my side, she jumps to try and catch a wisp, but the spirits always manage to flutter away before she may capture one. Their soft, eerie glow illuminates her lovely face. I revel in her expressions, how every sensation is new and hauntingly beautiful to her.

What sort of girl loves monsters and plays with the dark creatures of the world that go bump in the night?

So much remains a mystery. All I have are fragments as my magic only grants me a glimpse of a child's life. Twyla was untouched by Klaus. That much I know. But she is also an enigma to my kind. As if she's hidden behind a veil her whole life. A veil that has suffocated her up until the worst of all demons kidnapped her and brought her to his realm.

Frostwraiths perform in another nearby square, drawing Twyla's attention. Formed of ice and mist, the spirits come together to create a group dance of flawless choreography. The stuff of which the most wondrous of ballerinas and choreographers have drawn inspiration without even remembering. My kind are often known to play with gifted humans, to grow such gifts, drink human emotion, and move on. Demon-touched or Fae-touched—we are similar in that regard.

On the opposite side of the square, the ember shades perform their own dance of flames and light while ensuring the firelight throughout Krampus Haven remains lit and warm—from the smallest candle flicker to the roaring fires of the metalworks factory at the edge of the kingdom.

I treat Twyla to a savory stew in a hearty bread bowl, which she consumes on the go—too excited to pause for food. She wants to visit everything. Never tiring. Never showing any boredom or fear, min kjaere stops at every vendor selling their wares. Crafts of delicate, macabre jewelry, carved Krampus figurines for children, intricate tapestries depicting our folklore, and paintings depicting me in all forms, from fearsome beast to misunderstood protector.

"You don't have to buy me everything, Krampus," Twyla scolds me, but she can't hide that charming smile or the blush reddening her cheeks. I've purchased anything that her eyes show longing for and anything her fingers touch, which includes a fair number of dresses, skirts, and hair accessories. I imagine it's the fulfillment of a cosplay dream for her. One I am more than happy to gift.

One thing Twyla truly seems to love is when some demon children scamper toward me, wearing their masks and showing me their Krampus-themed ornaments, which will be added to the town square tree. Despite how the little ones climb on me after I've squatted to greet them, I keep much of my gaze on Twyla. Instead of laughter as one would expect from the amusing sight of the children butting me with their antlers or goat horns and tugging at my fur as I spin them around, my lady is quiet. She still wears a smile, but it's softer. Reverent. Yes, a deep reverence for this moment.

While part of me wonders if it's more than the irony of these moments, considering my reputation, another part may be curious regarding any other thoughts or feelings she may hold. After all, I am a demon. I can buy her whatever she wishes. I can give her a castle. A throne and a crown and the honor and adoration of my people. I can give her pleasure beyond her wildest imaginings.

But I cannot give her a child. At the very least, I cannot give her one her mortal form would be able to bear. And if she desires a child, how could I possibly deny her? To kidnap her, keep her here, but ruin her chances of having a family. Of having a child birthed from her very own womb.

The crowds have not stopped following. No, they've only grown. Not that I can blame them, considering humans rarely come to Krampus Haven. No more than a few in our vast history—ones with far Sight who slipped beyond the magic veil or 'tween traveling seers. Such humans were already demon-touched from birth.

Twyla is new. Twyla is rare. Twyla is special.

The outpouring of her emotions presents a veritable smorgasbord for our kind to consume. I won't deny them the opportunity to feel her whimsical jubilation and heartfelt longing.

When the children finish with me, they surround her. My turn to show reverence as she kneels before them.

"Can I touch your hair?" asks a little boy with large deer ears and small antlers.

Twyla smiles and leans toward him. "Can I touch your horns?"

After the sweet bargain is struck, the boy runs his fingers through her golden curls, which may as well shine like a constellation in the world of Krampus Haven. The boy giggles as she does the same with his horns. I'm well aware of the sensitivity of my own horns. And my many fantasies of Twyla touching them—and gripping them while screaming my name and riding my cock.

Pressure tightens my groin the more I watch her with the children until they've tackled her. She doesn't give one thought over her dress. She simply plays with them as I did.

Fuck, I desire her with every fiber of my magic and monstrousness. I need her. Need those bouncing curls to shower my face with their scent. Need to explore every inch of her body, count her eyelashes, and raise all the hairs on her skin. She possesses my every thought and haunts my dreams.

Once the children have dispersed, Twyla jumps at the chance to have a scryer witch read her fortune through the tarot. No more than a three-card reading.

The Page of Cups is quite fitting, given her free emotions and the inspiration all around her. A card of perseverance, creativity, and intuition.

The Seven of Cups is drawn second. A card that presents several options and advice when confronted with visions and fantasies. A card that shows how treasures and wonders await her, but so do monsters and shadows. A card of caution to separate truth from fantasy and to use care with each choice vs. imagination.

Fuck. The Five of Pentacles is drawn last. Twyla knits her brows into a confused little frown as the scryer witch reveals the card's meaning. One always associated with loss, abandonment, and adversity.

Twyla shakes her head. "That can't be the end. Please…could you draw one more card?" she asks the witch while leaning against me. She seems smaller than ever, barely arriving at my chest. Her breath hitches as the scryer obliges her with a fourth card.

"The Seven of Swords," announces the scryer, flipping it over to finish, "Reversed. The end of lies and deception is soon to come. The truth will be revealed. All will be brought into the light. And one will confess."

Twyla blinks. "What truth? Who will confess?"

The witch merely smiles. "The cards are never so specific, min freyja. Do you wish for me to draw a fifth?"

At first, she bites her lower lip, considering, but ultimately shakes her head. "N-no but I appreciate it."

My lille Virgo. Artistic and kind, of course. But she is not a risk-taker. But as Twyla is distracted by the midnight processions of dancers in full costumes with their antler horns and bone masks, I nod a silent command to the scryer. For, I wish to see the final card. And when it is drawn, I shake my head with a quiet chuff of a laugh. One of disbelief, of wonder, and amusement.

Such a revelation I believe I will keep to myself for now.

After exchanging a knowing smile with the scryer, I depart to join my lille stjerne for the procession as she loses herself in the dance rituals of my people, the haunting rhythm of drums, and the sacred ancient chants of our land.

Just as the well of emotion glistens tears in her eyes, I draw her closer until her back is secure against my chest and pelvis. She leans back, digging her fingers into my fur, which I've allowed to grow more heartily along my arms and sides. Her tears fall onto my hands where I've settled them upon her chest while toying with the ends of her curls.

The fire and ice dancers hold her gaze, but then she swings her eyes to mine. I tilt my head, offering her a smile of approval before wiping the tears from her cheeks. I wish to be here…at her side, always ready to wipe away those tears. Ones of joy. Ones of woe. Ones of hope. It is where the last card left her. Fear of lies and deception but hope for truth and light.

When she lifts her hand to cup the sides of my face, I battle with my raging erection. I swear all the crowds have stilled to watch us, but nothing holds my attention beyond those beautiful brown eyes—intoxicating with their witchlight and wonder.

Slowly, Twyla turns to press herself against me, her body melting against mine. I memorize how she shudders against me, how her eyes never stray from mine, regarding me with affection, gratitude, and tender worship—the likes of which I have never beheld. And ultimately, a heated hunger. Her parted lips, neck arching, and heartbeat thrumming quicker all testify to her desire. A simple kiss of thankfulness.

In the eye of this moment that I wish would last for eternity, I want her more deeply than I have ever wanted anyone or anything. She is the compass of my mind's comprehension. She is the essence of my heart. She is the matter of my very soul. The only one who could ever possibly hold it—and not run in fear.

Aware but careless of the observing and adoring crowds holding us in their gaze, I lower my head to grant Twyla the kiss she longs for.

A scream pierces the magic. And plunges us from the eye of eternity into the walls of a ruinous storm.

17

This is the Krampus of legend. The stuff of children's nightmares.

TWYLA

My first instinct is to reach for Krampus. But he's already brought me into his arms, lifting me with ease as if I weigh no more than tinsel.

"Draug! Draug!" the voice splits the night, freezing all festiveness and revelry—chaos and panic in their place. Whatever the word means, such a response is enough to send fear shuddering through me until I'm clinging to Krampus's fur, wishing I could disappear inside it.

With a deep growl, Krampus strengthens his arms around me and charges through the frenzied crowds. Monster mothers snatch up their children while fathers lead them to safety. The frostwraiths spirit away, becoming one with the ice sculptures. In seconds, ember shades snuff out all firelight from lanterns to the smallest candle.

"Lord Krampus!" a rimefang drake thunders through the chaos, tail swinging like a whip behind him. "Elves have breached the West Woods of the city. A draugr is with them."

The sound of a horn ruptures the night, blaring a warning to the entire town.

Seconds pass while all this happens. The next thing I know, Krampus is forcing the door to a nearby shop open and sets me down in the entryway. It's a costume shop from earlier, where he bought me a Krampus-themed black cape. Run by an old and blind gargoyle with cracked stone skin whose voice echoes her sage but decrepit appearance.

"Nyrith, Azarok, Morvain, Thalgrim!" he bellows the names above the sounds of the town horn, and four rimefang drakes stand at attention, bearing longswords formed of pure ice. "Form a perimeter around this shop. Do not allow anything inside. Varða min freyja."

"Krampus…!" I cling to him tighter. "Please don't—"

He cuts off my speech with a fierce crushing of his mouth against mine. A kiss of such ferocity and possession, I nearly fall back from its power.

"Stay here. Stay inside. You will be safe."

He shuts the door, and a gust of cold wind lashes my face from the motion. Nothing but darkness and the familiar scent of fabric and leather surround me. And my own thundering breath escaping like little tattered ghost orphans. Fear shreds my pulse.

"There now, my Lady," Sythara's voice cracks behind me right before I feel a soft and warm robe placed around my shoulders. I rub my bare arm as her stony fingers fasten the clasp around my throat. "A few elves and a draugr are no match for our Lord Krampus. All will be well soon. It's not uncommon for the elves to disrupt our solstice parades."

"And a draugr?" I wonder, turning to where the gargoyle busies herself—sorting through a nearby rack of clothes forsaken by customers, abandoned for other selections.

"Much rarer, thank Hel. It's quite possible he was drawn to your scent, my Lady. We've never had a human such as you in our Haven."

I marvel as she seems to know exactly what every piece of clothing is and where it must go. But I imagine she's had lots of practice with the various textures and shapes.

Approaching her from the side, I grasp a set of silk pantaloons and ask, "What is a draugr?"

Sythara pauses but returns to her busy work. "A draugr is a revenant who has come back from the dead. But neither ghost or living. Pray you never come to meet one, min frejya. They are dark creatures of death who feed upon live flesh.

They will settle for demon flesh and blood, but human flesh is their favorite delicacy." When I shiver, Sythara must sense it since she reaches over to cup my shoulder. "But you should not concern yourself, Lady Twyla. As I said, Krampus will set things right. I wager it will take no more than a half-hour to drive the elves away and deal with that draugr. The procession will resume soon after. Ack! You useless cinder britches! How did you get out?"

I lower my brows as three little demon creatures with spindly arms and legs, large ears, and tiny wings chase each other around Sythara's legs. No higher than my knee. Their taloned paws leave prints of soot all over the floor.

"Forgive me, min freyja," Sythara huffs and snatches one of the creatures. "I must deal with these sootstoking imps. They are good at keeping house for the most part, especially cleaning chimneys. Ack!" she says, managing to grab another. They kick their legs and fuss in her arms, but the gargoyle is far stronger than they. "But as you can see, they like to cause mischief at times."

The third imp scuttles around my legs, casting cinders and soot along my boots and leggings. Giggling, I lean down and scoop up the little imp before it can manage to escape. It tilts its head, eyeing me curiously. I smile, musing on how its horns remind me of tree branches. The imp flashes its lustrous eyes like yellow flames and chirps and warbles at me. It arches its neck toward me, and I respond, leaning forward until—

"Ow!" I yelp from the creature latching onto the side of my neck with its sharp pricks of teeth. Before I can dislodge the teeth, it lets go and licks at the mark. Little more than a drop of blood. Barely a bite mark. But still, I hand the third imp to Sythara. "It bit me." The imp lolls out its tongue, warbling at me again. "And licked me," I add.

"Oh, soot, that's just their way of saying 'hello'. Must like you, min frejya. They rarely ever bite my customers."

I chuff a laugh. "I'll consider that a good thing then."

"What a mess." She tightens her grip on the imps clutched in her arms. "Excuse me, my Lady. I'll tend to these and be back presently. The pantaloons belong on the second level just up those stairs."

Before I can ask specifically where upstairs, Sythara disappears around the corner of the shop. Shrugging, I approach the nearby staircase and follow the winding wooden steps with the banister of twisted branches to the second-floor landing. The second level is even bigger than the first, and I spend a minute or two hunting through all the clothing racks and shelves for a matching place.

In the corner of the shop, between a wardrobe and a door, I finally discover the small rack for the silk pantaloons, reminiscent of pirate costumes.

Just after I put them away, the sound of crying, of whimpering reaches my ears.

"What?" I wonder softly and hunt through the darkness of the shop, wishing there was more light to guide me, aside from the dim milky moonlight streaming through the nearby windows. "Who's there? Who's crying?"

"M-me," a soft, little voice says from a few steps away.

Several clothing racks lie before me, bundled so closely together, I must hunt through the fabric which thickens in layers to hide whoever belongs to the voice. I follow the sound of those shuddering breaths and whimpers until another sweep of fabric finally reveals the source.

"Oh, there you are…"

My heart goes out to the little one. Her big slitted eyes shine in the darkness like a cat. Her lithe little tail between her legs, the fur sprouting along her body, and her tall ears pricking up all bear similar cat features. While I have no basis for understanding of demon ages, she looks like she's no more than six.

"What are you doing in there?" I ask the cat-like child who sniffs and rubs at her whiskers with clawed fingers.

"I was playing a trick on my mamma, and I hid in here. But then, the horn went off, and everyone left. And I don't know what's going on."

"Your mother left you?" I lift my voice, shocked at the statement, considering how close the families of the village seem.

"We live just down the street," she sniffs and curves her ears low, "and I-I snuck out and followed her here. I was going to pop out and scare her with my new Krampus mask." She taps the little mask on the floor next to her. "I don't know what's going on. I was s-scared, so I just h-hid."

"It's okay. You can come out now." I gesture to her, giving her a soft smile. "Sythara said everything will be fine." I cite the gargoyle's name, hoping the familiarity will help the child.

It seems to work since she flicks her tail out of her legs and crawls out from the layers of clothes. "That's right," I commend her. "Nothing to be scared of now. Krampus will take care of those elves and nasty draugr."

"A draugr!" the cat screeches as soon as she's in my arms, panicking, claws scraping at my dress.

"It's okay!" I try to dispel the frantic cat, but she wiggles her flexible form out from my arms. "We must stay inside. We will be safe," I repeat Krampus's words.

"Nooooo!" she mewls while hissing the more I try to hold her. "My mamma will be outside. She will be looking for me. The draugr is gonna get her. Mamma!"

The cat yowls and lashes her claws at me. Pain splinters through the skin of my upper chest as those claws sink in, causing me to lose my grip. Before I can reach for her, she hisses and scampers away, escaping from me.

"Wait!" My breath is rushed and panicked as the little cat-girl tries the back door, twisting the handle, opening it, and disappearing into the darkness of a back room.

Even as I lunge after her, I half-consider turning back, asking for Sythara's help. Or the rimefang drakes. But she's just a scared little girl. My chest lurches. Nerves rioting with my thoughts. I could never forgive myself if something happened to her. The draugr might not be anywhere nearby. But if any of those elves manage to slip through, a little one like her won't be any match. If they brought the draugr, they could be hunting for any demon flesh. Her little claws won't protect her from a revenant who feasts on flesh.

Then again, nothing will protect me.

I'm slower than her. And I imagine her eyes are far better at seeing in the dark, so I stumble around in this back room that I first think is a storage room for more clothes. But the little flight of stairs leading up to another door is the only exit out of this room. A door that slams open from the little escapee. Cold air surges toward me.

Pushing through the aching of my lungs and the stinging lash marks on my chest, I take the steps two at a time, three at a time before plunging into night.

My eyes adjust to the pale moonlight and thicket of clouds above my head. A scurrying sound to my left catches my attention.

"Wait!" I shout at the little girl as she jumps from the shop's rooftop onto the next one—no more than a few feet of air between them. Simple for a cat, of course.

Blood hammers in my ears, but I hurry after the child. "Please, it's not safe. Come back in. We will find your mother after, I promise!"

She pauses on the next rooftop, her tail flicking manically, her moonstone eyes blinking rapidly. Nothing but fear rules them. My heart curls up in horror because I've seen that look in her eyes. It's the same emotion I felt so many times growing up. Nothing but terror over unseen things preying on me every night when the sun went down.

I was taught to fear the monsters under my bed. I never imagined they would have their own monsters, too.

She darts away.

I leap from the edge of the roof onto the next. Tremors rip through me, but I don't stop. I follow her from rooftop to rooftop until a wrought iron staircase mercifully winds down to the ground. My heartbeat thrashes in my ears as she scampers down the steps. Neither my heartbeat nor her steps can drown out the bloodcurdling sound of guttural growls and the clashing of swords no more than a few hundred feet away from the houses.

Out of the corner of my eye, I catch a glimpse of a battle in the town square. A violent scream claws at my throat, but I hold it in, letting every fiber of terror crawl through me like thousands of spiders beneath my skin. Those are *not* normal elves.

They are not small. They are not old. They are not cute.

These elves—there are so many. They are so pale, their skin is almost translucent. Long dark plaits of hair twist down their backs. They hold swords, clashing them against the weapons of several rimefang drakes.

And there he is. In the middle of the square, dozens of elves with swords raised close in on him. *Krampus!*

I push my horrified scream down, down, down—too afraid of what could happen if I distracted him.

But when he changes, a new scream pierces every thought in my mind and detonates in my ears. Gone is the Krampus I've spent the past three weeks with. Gone is the sexy daddy demon and masculine monster. Yes, I knew he was powerful and had magic. But I never could have imagined he would turn into…this.

When Krampus transforms into this…savage beast, growing more massive and monstrous than I've ever seen, it's enough to strike a thousand birch branch whips of fear into my heart. The kind of fear that is more awe than terror. The fear that demands respect. Long, jagged fangs rupture from his mouth. His tail lashes the air like a whip of powerful corded muscle. His shadow dominates all others. Fur and muscle bombard every part of his body. And his eyes go from the wintry iridescence I love to a carmine blood-red—vowing violence and death upon the elves who have invaded his kingdom.

This is the Krampus of legend. The stuff of children's nightmares. The shadow fiend of Christmas snarling his predatory warning to all. This is who I've been sleeping next to every night for the past three weeks.

Seconds must pass because the sound of the cat girl's footsteps echoes on the wrought iron steps, jarring me to attention. The last thing I make out is the sight of Krampus crushing elf skulls and shattering swords while unleashing a great roar of thunder throughout the city. Ten times louder than the warning horn.

I take off after her.

By the time I make it to the ground, she's rushing around the corner and down a side alley. Her long tail swings behind her, much like the robe Sythara gave me. The robe is already torn thanks to a sharp pinion on the wrought iron stairs.

The tail is inches from me now. I'm so close to grabbing it, prepared to haul the little girl into the nearest building.

At the last second, she careens to the left through a thick group of gnarly trees. All rational sense tells me to turn back. She's not my responsibility. I've given her every opportunity to turn back. She is fast and can run away better than I can defend myself…much less catch her.

I'm placing myself in too much danger. I'm disobeying Krampus.

I shiver, my blood chilling at the thought of coming face-to-face with the draugr. But the thought of something happening to the little cat-girl pierces me to my bone marrow. She may be fast, but if that thing grabs her…I can't. I can't leave her.

I've already left too many behind.

The trees become far more than a grouping. Apprehension floods me with the knowledge that this patch of woods has transformed into a whole forest. The twisted, macabre trees are like black ghosts clawing for me. Their branches lash at the robe and my dress, biting, ripping, piercing.

A whimpering mewl splits the night a few feet ahead of me. Somehow, I've managed to keep the girl's tail within line of sight this whole time. But I'm closing in on her. If fortune and Christmas spirits are on our side, I'll be able to snatch her and drag her back to a safe hiding place. If the draugr can't climb trees, my next plan will be to get as high as I can. And scream to the almighty heights for Krampus.

For some reason, the scryer's tarot reading flickers in my memory—the Seven of Cups urging me to separate fantasy from reality. And remember that rescue is unlikely. Because I must depend on myself for strength and rescue myself like I always have. Survive like I always have. They always said I was too weak, too little, too emotional.

Blocking out those dark voices of my past, I focus on the girl who swings to the right. One glimpse back shows me just how far we've strayed from the city. No firelight signals its presence, but I can make out the chimneys and watchtowers.

I stop dead in my tracks. Because there is no way this girl is leading me to her home a block away. These woods are so dense and foreboding, the moonlight doesn't even shine here. The scent of decay thickens the air.

When a low, deep growl off to my right shivers all the nerves in my system, I take one step back.

"Please do not run, Twyla Eyres," a familiar voice emerges in the darkness, close to the source of the growl. "While I maintain control over every creature in my realm, not even I can control a draugr in the middle of unquenchable blood thirst if he senses prey. If you run, he will have no choice but to hunt you."

I search the haunting trees with eerie skeletal branches stretching out as if eager to imprison me. "Show yourself," I demand, but my voice is too soft to be intimidating.

I'm not surprised by the crimson-red robes like waterfalls of blood. Or the wrinkled skin and white beard of an old man. Or even the twinkling blue eyes and hearty red of his cheeks. Klaus is much taller than me, and despite his jolly-seeming presence, it's still intimidating and off-setting enough to have my chest squeezing and my hands rushing to hold myself.

But it's the draugr next to him that strikes terror into every last heartstring. The undead revenant is little more than a reanimated corpse with decayed flesh clinging to its bones. But the spectral glow of its eyes, pale and blue as deathly lips, proves the sense of an otherworldly predator. One with supernatural strength. It's more than just a creature. More than just an undead monster. It's a harbinger.

And I've fallen right into its trap.

With the frosted wind echoing its eerie whispers and projecting the draugr's heavy breaths like foul vapors to drift toward me, I want nothing more than to scream at the top of my lungs for Krampus. But I'm not stupid. Screaming would be equal to running for this dark creature. So, I hold myself together as much as I can. Staring down the superior power next to the revenant.

A movement to the right catches my attention. The cat-girl appears from behind a nearby tree, swinging her tail.

"Get out of here!" I cry out, only for my spirit to sink from the confirmation of my suspicions as she bounds toward Klaus.

"Excellent work, Nyctra," Klaus commends the cat-girl, who purrs her appreciation. I lower my brows, hurt and frustration filling me as Klaus drops a velvet pouch into her paws. When she opens it, her eyeshine lights up, reflecting off the gold in the pouch. "Run along now."

I narrow my eyes upon her, but when she meets my gaze for a fleeting moment, something in me softens as if remembering she's just a child. But it still doesn't stop me from saying, "I hope you hack up a thousand hairballs when karma comes for you. Bad kitties shouldn't get presents."

She snarls low and answers, "They also shouldn't get beat with birch whips and tied up in a sack and dragged to the underworld, which Krampus did to my older brother. All because my family was poor and couldn't pay his demon tax. And because we left all his dark, evil beliefs behind. Heir Klaus gave us sanctuary in his kingdom. And he still is." She hisses and scampers off into the night, tail disappearing behind her—in the opposite direction of Krampus Haven.

Her profession leaves me bewildered, and my eyes lower to the ground. I don't want to believe it. Krampus said he was forced to do all this. Never wanted to do any of this. I remember his conversation with Klaus, how I eavesdropped before Krampus beat him bloody until I ran. He's never mentioned anything about a tax. Or anything about those who choose Klaus over him.

My eyes flick back to the draugr whose nostrils flare as he scents me. "So, what now? Will you send my body back to Krampus in pieces after he's done with me?" I gesture to the monster next to him.

"Believe it or not, Miss. Eyres, I do not wish you any harm or ill will. I apologize for the deception, but I knew you had a good heart and would follow the little one. And my magic, much like Krampus's, operates within the world of bargains and gifts. And I wish for nothing more than to give you a gift. If you accept, of course..."

I cross my arms over my chest, huddling into the robe for warmth. "I can assure you I like Krampus's gifts much more than yours. Especially since you never bothered to show up during my whole childhood." Frustration laces my tone because it's easier to feel the heat of anger than the cold, raw grief.

"True, but neither did he. Who do you think kept him away from your family all those years, Twyla? Your family was so dedicated, so committed to abiding by the purest and most sacred ways, they refused to take part in any traditions...no matter how watered down and commercialized. Those traditions became the compromise my followers chose, all so they could reach more who belonged to Krampus. They even tried to banish him, but I refused to hear of it. A being as powerful as Krampus cannot be swept under the rug and merely forgotten."

"No, you just preferred a caricature," I spit out.

Klaus heaves a sigh, shoulders lowering, palms out. "He was always a caricature, Twyla. That's why he was created. A monster to frighten all other monsters. A demon to rival all demons. More fearful than any Hallow's Eve ritual or mask. I never wished to destroy such a belief. I do not wish to destroy him now. Just the opposite. Our interests are far more aligned than you know."

Livid heat reddens my cheeks, and I clench my hands into fists. "If those interests involve attacking the innocent within Krampus Haven, I'd rather not align with you at all."

"I assure you that sacrificing my elves solely for the opportunity to speak with you alone was no simple choice, Miss. Eyres. One they agreed to, knowing they would go to their deaths. Krampus is too strong to be conquered, and I summoned the draugr back after the horn was sounded. And because I believe you have a good heart and do not wish for any sacrifice to be in vain, I will beg you for a few moments of your time."

"For what?"

"Simply to listen. I ask for nothing else. I will not force you to accept my gift. I will make no threats. Upon my honor as a bishop, which I have carried for centuries, I will not lie to you. After I've shared my gift with you, you may turn around and return to Krampus with no ill emotions, delays, pressure, or force to make you stay." He deepens his eyes, and every wrinkle in his face seems to soften.

At first, I consider turning around right now. But he is right about one thing. If he did all this on my account—no matter what I may assume about the nature of the elves battling Krampus—I will not let blood be shed in vain. In any case, it will be a good test to determine if he keeps his word. If he takes me by force at the end of this, nothing will stop me from screaming for Krampus. And if I bide my time and keep him talking, the greater the chance that Krampus will find me. If nothing else, he could destroy this very draugr while ordering Klaus to leave me alone.

So, I drop my arms to my sides, and bristling, I deadpan with him to say, "Go on."

Klaus first looks to the draugr and lowers his voice in a deep command, "Return to the Shadows."

With a menacing growl and those spectral orbs shimmering my way a final time, the revenant turns and stalks away into the night, vanishing into thin air. Gooseflesh still prickles my flesh in the ghostly corpse's wake.

"It is true, Twyla," Klaus begins. "I am ultimately responsible for the era when Krampus became the tool used to frighten and punish children. It was a far better and more effective method than allowing evil to reign."

I wrinkle my nose. "And who gets to determine whether beating a child will result in preventing evil…or creating more of it?"

"For centuries, I believed in this form of justice and discipline. After all, if you knew that a disobedient and horrible child would turn into a genocidal dictator responsible for the Holocaust, wouldn't you apply a firmer hand? Wouldn't you want the child to know right from wrong and understand evil deeds have consequences?"

The words dig like barbs deep into me, bleeding me open with words I learned every day and night of my childhood. A thousand memories splinter through my thoughts. I try to hold them back like a dam with reminders of how I left all that behind me and carved my own way in the world just as several of my older siblings did. I left home. I worked hard for a journalism scholarship and a paid internship with Colton Enterprises. I got my own apartment when all my friends lived with roommates to share the load.

I did *all* of that. On my own.

"Regardless of your answer," Klaus continues and steps toward me with his body to the side, non-threatening, mouth and jaw soft, "not even I am immune to growth and change. Just as my followers have changed and thrown aside so many of their rigid and strict belief systems. I wish this was the case for Krampus. But the ancient ways of the world are much more difficult to change. But I still gave him a chance. One hundred years of them."

He then turns to me, fixating his eyes on mine as if to prove their truth. "He entered the bargain of his own free will. I have given him nearly a century to redeem himself. He used it to create Krampus and Christmas World, choosing wealth while imposing taxes to fund those amusement parks. While entertaining, such parks are not enough to hold back the ancient evil of his bloodline.

"Krampus is a demon, a monster—something he has never denied. And while I have given him nearly a century, evil cannot truly sleep. It is always there, waiting to rise again."

"He's not evil." I shake my head in denial but find myself wrapping the robe tighter around my frame.

"He will be."

Klaus steps toward me. I flinch, almost stepping back until he lifts a small snow globe to my face. With one wave of his hand, the snow flurries swirl, then clear to show Krampus. The Krampus I saw upon the rooftop. But even worse. The most hideous and horrific monster to ever walk the earth.

This Krampus does not merely scold and scare naughty children. This Krampus is worse than the Bogeyman, worse than the Devil himself. A demon who preys on children in their beds and gives them living nightmares. A monster who destroys every light and turns Christmas into nothing but darkness. Like the cold, dark Christmases of my past.

Tears sting my throat and cut through my eyes. "That's not him. That's not Krampus," I whisper.

"No, it is not, Twyla. This is *your* Krampus."

"What?" My voice cracks through my tears.

"Once the bargain ends and the curse of hell reverts to Krampus, the curse I've held back with my own blood all these years, it will be far worse than what it could be. Because of you. None of this is your fault, Twyla. Please understand that. You did not ask for this." He closes the distance between us. "Krampus kidnapped you and brought you to this realm of monsters and shadows."

Monsters and shadows...just like the Seven of Cups card. I shiver as Klaus draws me into his arms and embraces me. He smells like gingerbread cookies, fresh milk, pine, and all the things you'd expect of Santa Clause/St. Nicholas.

"But if a demon like him experiences any fraction of light and love, when his old nature returns, it will create such grief and rage inside his soul, no force will stop him from unleashing a new Dark Age upon the world."

I part my lips, a gasp catching in my aching chest. I don't want to believe it.

"Do you understand why all the monsters of Krampus Haven adored you so? It is because you are the first human in their realm they could feed upon. Krampus and his kind feed on emotions just as the draugr feed on flesh. And human emotion is the sweetest treat for them."

Bile churns inside me as my stomach twists and turns. That is why so many followed me and stared at me. And...I let them. I felt it. I wanted to give so much of myself to them...as I have given myself to Krampus.

"Yes, you see now, Twyla..." Klaus continues, his lips pressed into a firm seam. "Krampus has been feasting ever since he met you. After such a feast, he will want more. Darkness always wants to feed on light. Evil always wants to feed on good. Your emotions will not be enough. So, he will take from every child he can find, for children have the most potent emotions."

My throat burns from acid. And I cover my mouth to hold in the sobs.

"It is why I am here, sweet young Twyla. Because you do not deserve this."

He leans away only so he may cup my chin. By now, I'm shaking, shattering at the vision I've just seen. Nothing but the weakest of stitches holds my heart together.

"When?" I whisper.

"By the time the sun rises on Christmas Day."

My heart sinks to my stomach. Because it's already Christmas Eve.

"It is natural to dream, Twyla Eyres," Klaus assures me. "You have been dreaming all your life. And no one appreciates and loves a dreamer more than I. But not even I can make certain dreams a reality. At some point, one must perceive reality from fantasy and come back to earth. One must choose what is right and not what one wants. Sometimes, there is no happily ever after. Sometimes, nothing but darkness waits for you in a land of monsters and shadows."

The Seven of Cups. Monsters and shadows. If I don't differentiate between fantasy and reality, if I don't use care with each choice, if I don't stop giving into my imagination…it will be the Five of Pentacles. Darkness and adversity.

Ice fills my veins and chills every drop of my blood. All I want to do is fall to the ground.

"Hope still remains, Twyla. Just as you never lost hope every Christmas Eve of your dark childhood."

"H-how?"

"Take this with you." He offers me the snow globe. "If you shake it before midnight at the Krampus Eve Ball, all of this, from the moment you entered the gates of Krampus world, will be but a dream to you. Krampus will have no memory of you. You will have no memory of him but a figment of your imagination. There will be no loss. No grief. No rage. No dark emotions. This dream will end. But…some dreams are within my power to grant."

He waves his hand. Again, the snow flurries, swirls, and reveals a new dream. The one I've worked so hard for. A good job. The byproduct of hard work and years of education while living in a shitty apartment and surviving but never truly living. This time, there would be living. A living wage. A journalist title at Colton Enterprises. Congratulations and cheers from my friends. Pride and respect from my parents who said I could never make it on my own.

"How do I know this is true?" I test Klaus. Everything he says makes sense, but I'd be a fool not to try and confirm.

"Ask him yourself, Twyla Eyres. Ask Krampus if he made a bargain with me and if his curse will return. He will resist sharing with you because he is bound by blood to speak the truth. But do not stop until he confesses his curse to you."

He takes my palm, opens it, and places the snow globe inside. "Then, all you need to do is shake it at the ball, and all will be revealed. Krampus will have no power over you. He will have no choice but to let you go.

"This is the truth, Twyla. *Your* truth. The light in the darkness waiting for you. Look deep into yourself, Twyla. Isn't this more realistic than a mortal girl yoked to the monster of all monsters and living happily ever after as a human queen of demons?"

With every word he's spoken, pieces of my heart have shattered. Like the Seven of Swords – Reversed has splintered its power into me, cracking my imagination and fantasies and the lies I've been believing for the past three weeks.

Who am I kidding? All this time, it was a dream. A sweet and dark holiday dream. But the holiday always ends. And the day after Christmas, the Christmas spirit grows dim. The magic fades. The fantasy must end.

It's all been a lie. A lie I've been telling myself, wanting so much to believe. But I don't belong here. How could a monster like Krampus keep a human like me for a queen?

If the vision of the new Dark Age is true, how can I possibly risk such a thing all because I'm living in an impossible dream that can never come true? Klaus is offering me a real dream. One I've spent the past eight years working toward.

"The last thing I want is for you to be hurt," Klaus tells me, tapping the snow globe and tucking a curl behind my ear. "But if you stay with Krampus when dawn appears on Christmas Day, when the curse and his blood return, nothing will stop him from trying to destroy the only light shining in the darkness of his realm.

I am truly sorry I could not come to you during your childhood, Twyla. This is my way of making amends. I owe you so much more. You deserve so much more. But this is the one gift I can grant you. By the laws of my blood and power, all you need to do is shake this globe.

"It's time to wake up and let go of the dream. I know you will make the right choice. You have a good heart." He cups my shoulder, squeezing it and spreading a warmth into my chest. "You wish to spare him any pain and loss as much as yourself. If he doesn't remember you, he will have no memory of those emotions. And perhaps, I may even form a new bargain with him. He can return to Krampus World and feed on the emotions of the adoring public as he's done for nearly a century. Is everything…clear to you, Twyla?"

I don't look up. I keep my gaze on the frost and dark tree roots along the ground. But I nod. Then, I place the snow globe in the inner pocket of the robe since it's small enough to fit and conceal.

"You're a good girl, Miss. Eyres. I must leave now, but I will be nearby to help you find your way home."

Klaus turns away. I hear his footsteps crunching on the frosted ground. I don't look up from the ground. But I hear the familiar pounding of the earth, signaling *his* approach.

I wrap the robe around myself as much as possible, dry my tears, and put on a mask of relief as Krampus thunders his way toward me, growling through his rushing footsteps. He's not the monster I saw in the square. But he's close between his fangs still showing and the blood mottling every inch of his fur.

"Twyla!" Relief mirrors his features, but a moment later, they twist and bleed to rage. "I fucking told you to stay inside!"

"Krampus, I—"

Before I can finish, he plucks me from the ground and hurls me over his shoulder. I don't fight him. I give him no excuses for running off. I'll take whatever punishment he wants to give me. One I know will be different than all the others.

It's not like I'll remember it anyway.

With tears falling below me, I hold tight to the monster of monsters. And count the moments until the fantasy ends and I find my way home.

18

She must understand what it means to be mine.

KRAMPUS

I don't take her back to the castle.

I can't let this go. Not this time.

All my muscles cord tight as war drums and hotter than coals in hell as I carry her deeper into the forest. A power imbalance exists between us, unlike at any other time. Her blatant disobedience, regardless of any circumstance…she doesn't understand how close I came to destruction. One glimpse of her on that rooftop as she was running away from me nearly ended with a dozen elf swords cleaving me to pieces. I still feel the sharp fire of their weapons piercing my flesh.

It was nothing compared to how she pierced my heart at that moment.

Her breathing is heavy, reaching my ears from where I hold her little body still hauled over my shoulder. I'd expected more of a struggle, but she is mercifully still and quiet—apart from the occasional whimper that pulls at my heartstrings, straining the strands holding the cursed organ in my chest.

She must understand what she did tonight—how she put all of Krampus Haven in danger. And what she did to me. Faen! I could consider nothing else but the vision of her golden curls fluttering behind her like butterflies of starlight. My blood still burns like sulfur. Muscles, still primed for a fight.

In some ways, this battle will be infinitely worse.

"K-Krampus?" Her voice is so weak, it's barely above a cracked whisper.

"No," I growl the one word.

"P-please, I-I just want to know…are they all right? Was anyone hurt?"

I pause in my tracks but don't lose sight of my goal. Nor the responsibility and authority I must command over her. But…

Faen. Faen. Faen. *Fuck. Fuck. Fuck.*

Hun vil være døden for meg. *She will be the death of me.*

"No," I say in a low voice, lower and deeper than any I've used with her. One that triggers her to shiver. "No one in Krampus Haven was hurt. But you will be tonight, Twyla. Do you understand?"

"Y-yes."

Flink pike.

I don't stop until I've arrived at the ruins. The temple that once existed to worship the Goddess Hel. My mother.

Now, it stands as a desolate ruin of cracked and weathered stone. Solemn decay. Haunted honor. A melancholy beauty.

By the time I approach the soaring arch that stands as a testament to the entryway with its intricate carvings depicting souls in various stages of passage, Twyla has broken down. She has become trembling flesh and tears staining her cheeks.

Tonight, I will break her further. She must understand what it means to be mine.

I embark past the threshold and carry her deeper into the heart of the ruins, where a cavernous expanse awaits. Ancient altars, crumbling pillars. Moonlight splinters through the shattered windows, bathing the surroundings with eerie yet ethereal beams. Frost gilds every stone, shimmering crystalline radiance in the moonlight. To this day, the faint aroma of incense drifts in the air. And ravens still caw their deep and lyrical calls in memoriam of Hel.

I take my lille stjerne into the central chamber. When her whimpers grow quiet, and the trembling fades, I wonder if she senses the reverence of this place. And what it means to me. My mother's likeness shows itself within the grand mosaic with the duality of her nature. Radiant pale skin like moonlight on one side with a silvery cascade of long hair.

Her other half is the living corpse. Skeletal features of rot and decay and shadows dark and deep as the abyss. She never loses her cold and pitiless expression. One that represents her sole dominion over the living and dead—neither good nor evil. She simply is. My mother… always reminded me of light in the darkness and the duality of life and death. The beauty and morbidity that define all souls.

Tonight, I will strip Twyla down to her roots, unveil them, expose them, and discover how she will shine within such darkness.

I slowly lower her to the ground, facing her toward the great altar. While all of nature has laid claim to the temple, the altar remains an ode to the sacred energy of life and death which still defines it. I already sense the hairs prickling to life upon Twyla's skin, a sign she can feel that energy from which none may hide.

No matter how much I wish to prepare her, encourage her, or comfort her in some respect, I cannot. Resisting the urge to so much as comb my fingers through her curls, I lower my head to her ear and command in the voice I dredge from my birthplace in the Underworld itself, "Turn and face me."

She does. Not once do her eyes lower despite their obvious struggle with the film of tears swelling within them.

"Remove your clothes, Twyla. Now."

A tremor rips through her. At first, I'm concerned she will try to run. But she steals my breath with the sight of her sweet submission. A trust she still bears for me as she immediately undoes the clasp on the velvet robe and slowly lets it pool to the ground next to her.

Her quivering fingers inch to her back where she works at the laces of her bodice. It's one time where I don't help her immediately. No, I test her.

She holds my gaze the whole time. In and out of minutes until I imagine her fingers ache. Her breaths turn ragged, her pulse thrumming chaos in her veins, but not once does she look away. Those brown eyes, somehow manage to glimmer like a gloaming in the darkness.

At last, the bodice is loose enough for her to tug it free. Nothing more than strapless slips of transparent lace hold her swelling tits. I watch the chiffon sleeves slip down her arms and the bodice catches on her abundant thighs beneath her skirts.

Now, I close in, reveling in how she flinches. She is right to fear me. But she also respects me. It's why she does not look away as I help her with the skirts. Yes, I will stretch her boundaries to the breaking point. Yes, I am a monster. But I am *her* monster. Bound to her with every breath in my lungs and every beat of my heart.

A few moments later, she stands in nothing more than the leggings and boots and lace covering her breasts and her cunny—already damp from her juices…and endorphins no doubt. One hand touches her wrist as if centering herself, keeping her rooted to the ground as her eyes remain rooted to mine.

I imagine what I must look like to her. My beastly shadow devours hers. Halfway between the monstrous warrior she must have seen from that rooftop and the demon of the Underworld. The craze in my pale spectral orbs. More creature of the abyss than the demon man of muscles and fur she has slept with every night for weeks.

Her beauty and bravery in this desolate place astound me. Hunger tightens a hideous pressure in my groin. Du er så vakker. *You are so beautiful,* I wish to tell her. But I won't disrupt the ritual of these moments.

"Your boots, Twyla," I direct her.

The moment she bends to reach for them, I seize her wrist. Just enough force that she gasps but tender enough to show her who I still am. And what she means to me.

"Lean against the altar. And give them to me," I command.

When her dainty hands cling to the edge of the altar, it prompts her back to arch and her breasts to thrust into the air. She obeys my word, lifting her first boot, which I slide off her small foot before doing the same with the other. I love how she trembles most when I set my fingers on those leggings and slowly peel them off her hips and slide them down her legs.

Gazing up at her the whole time, I print my lips to her belly, her hips, and the ripe, thick thighs I adore. I memorize the sight of her breath cleaving and heaving as she stares back at me, her lips parting, her brows lifting in astonishment. Perhaps she believed I would simply claw the clothes off her body and beat the hell out of her.

I fully intend to whip her ass until her flesh nearly bleeds tonight. But she needs to witness the monster that is Krampus in his unabashed form—holding complete control and sovereignty over her. Tonight, she will bare herself in ways beyond skin and flesh so that I may reinforce the connection between us.

Once I break her down and shatter her old self, I will build a new foundation where she will rise and shine…for me and her.

At last, she stands before me, pale and naked in the moonlight. My silver star in the darkness. For a long moment, I simply stare at her, treasuring her body, worshiping every curve, every shadow, every shiver dragging gooseflesh to the surface of her skin. Her eyes seek mine. They blink once, freeing a trail of glittery tears.

I close in again. Her breath hitches as I back her straight up against that altar and lower my mouth to the curve of her neck. Her pulse gallops to my touch. My fur tickles her belly, her breasts until she's flush against me, melting against me.

I claim her mouth. Sealing my great one over hers, I consume all her breath and tattered moans and lay siege to her tongue in pure conquest. A hint of what is to come. Tonight, I will take Twyla Eyres's heart and soul. And on Christmas Day, I will reward her and take her on my cock. I want to bury it inside her now. Fuck her amid this sacred beauty because she is the one being worthy of it.

When she parts her lips and tips her head more, it's a sign of her trust. So, I slip my tongue along her jawline, down the curve of her throat, and arrive at my target where the line of her neck meets her shoulder. I sink my teeth in. I bite. A desperate hiss escapes from her throat, followed by a needy whimper. I bite hard enough that it draws a faint prick of blood. A print I seal with my tongue, kissing the wound but lacing it with my venom. It will forever leave a scar.

Finally, I swing her around to face the altar. "Put your hands at each corner."

She stretches them until her limbs nearly protest. Her golden hair ripples down her back like a curled constellation.

"Spread your legs. Wider. Wider. Yes," I commend her once she is in position. "Now, drape your upper body upon the altar."

When she hesitates and inspects the stone as if wondering what sort of offerings once graced it, I unleash a low growl, fist her hair, and firmly lower her form onto the dust-coated stone.

Now, I bind her. I always bring rope with me. And it requires no more than a single thread for me to grow multiple lengths with my magic. It takes little time for me to tie her to the altar. To avoid any damage to her flesh and muscles, she must be firmly in place for the punishment I will inflict upon her.

Next, I secure the red leather gag in her mouth, latching it around her head beneath her strands to protect her teeth.

She shivers when I catch hold of her hair. After breathing in her scent, I scatter her curls along the altar like twinkling treasure—then press my lips to the back of her neck, then her shoulders. And trail my breath along her back, following the curve of her spine. The plump globes of her buttocks tighten in anticipation of my touch. She does not revile me. That is significant.

When I rise, I notice her hard swallow, her throat constricting. A cold sheen of sweat breaks out along her body, glistening her opalescent skin. She tenses more, so I wait.

I stroke her curls and wait for her to melt. The more relaxed she is, the less pain she will bear. One hand sifting through her hair while my other stations at the base of her spine, anchoring, centering, grounding. I touch her as if she's a sacrament—she is the most blessed one.

Finally, Twyla's breaths deepen. Her limbs turn from locked to loose. She touches her cheek to the stone and closes her eyes with a heavy sigh.

I crack the birch whips, striking without mercy or warning. No warm-ups. After the first three, she wails through the gag. I rain down a barrage of Underworld fire and ice upon her ass, vibrating clear through to the bone. Her heartbeats skip between each blow.

Despite how I observe her vision blurring, her sobs, her aching groans, I memorize the way she shudders, how her burning tears fall, and the sight of her skin flushing. Each welt creates beauty upon her flesh. A swollen, burning mosaic on her backside. A masterpiece of inflamed art on her skin—one only an expert like Krampus can perform.

After her perfekt rumpa, I lash her thighs. Slick has already gathered on them. Her pussy folds drip with each burning strike of my birch whips. Jævla gjennomvåt for meg. *Fucking soaked for me.*

A few stripes on her back.

As her breaths turn staccato and saliva trickles from her mouth, I pause. And let the blistering lashes breathe. Twyla's eyes turn vacant—lost in endorphins. Before her eyes can roll to their ceilings, I unlatch the leather gag and remove it from her mouth.

Her teeth chatter as she opens her mouth. "Kr-K-Krampus, I'm s-so—"

I whip her again, transforming her sob into a high, shrill wail. From her hips all the way down to her thighs again, I strike the smoldering whips. This is different than all other punishments. I always wove pleasure into the pain as those were discipline. This goes beyond discipline. It's to teach her a lesson.

She will feel my anger searing into her with every strike. I saw a glimpse of her—running away on that rooftop. Just like the other night she ran from me. Every cell in my body and every fiber of my being centered on her. Like my gods-damned touchstone.

Jeg kan ikke leve uten deg. *I can't live without you.*

She is the center of my flesh and blood. She is the ghost haunting my every thought. She is the dream of my heart who lights up my darkness like the last bright star before dawn. And the salvation of my soul.

Jeg er forelsket i deg. *I'm in love with you.*

Words I don't speak but ones I preach down to my cursed soul and will her heart to hear them.

I reduce her to a quivering, catatonic mess of adrenaline stoking her hot blood, raw nerve endings, and a liquefied pussy. Damn right, everything is mine.

The second I touch her flaming cunt, she throws her head back with a squeal. I descend. Kneeling before her, I take my place on the threshold below her and tongue the blazing globes of her ass, licking at the hurt. More juices drip from her slit. She flexes her weary muscles.

I do nothing more than touch my fingers to her slippery cunny. It's obvious she desires my tongue, but I will have hers first. "Twyla…" I tease my finger around her drenched slit, summoning her attention.

"Krampus?" she whispers, her cheek not forsaking the stone.

"You will give me your darkness tonight." I press my lips to her inflamed skin, savoring her shiver.

Why did she climb onto her roof every Christmas Eve to wait for a holiday miracle that never came? Why did she hide a little snow globe behind the vent in her room? Why does Twyla Eyres shine with wonder over everything related to the spirit of the season, from the light to the dark?

"I…I…I grew up in a cult."

Almost awed by the ease of her confession, I continue to lick at the wounds. For every word she shares, I will fuse my magic into the hurt and heal the marred skin. A testament to how she may find her refuge, her haven in me. I will care for her as greatly as I torture her.

"Not the kind with black robes and blood rituals. That would have been too interesting. Too validating to others." She moans from how I suck the base of her buttocks. "Ours was the cult that never ate pork, never went dancing, and never…celebrated…one…holiday," she finishes in a gasping string of breaths.

I reward her profession by capturing her swollen clit with my fingers. Gasping, she rolls her hips, struggling and begging silently for her pleasure.

"Go on, Twyla."

"I was the bad girl who never got caught. You see…we weren't allowed to know about holidays. I was pulled from school if there were any Halloween or Christmas-themed activities. My mother would burn any crafts I brought home. I couldn't participate in cookie exchanges or Secret Santa gifts. My dad slammed the door in carolers faces. Our house was the darkest on the block, in the neighborhood. From hell, all holidays came, and to hell, they could go."

I increase the pace and pressure of my fingers, stoking her blood to mirror my hot rage. A sharp wind spreads her curls around her face, where they cling to her cheeks—damp from her sweat.

Wherever religion is spread, there are always weapons of fear and shame.

"It just made me more curious, Krampus. I was the little rebel who tried to hide a book on the pagan rites and customs of popular holiday traditions. When my father found it, I was spanked and sent to bed without supper. Things like that…happened a lot. One year, it was candy canes. Another year, it was mistletoe. My snow globe was the only thing they never found. And my journals…my stories. I wrote down whatever truths I could find and hid them beneath the floorboards of my bedroom. They're still there."

A born investigator. So determined to sort the truth from the lies, ever seeking the light in the darkness.

This time, I pump my fingers inside her, and she lurches. Her inner muscles spasm. She's on the verge of convulsing.

"Why?"

"Mmm…I guess when I left home, when I left my family, got my scholarship, worked two jobs, and gave up all semblance of a social life for years, I guess it was my way of leaving a piece of myself there. A piece the cult could never take away. Like…a…"

"A little light in the darkness," I finish for her and touch my lips to her pretty wet folds. I trail the tip of my tongue along her plump labia but stop short of her clit. "And when you grew up, min kjaere?"

As she tells me how she worked toward her journalism degree, only to end up as an intern at Colton Enterprises, I edge her. Anytime she clenches those muscles, cresting the peek to her orgasm, I rip it away until she thrashes and moans, straining at the ropes binding her. Her breath bursts, competing with the wind.

“I was finally getting back to something close to living. The daily grind, just so we can pay our bills never gives us life. It’s all the little things. Like crafting a beautiful costume and eating roasted chestnuts and sipping eggnog and…reading monster romance.”

Min vakre jente. *My beautiful girl.*

Somehow, she’s managed to find the silver linings no matter how thick and dark the clouds. If I could, I would rip every star loose in the sky, grind them up, and place them in a new snow globe for her to shake to shimmery life whenever she desires. All she’s ever desired is a happily ever after.

Hers begins tonight.

I bury my face in her drenched pussy. And listen to the sounds of her whimpers and sobs transforming into wails, shrieks, and screams. Again and again, I bring her to that razored edge. Faen—a diamonded edge. My cock has never been harder. Harder than ore in the Underworld.

I peel the hood back and work at her swollen nub, stroking and flicking it back and forth with my tongue. And coiling the organ around it, maintaining its pressure while sliding the tip into her inner channel. So fucking hot and wet, spasming with desperate need.

At some point, she loses her voice from the cold wind lancing her vocal cords. She becomes nothing but frazzled breaths, ragged whimpers, and thick, raspy moans.

“Please…for the love of all Hel, please, Krampus!” she begs me.

Oh, faen! The sound of her invoking my mother’s name in her temple and on the altar has my cock breaking through the barrier of my pouch until it springs free.

Electricity volts through me. Another vicious tremor ruptures through her.

I rise. Flattening my chest to her back, I whisper in her ear, “Come,”. Now, I coil my tongue around her luscious thigh and train all its attention on her soaked, ripe clit. And the moment she throws her head back against my shoulder, I rub my crown along her puffy, wet folds.

"Krampus!" she screams her release at the top of her lungs.

She unravels me. A deep guttural groan leaves my throat, followed by a snarl as I press my cock against her center, jetting my cum along her labia, down her thighs, and across the very threshold beneath my mother's altar. I smirk at the thought of how I just raised my personal naughty list to a whole new level.

Once she meets Twyla, I suspect she will forgive me.

For now, I untie my stjerne, lift her languid puddle of a body into my arms, gather the fallen robe and gown, and return to the castle. Twyla falls asleep before I tuck her into bed.

19
Fairytales aren't real. And I don't belong here.
TWYLA

"You are always beautiful, min kjaere, but you are so beautiful tonight, you shame the definition of beauty."

I can't bring myself to meet his eyes as I gaze at my reflection, unable to fathom it's mine. Because I'm an imposter. The girl in the mirror shouldn't be wearing such an exquisite gown. Red as holly berries or winter roses in full blood. The sweetheart neckline dips to show my fair skin, which the chandeliers have gilded to a pale golden alabaster. With delicate gold filigree adorning the fabric, the form-fitting bodice hugs my curves, accentuating my figure, along with the off-the-shoulder sleeves. The bodice flows seamlessly to layers of sumptuous red silk skirts. Embroidered gold snowflakes decorate the skirts that fall all around my feet.

The girl looking back at me should be wearing appropriate office work attire while hoping her boss doesn't know they're hand-me-downs or thrift store finds. Or by all that is holy, you hope he doesn't notice the white blouse is a little transparent and take it as a ploy for attention.

Little more than two gold combs pinning one side of my curls decorate my hair. Other than the glitter-shine Krampus sprayed upon my hair.

My breath catches in my chest when he retrieves something from the inner folds of his robe. Folds I'm convinced are magical as he seems to have the ability to manifest anything he desires.

“Holy holly berries, Krampus! No…” I cover my mouth with my hands, shaking my head and holding back tears. “I can’t accept that.”

With an annoyed grunt, the demon of Christmas stands behind me—spanning far above my height—before he slowly lowers the gold and silver tiara with three crystals shaped like six-pointed stars onto my head.

“It is a mere trinket compared to the stardust curls gracing your fair head, min stjerne,” he responds in typical Krampus fashion.

It won’t do any good to argue with him. For a moment, I consider it, knowing he would bend me over the nearby bed and give me a good spanking. The distraction is so tempting, but it’s pointless to play games. After tonight, I won’t remember them. And he won’t remember giving me the crown. My heart grows cold at the thought, wishing I could numb myself for the rest of the night.

But the gown is too warm, the lights are too bright, and Krampus is turning my blood hotter by the moment with how he slides his big arms around me from behind. At first, I flinch but then lean into all his warmth. He no longer feels the need to return to the state in which we first met—back when he was more demon man than monster. I still giggle when he flicks his tongue along my cheek.

I woke up to that tongue this morning—buried in my pussy and bringing me to orgasm barely before I had a chance to adjust my blurry eyes. The last thing I remembered was falling asleep in the bathtub. I was so worn out, he said a bath would be more fitting than a shower. His big hands massaging and scrubbing me from head to toe put me to sleep within no time.

Pieces of my heart broke off like cracked ice when he escorted me to the kitchen, where he made breakfast. Not a servant. Him. Krampus wouldn’t let me lift a finger. He just told me to sit at the table and wait like a ‘flink pike’ while he made me Grøtris—rice pudding with butter and brown sugar.

And when I found the almond in the dish, I won a marzipan pig. Krampus in the kitchen with an apron is quite possibly the cutest *and* sexiest thing I've ever seen.

Especially since he saw fit to swat my hand with his tail anytime I tried to get up and help.

Kransekake biscuits were added to the menu for a snack between breakfast and lunch. I'd never seen a more beautiful display of the wreath-like pastries. Later, Mephisto shared, in passing, how Krampus had stayed up into the wee hours of the morning to make it.

Tears pierce my throat at the thought of how I will forget all this…forget him. It won't matter if everything Klaus says is true. If the scryer's cards are true. I still haven't brought myself to ask Krampus for the truth. I've held back all day—too swept up in how sweet he's been following last night's punishment.

Soaking in all his attentiveness when I know it's the last time is only natural. But…my stomach twists because I can't hold back any longer. The Krampus Eve Ball will begin soon. I'm running out of time. And the little crystal snow globe is practically burning a hole in the pocket folds of my gown.

"Min kjaere…" Krampus presses his belly to my back—on account of how tall he is—, and I feel his massive hardness pushing against the pouch and prodding my ass. He breathes me in as I swallow my clump of tears like they're poison. "You are sad. Do you not like dress?"

"No…" My voice cracks when I try to respond. I lower my chin, unable to face myself. "I mean, no, Krampus, it's not the gown. It's perfect. Everything is perfect. It's like a dream. The most beautiful dream anyone could ask for."

"It's Christmas Eve, Twyla. What must I do to make you happy?" He strokes his knuckles across my cheek, shivering all my nerves.

"Do you…feed on emotions? On human emotions? On *my* emotions?"

When I lift my eyes to his in the mirror, he blinks before his whole body language changes. His shoulders sink, his eyes lower, and he sighs. Hot breath blankets the back of my head from that sigh.

"Yes. To all three, Twyla."

Pursing my lips, I look down and shuffle my feet below the gown. "They were all feeding on me in Krampus Haven, weren't they? It's why they followed us the whole time, but they were more interested in me?"

I feel his hands descend upon my shoulders. It doesn't take him much to urge me to turn and face him. My chin trembles when he cups it and tilts my jaw so he may meet my eyes. His are more iridescent than ever—silver as a moonlit snowfall.

"Demons have very little control, min stjerne. It is our nature to feed upon the emotions of mortals. Fae, vampires, shifters…we are all equal in this manner. But make no mistake, Twyla Eyres…" he deepens his voice and leans closer to me, his muzzle nearly brushing my nose. "They fell in love with you. All of Krampus Haven loves you. My castle staff feel the same. You are the brightest Christmas gift to ever grace my halls and my realm."

I part my lips to ask my next question, but he takes it as a signal. My speech, my breath is crushed the moment he dives in for the kiss. As much of a kiss as it can be with his stupendous supernatural tongue burying itself in my mouth and licking all over the insides while his jaws open around my face. He tastes like ginger and sugar from our earlier pastries. That tongue is like an extension of his body but more powerful and flexible than anything.

My cheeks heat from the heady kiss. His deep groan vibrates into my mouth and resonates in my chest. I'm certain it's thrummed into my heart where I'll feel it forever. His kiss in full Krampus form is far more intense than any he gave me as a demon. My head spins from his devilish tongue. I arch my neck and rise on the tips of my toes to meet him, pressing the tips of my fingers to the ridged muscle on his upper chest.

Slowly, I inch out my tongue to draw it along his. A live wire electrifies my nerve endings. And a low growl builds in his chest.

Seconds later, Krampus has me up against the wall, his hand wrapped around my neck. Not choking. No, he presses with just enough force to anchor me here with his fingers centering on my galloping pulse.

"Oh, Krampus..." I moan as he flicks that tongue along the curve of my throat. "I thought you said the ball was starting soon."

"I'm more concerned about other balls at the moment, skitten jente," he teases, grinding his pelvis against my belly, so I feel the full weight of that iron-hard cock.

His tongue twists and curls along my collarbone, and I know if he gets it past my neckline and into the bodice, there's no chance I'll be able to stay sane.

"Did you make a bargain with Klaus?!" I blurt it out, but my voice is weaker than a whimper.

He pauses. His tongue retracts. And Krampus rises to his full height, dwarfing mine—enormous shadow scooping me up. His brows draw low, eyes turning cold and hard and dark as black ice.

I resist the urge to cow because this is my last chance to get the truth.

"Who the fuck told you that?"

"He told me to ask you. He said you wouldn't lie to me."

It can't be helped. My throat constricts as he presses his hands to the wall on either side of me, trapping me—unable to so much as budge beyond him. The livid heat rolling off him practically sears into my bones. His eyes turn from lustrous silver to fiery orbs.

"When was this, Twyla?" he asks in a voice like deep shadows.

"I-I didn't tell you why I ran. It wasn't because of you. I was following a little cat girl from the shop. I didn't want her to be hurt. But she led me to Klaus." The more I speak, the tighter his muscles become, the more his veins throb. "He promised not to hurt me. He just wanted to talk."

"I bet he did."

"Krampus, is it true? Will the curse return?" I hold my breath, my lungs themselves shriveling.

His breath is fast and heavy from his nostrils—the only sound thundering in the room for a few moments. The tension thickens in the air between us. He's not going to tell me, is he? With his teeth bared, he looks more like he's about to erupt into the savage beast I saw that night.

"Yes."

The one-word answer of truthful surrender is great enough to collapse the heart in my chest. All these weeks, he's consumed my emotions, he's kept the truth about this curse from me, and he's spent his remaining days with me. Every waking and sleeping moment, he's gorged himself…on me. He should have been finding ways to stop the curse, to bargain with Klaus. Or crawl back to the Underworld and stay there.

I don't want to imagine what could happen if he unleashed a new Dark Age. Or what children would be the punished chosen ones.

It's the second time I can't bring myself to look at him—but for a whole different reason this time. I hug my arms, holding myself together and finding a way to give voice to my next question. "It's been a hundred years since you did those *things*. But would you…would I have been one of them, Krampus?" It's no more than a withered murmur, though the words echo in my mind like thunder cracks.

When he doesn't speak, and it's just those wordless breaths drifting around me, I don't swallow.

For the first time, I let the tears come—tears I haven't shed in years from the torrent of dark memories of my broken past. All the times I was caught sneaking glimpses of erotic books at the library, or when I couldn't remember the words to certain verses, or when I asked too many questions. Because I shouldn't question things that were "black and white" in a world that otherwise seems the epitome of every shade of *gray*.

"Twyla..."

I flinch when he cups the side of my face. The hurt in his eyes has my heart pitching in my chest, making me long to throw myself into his arms. But I don't. He flexes his fingers before lowering his hand, balling it into a fist at his side.

"What about all those in Krampus Haven? What will happen to them when you fall under the curse again?"

He lifts his other hand to knead his brow. I'd swear even his horns droop when he confesses, "They will be forced back to the Underworld."

I press my back against the wall, wishing I could disappear inside it. "You should have told me. You should have been figuring out a way to stop all this. Not spending all your time with me."

"If the ball were not beginning soon, I would bend you over the bed and spank your fine little rumpa for not telling me all this until now. All I can offer you is my vow that the truth will be revealed tonight. And I will prove my love to you, Twyla Eyres."

"It doesn't matter!" I cry out, lurching but in anger this time. Heat rises to my cheeks as I narrow my eyes into a glare and confront him, "You made me fall in love with this place. You took me from a life I loathed but one that was within my control, manageable, and practical. And you brought me here. You gave me gowns and food and gifts, and you saved my life and made me fall in love with Krampus Haven. You made me fall in love with everything!" I take one step forward, astonished when he steps back despite all the fur rising on his hackles. "And now I'm going to lose everything."

"No," he growls. "You will see. You must, Twyla. For you are my kjaere, my bright stjerne in the darkness. I will prove it to you. Then, you will know."

Before I can protest, Krampus seizes my hand and drags me out of the bedroom so quickly, I nearly lose the tiara.

Doesn't he know how pointless it is? The very cards testified that I need to get my head out of the clouds and come back down to earth. So does Krampus.

Before the clock runs out, I must shake the snow globe and prevent this Dark Age from happening.

The Krampus Eve Ball takes my breath away!

The Northern Lights paint a celestial spectacle upon the night sky far above my head. Light and color create a symphony beyond the great crystal-domed ceiling, weaving wonder across the dark velvet sky. Like silken robes of ethereal dancers, they create a cosmic ballet of quiet magic. Snow falling in a silvery curtain completes the beauty as if the angels wish to shed their crystalline robes while holding their breath through the luminous performance.

Inside the castle, the atmosphere is quite different with its dark mystique and old-world holiday enchantment. All over the Great Hall, tapestries depicting Krampus in varying forms cascade down the stone walls. Candle sconces surround the hall, casting a warm, golden glow to contrast with the icy winter night.

A towering Christmas tree stars as the centerpiece—decorated with twisting vines, holly, gilded ornaments, and handmade trinkets.

Many gather around the grand tables, laden with traditional and modern Norwegian dishes. Even from our place just beyond the entryway, the scent of mulled wine, steamy cider, and festive spices fills the air.

As Krampus leads me through the grand archway, the musicians serenading the audience with dark carols abruptly quiet their instruments. Dancers pause mid-step, face the entrance of the Great Hall where we stand, and promptly surrender into a graceful bow. Countless horns parallel the floor.

"His Malevolent Majesty, the Lordship of Yuletide and Guardian of the Solstice, Krampus!"

I snap my head to the demon next to me, awed by the proclamation. Of course, he lives in a castle, and his servants and citizens have addressed him as Lord Krampus. But fear and wonder strike like hot iron in my nerve endings at the knowledge of how he's never retained or assumed a title with me. And how I'm on the arm of a true legend who dates back in time before the Middle Ages—one treated in this land of monsters and shadows like a…King.

The instant I stop in my tracks, Krampus turns, tapers his brows, and shakes his head. "Too late for cold feet, min kjaere. And if you don't move them now, you will discover how hot I can redden your perfekt rumpa…in front of the very host before us." A muscle bounces in his jaw. His eyes gleam with the assurance he would make good on his word.

So, I swallow hard and follow a mere step behind him as we progress down the center of the Great Hall with a multitude of eyes fixed on our every move. I avoid those gazes like my life depends on it. Because I recognize several from Krampus Haven. Are they sensing my emotions even now? Feeding on me? My skin crawls at the notion, making me want to fold in on myself until I'm too small for them to notice.

After passing the enormous tree, we finally arrive before the grand dais, where two throne-like chairs sit before another long table covered in a velvet tablecloth. A feast already prepared for us.

Like a perfect gentleman, Krampus pulls out my chair. To my astonishment, my shoes touch the floor! It's the first time I've ever sat in a chair in his castle where my feet don't dangle, given how I'm the most petite of all beings in his entire realm. I flick my eyes to his, searching his expression, wondering if he commissioned this chair just for me.

He offers me nothing before pushing the chair in and resuming his place next to me. Curiosity tickles in my prominent thoughts when he gives no speech. No toast. No words. Nothing.

The moment he sits, the musicians bring their instruments to life again. The monsters of the realm carry on with their dance. Children participate in Krampus-themed activities, crafting masks they will use to play, ornaments to add to the tree, or twisting greenery to form wreaths so they may decorate the hall. From beyond the sweeping glass doors on one side of the room, I make out an immense bonfire where others have gathered round to warm their hands—or paws—, and I imagine they are swapping ghost stories.

Dark magic and haunted lore shroud the evening. So beautiful and eerie, it could only ever be a dream. A dream I wished so terribly would last beyond the holidays.

But sometimes, what begins as a dream can end in a nightmare. At the end of it all, I will have no choice but to wake up. Better the practical future Klaus informed me would come to be for me instead of risking all the punishment, the hurt, the darkness that could be for thousands…millions of children.

If I could spare only one from such darkness, I would sacrifice all this in a heartbeat. And know my heart would break in the process.

Except, I won't remember.

For now, I maintain an eye on the grandfather clock in the corner of the hall while my fingers fiddle with the snow globe in my pocket. Black candles flicker, forming shadows upon the table…and Krampus.

He serves me. Just as he did at breakfast, Krampus gives me succulent meat, sides of roasted root vegetables, seasoned with fresh herbs and drizzled in a hearty sauce. Rich and steamy soup with warm bread twisted into the shapes of ravens come after. Even the dried cod with potatoes drenched in olive oil has my mouth watering. Finally, it's all sorts of delicate pastries, which pull tears from my eyes. They flood the memories of our time in the cabin when he read monster romance to me and ate such pastries off my…rumpa.

Krampus says nothing as we eat. But now and then, his tail strays toward my side, flicking to show his interest. In the background, merriment fills the hall from the gathering of souls and ancient carols—so ancient, they could originate in the Underworld itself. A cauldron of emotions stirs inside me. Light and darkness war inside me.

And I can't stop staring at the clock, counting the moments because they say it's supposed to make time pass slower. So far, it's not working.

Once I've helped myself to a second glass of spiced wine, Krampus touches the back of my hand, startling me. Scooping up my palm, he rubs his muzzle along my knuckles and says, "Come with me, kjaere."

My breath staggers, and my heart skips a beat as he pulls out my chair and escorts me down the dais and onto the main dance floor where all clear the area.

Because the Lord of Yuletide pauses in the center, bows to me, and wraps one hand around my waist. Commanding and magnetic, he towers over me with his very form absorbing the darkness even as the firelight seems to pull to me.

A hush falls upon the crowds as if they are hanging upon every string of breath, every slight movement, and every thread of emotion I may grant them.

You won't remember. You won't remember, I chant to myself.

Otherworldly energy pulses in the very air. A haunting melody echoes in the background, but it could never prompt me to the degree that Krampus is.

Slowly, I lift my trembling hand and stretch it high to cup his boulder-like shoulder. I take his other palm, open to me, and fold my hand into his. Cold as the winter wind but electrifying as every twinkle light in the hall, it devours mine. Dark consuming light. Our eyes crash together in a crescendo of heartbeats. Iridescent silver meeting chestnut brown. He holds me strong. He makes me feel safe and warm and wanted. Like a holiday haven.

But that's not real life. Life is never safe and warm. Life is survival. And you live for all the small moments in between.

An infinity of moments, trapped in a single second of time, pass. A thousand secrets held in the silvery gleam of his eyes. A thousand words trapped on the tip of my tongue, unable to breathe.

The music plays. And Krampus sweeps me into a dark waltz.

Such a fusion of grace in his movements, I'd swear he is the one giving life to that energy humming all around us. The firelight dims to mere candle flickers casting moving shadows wherever he steps. He doesn't carry me. My skin tingles with the deep awareness that somehow, Krampus is commanding magic to weave into my being, locking me into a flawless rhythm to mirror every necessary step.

"You dance?" are my first words to him since before we entered the Great Hall. More than any other time tonight, I meet his eyes, discovering a depth of emotion that defies every horror story ever spun about him.

"Ja. Dansekuntsen—the art of dance—is an ancient custom of my realm and race. Who do you believe taught mere mortals how to dance?"

My spirit is mesmerized by him. With every word he speaks, his dance becomes more intricate, more passionate.

"Dans is magic," he says, lowering his head toward me, fueling the unspoken desire between us. My heartbeat races as I fall deeper into his enchantment, wishing more than anything that I could lose myself in the eye of this waltz, the magic I want to be real…for me. For us. "Dans steals one's mind and body and has the heart hanging onto the embodiment of the art until it transcends the very soul. It is why mortals will beat their feet bloody to master it. Longing to become part of the magic. To steal a piece of the gods, own it, and give it back to all mankind."

He twirls mc as if he's mastering an instrument, treating my body like a prized treasure. Just as he's done with me since the beginning. Dramatic swirls from his hands, his monstrous form carries me all over the dance floor as the rhythm intensifies. Heat radiates off him, blanketing me, protecting me.

The very stones of the castle and the snow falling outside bear witness to our dance, but we exist in a space of our own. Every note rising to a crescendo testifies to the moments we have shared. A love as forbidden and dark as any. The demon and the human. The monster and the maiden. Beauty and the Beast.

This is not a fairytale…no matter how much I want it to be, dream it could be, believe it is. Fairytales aren't real. And I don't belong here.

When the crescendo crashes, thundering into the very floor beneath us, I'm breathless. Gasps echo in my ears as I stand before Krampus. No other sounds. Not one being dares to disturb the magic and wonder. He still holds my one hand while his other lets go of my waist so he may brush his knuckles across my cheek. A tender, intimate caress.

In the darkness of the Great Hall, with nothing but the beautiful Christmas tree shimmering its lights upon us, I stand before His Malevolent Majesty, the Lordship of Yuletide and Guardian of the Solstice. He lowers his muzzle toward me. A thousand heartbeats hold their breaths between us.

And just as he leans closer, I close my eyes to welcome his kiss—the last one we will share before everything fades. Because the clock is ticking down. Midnight is coming. Even now, I lower my hand to the pocket of my gown, fingertips lighting on the snow globe. It feels cold as a nightmare.

Krampus doesn't kiss me. A rush of air instead meets my lips as he moves away. Confused, I open my eyes to find him rising straight and tall, extending one arm, reaching into the air. He faces the dark demon host before us, squeezes my hand, and proclaims in a thunderous voice that shakes the very walls, "I present to you, your new Queen, her Amorous Majesty, the Lady of the Winter Star, and Monstrous Mistress of the Solstice…Twyla Eyres!"

No. Oh, gods, Krampus! He can't! Every eye in the castle centers on me. And the moment they all kneel, the moment Krampus lowers himself at the waist in a regal bow, I don't hesitate. With more resolve than ever—because a human could never be the queen of monsters and shadows—, I clasp my fingers around the little snow globe, lift it from my pocket and into the air, and meet Krampus's silvery eyes one last time. The snow globe glints, twinkling and reminding me of a sinister Judas kiss.

"Twyla! Wait!" Krampus shouts.

It's too late. Pulse pounding, heart breaking, soul shattering, I shake the snow globe.

The Great Hall evanesces. It feels like I'm falling into a giant snow globe. Shades of winter white flurry all around me, transforming into a vortex and spinning my body, spinning my vision, spinning every thought and memory of my world…until everything fades. And darkness swallows me whole.

20

"You should know monsters don't get a happily ever after..."

KRAMPUS

Fear knifes through me—colder than a thousand icy blades at the sight of her holding the snow globe. "Twyla! Wait!"

It's too late.

She shakes the damn ball. Tears fill her eyes as she gazes back at me. My chest collapses. My lungs lose all breath as I reach for her at the same time that suffocating darkness eclipses my Great Hall. And my hands collide with cold, cruel air and not my warm Christmas star.

Not my Twyla.

Faen! Faen! Faen!

Oh, Hel, save me from this fate! I thunder the prayer in my mind, wishing I could reverse time.

Her loss is so great and mighty, I fall to my knees, cracking the floor beneath me. I hold back the silent tears shivering to the surface and bury my head in my hands as a thousand memories come to me. They spear me. Like shockwaves, each holds the power to rupture the very fabric of my heart. Splintering it within seconds.

The sweet 'thank you' slipping from her lips that gave birth to the magic between us. The sight of her golden stardust curls falling across my bed. Her perfekt rumpa glowing red beneath my palms. Eyes melting in the heart-shuddering knowledge of what I was doing when I suspended her in the gazebo.

A million more memories, glimpses of moments of our time together.

I remember the relief sinking my heart when I pulled her from the ice and warmed her before the cabin fire. How she pulled my fur and tested me until we turned the corner of the next page. Oh, faen—How she took me into her mouth, willingly, beautifully, powerfully! How she asked me about my history and traditions, played with me, and took her punishment like such a good girl. The table and treats on her sweet little ass as I read to her.

How she loved Krampus Haven. And how all my realm fell in love with her.

Oh, gods, every god in the Underworld, every god in every realm and world—all I ever wanted was to show her the treasure, the princess, the star she truly is. Ready to make her Queen, my Lady of the Winter Star!

The pain is too much. My horns themselves are ready to crack. Her absence draws all my magic, power, and emotions from me—my very essence bleeding to nothingness.

This raw sense of numbness takes over until I'm shaking, prostrate on the floor. A fallen lord. A broken King of the Solstice.

Twyla was the one time in my entire existence I gave all my power to when I confessed my love to her. The one sweetheart and good girl in the world who could love monsters and embrace demons.

Now, she's taken my heart with her. Where I cannot reach her.

A hundred growls thunder in my once great hall, reverberating blood-curdling horror into each and every being. The spectral eyes of the unholy revenants surround the expanse. The terrified screams of my people, of families huddling together, are enough to rip me from my grief-induced stupor.

"Come now, Krampus..."

Klaus's sick and twisted cackle stabs me in the back. "You should know monsters don't get a happily ever after.

You work for me, and you have ever since I crawled into the Underworld and claimed your soul tether."

Snarling, I spin around and grip Klaus by the throat, squeezing beyond the limitations of what any mortal could take, squeezing so hard, it would snap vocal cords. Klaus simply laughs. That maniacal and disturbed laugh of someone far worse than I could ever be. Because Klaus possesses a soul. His is simply rotted beyond redemption—nothing but black decay.

"Don't unleash your anger on me, Krampus. After all, I simply offered your little Twyla a gift she could not refuse. Just as I will you now."

I don't let go of his throat, but I do rip the cross from his gods-damn neck and crush it in my hand. "What fucking offer?"

"You have been hoarding again, Krampus. Tsk, tsk, tsk…and my draugr I have so blessedly brought back to life are quite hungry."

Horror ices my blood with the thought of the dozens of Draugr feeding upon my people. My pulse explodes at the thought—my need to protect them is still at the forefront of my mind. They are not mine anymore. From the moment Twyla shook that damn ball, it ripped the title from me. It stole my throne, my power, my people, everything. But I'd rather surrender every drop of my essence to eternal damnation than let Klaus have these demons.

"However," lilts Klaus in a casual tone, "if you are a good boy and come with me now, I vow I will spare your people." He crooks one corner of his mouth into a malevolent grin because we both know he has me by the balls. "We both know I could take what I desire by force if necessary. And my revenants will certainly feed on the emotions they have absorbed from your human throughout her time here and your pathetic little venture to find love. But their lives will be spared. Consider this your little Christmas gift from me, Krampus."

"Fucking hate your gifts. Always have. Always will."

"Now, now, Krampus. Do you truly intend to refuse my generous offer?" He cocks his head to the side. His bishop's cap barely shifts. More than ever, I wish to rip that cap off his fucking head and shove it down his damn throat. Not one strand of his ghostly white beard is out of place.

No, I won't refuse. It will be a dark Yule, the darkest my former citizens will have ever known. The draugr will feed to the barest dredges. My people will hunger and hurt, but they will live. They will return to Haven, not Krampus Haven, and they will do what they must to survive. Which normally means hunting for whatever souls cross into Purgatory. If I last the night, I'll get an earful for it from Eros after the new year.

But they will live.

Twyla would have fed them for years to come. If our souls had united…

"Well, Krampus?" Klaus interrupts my thoughts.

Slowly, I retract my claws, one at a time, from his throat. And remove my hand. I flex it once before dropping it to the side. Defeat sinks my shoulders.

After Klaus tugs on his robes and brushes them off as if wanting to rid himself of my stench, he strokes his beard and confirms, "Do we have an accord, Krampus?"

I set my jaw. "We do."

"Excellent. Thank me, then, Krampus. You know how bargains work."

Yes, I unfortunately know exactly how bargains work. Nerves more electrified than live wires, I grit my teeth around every word, "*Thank you, Saint Nicholas.*"

"Come, we have much work to do."

21
"Care for a drink with a stranger, my lady?"
TWYLA

The Christmas jingle ringtone of my flex-phone jolts me awake.

Vision still adjusting, I fumble with the photo frames and random objects on my nightstand until my fingers collide with the phone.

"Hello…?" I ask in a groggy voice.

"Eyres!" the familiar scratchy tenor voice greets me. "Hey, how is my favorite ace journalist who is willing to work on Christmas Eve itself?"

I catch the time on my alarm clock and groan. "Colton? It's six a.m. in the morning."

"I know, I know, but I wanted to tell you I pulled some strings and got you a stay at the Palace."

I flop onto my pillow, curious about how nice it smells. Like lavender. Huh…that's odd.

"The Palace?" I wonder and idly toy with the tassels on the wool throw on my bed. Brand new. Authentic sheep's wool. What?

"Yes, you're doing me a solid and getting the lead scoop on the Christmas World Ball tonight, so I figured I would treat you to a weekend stay at the Christmas World Palace Hotel. You'll meet with the new owner for a late dinner following the ball. It will be well after midnight, so I secured the hotel stay. You won't have to make a return trip. All sound good to you?"

I rub my eyes and fight a yawn. "New owner?"

"Sure, you remember the assignment. Christmas and Krampus World has a brand new owner. Some Gothic Greek-sounding name. Anyway, you're getting the scoop before anyone else since you're willing to work over Christmas. Did I mention it's a masked ball? And that I sent your holiday bonus a little early? Go buy yourself one of those fancy dresses you love for the ball. It's on me."

"What time is the ball?"

"Seven pm sharp. And we'll do a rush on it for print the day after Christmas. Readers will appreciate it after they've gone back to work. I've transferred all the credentials you'll need to your phone. Have fun!"

Colton hangs up, leaving me bewildered, threading my brows. "Ugh!" I groan again because he woke me up from the most amazing dream.

Annoyance prickles my spine because I know I won't be able to get back to sleep now. Pieces of the dream return to me. Of dancing in a grand castle hall with Christmas candles everywhere. I remember the taste of eggnog. And a warm bed with twinkle lights woven into a canopy above my head.

I remember big arms surrounding me, a chest so muscled, it was like a fortress. And the sound of purring.

Shaking off the glittery thoughts, I do my best to come back down to earth. I roll out of bed, feet hitting the brand-new fluffy rug covering my hardwood floor. The scent of vanilla and pine fills the air, and I smile at the random candles on the white ledge surrounding the apartment.

A joyful sigh eases from my mouth when I consider how far I've come. I have a professional journalism career. My debt is nearly paid off. My apartment is well on its way to being fully furnished. And a stack of small 'save the dates' for Christmas and New Year's Eve parties lies on the table in my adjoining kitchen.

But when I shed my pajamas and get into the shower, I can't escape this nagging feeling that something is…missing. Like other hands scrubbing my hair, washing my skin.

Even after I've dressed for the day and had breakfast, the sensation doesn't leave. My scrambled eggs don't taste like rice pudding with brown sugar, almonds, or warm biscuits with butter. Where did that come from? I wonder as I wash my dishes.

After doing my laundry, I resolve to sit down and watch TV to distract myself. But my fingers freeze on the remote buttons when I notice my little Christmas tree in the window.

"Where's the star?" I lower my brows. Confusion swirls through me.

For the next hour, I search through every box in my apartment, every nook and cranny. I look in my old hope chest. I search under my bed, in the closet.

I can't find the star.

Frantic gasps escape my throat, and I rake my nails over my scalp, tugging at my curls. Why is this so important to me? Why should I care about a missing star? I could just go out and buy a new one. My pulse thrums in my veins, and I consider what shops might be open on Christmas Eve near me.

My phone jingles at me from my nightstand. Chest squeezing, I approach it to find an alert with an e-mail from Colton. Oh, it's the VIP pass to Christmas World along with my reservation for Christmas Palace. Warm flutters erupt in my belly when I consider shopping there for a star. It would be the ideal place.

Unfortunately, another e-mail catches my attention. My stomach twists, and my heart aches in my chest. I know I shouldn't open it, but I still click on the e-mail from my mother. Most of the time, the words give me a sense of itchy frustration. Like one step down from pins and needles under my skin. Today, they sting a little more.

It's nothing new. They usually begin with a Bible verse or two. Next comes the 'we love you and forgive you' because I obviously committed some great transgression by moving away from home and getting my degree in a field they didn't want me to. The third section is about my sisters and how well they are doing with their multiple babies and homeschooling and church projects. A subtle reminder that they are on the right path in life while I am not.

She always wraps up the letter with a note about coming home, coming back to church, seeking forgiveness, and finding God—followed by a last Bible verse to hit home.

Hmm…call me crazy, but if my life is any consideration, God showed up more *outside* the church. It's not like it's difficult to find him out here. They just have blinders on, believing the best places are inside four walls with pews, crosses, and heavy hymnals.

Ironic, considering God spent much of his time *outside* and on the go when he was on Earth.

I spend the next hour packing my bag, watering the plants in my apartment, and finishing my chores. After putting on my hooded red wool coat, I grab my bag and prepare for my grand entrance to Christmas World.

A symphony of festive sights, sounds, and smells greets me as soon as I step beyond the gates. I take a deep breath of evergreen scents, gingerbread baking from the nearby pastry shops, and even burning logs from random bonfires where tourists gather to warm their hands. The holiday joy of everything spreads heat into my blood despite the blustery weather.

Above my head, the milky clouds shed a soft snowfall upon Christmas World. Enough to light on my eyelashes and cling to my black gloves—tiny crystals that fade too soon. The breeze stirs tiny flurries to swirl here and there wherever people walk.

Thousands of twinkling lights and oversized ornaments decorate the main archway of Christmas World. Thankfully, the Palace Hotel is located right near the entrance, and after a brief check-in, a porter offers to take my bag to my room. It's not like I brought much beyond a couple of small toiletries and a change of clothes for tomorrow.

Too excited to stay in a stuffy hotel room when I can shop with the knowledge of my holiday bonus, I don't even bother checking out the room yet.

Instead, I make my way out of the hotel and toward Holiday Market Street. After all, if I'm going to meet with this new owner, I'd better dress in something quite festive.

A thrill surges through my nerve endings as I stroll down the central cobblestone avenue of what reminds me of a quaint European Christmas Market. Charming stalls of vendors selling roasted chestnuts and hot cocoa or others featuring artisanal goods like hand-carved ornaments or festive clothing. More than once, I pass a troupe of carolers—some decked out in full Victorian clothing to echo Charles Dickens's *A Christmas Carol.*

The Market branches off on one side to a children's attraction. A whole life-sized village of gingerbread and colorful treats that reminds me of the game Candy Land. A sugar cube castle completes the village.

The North Pole-themed village is a few streets down. A line of children wait for Santa, participating in the various activity stations from toy-making demonstrations to reindeer-petting.

I can't fathom why annoyance prickles the nape of my neck to my toes, and a chill sweeps up my spine, sprouting goosebumps on my skin.

In some ways, it's too bright, too festive. More difficult for me to appreciate the full scope of the Christmas season with all this commercialization and...glee.

At last, I find the perfect shop for my gown, where I opt for something a little more whimsical but alluring—something that will echo the essence of starlight on a dark and cold night. Who knows? Perhaps I'll meet someone at the ball worthy enough to slide the straps down my arms and free me of the becoming bodice. My cheeks heat at my imaginings.

A mask matching the gown is a special find for tonight. The lace contours follow the curves of my face—as if it was designed especially for me.

After I purchase the gown and keep it on hold, I spend the rest of the day soaking up every experience possible in Christmas World. It will make a great feature for the article.

The Candy Cane Amusement Park welcomes families to whimsical rides and attractions, as well as a Land of Sweets-themed town from the Nutcracker.

I spend an hour or so at the Christmas Museum, where I research and learn more from the ancient Yuletide relics, vintage holiday displays, and antique ornaments from various periods of history. One exhibit features information on Krampus. The gruesome devil-like figure with his twisted, disturbing features and lolling tongue as he brandishes a bundle of birch whips shouldn't give me pause. But I can't escape the tickle creeping along the back of my neck and raising the hairs on my skin. As I study the cloven-hoofed figure swinging his tail and chasing after a naughty child, I can't help the chill spreading deep into my bone marrow.

It stays with me long after I leave the museum, which doesn't make sense. Weeks ago, I wrote my feature on Krampus World, which highlighted much of the German traditions and their origins, along with the resurgence of popularity across cultures.

By sunset, I've toured almost everything in Christmas World, ending with the mesmerizing, enchanted forest where twinkle lights adorn every branch, thick or thin. Luminaries direct visitors along snow-dusted winding paths. Now and then, I round the corner to witness a sculptor dazzling audiences with his ice carvings. Or a vendor displaying a holiday tradition from another country.

At the end of the forest, a phenomenal ice palace welcomes tourists to a small world that brings a winter fairy tale to life. Frost-covered ice caverns create an intricate maze with slides and tunnels for children and glowing ice bars for adults. Laughter and happiness engulf the air.

Something is still missing.

I feel it with every fiber of my being as I get ready for the Christmas Eve Ball, pinning my hair into an updo. The black base color of the gown with a lustrous sheen accentuates my golden curls all the more and reminds me of a starlit night. Lace forms in intricate patterns along the bodice, mirroring winter foliage. An illusion neckline blends seamlessly with the sheer long sleeves—perfect for the evening. Especially with the snowflake and vine motifs decorating them. I love how the illusion continues, spilling down my back to the base of my spine, patterned in that delicate lace.

Voluminous skirts cascade in elegant folds the color of midnight. With the tiny crystal beadwork all along the fabric—like moonlit frost—it feels like I've become part of a winter night filled with a host of stars.

A few loose tendrils frame my face, drawing attention to my smoky eye makeup and deep burgundy lip to complement my rich brown eyes. The lace mask completes the ensemble. Soft and lightweight, it molds to my skin, decorated in the same snowflake and vine motifs to mirror the gown. Black gemstones shimmer at the edges of the mask like twinkling stars.

Now, I am ready.

Invitation in hand, I follow the garland and holly-adorned golden lanterns lining the corridor, welcoming me into the majestic archway that marks the entrance to the ball.

Revelry and carols explode all around me.

The ceiling itself is a wonder, taking my breath away with its expansive backdrop of holographic lights creating a night of twinkling stars…and even shooting ones now and then. Crystal chandeliers suspended from the ceiling like miniature frozen castles. Sprawling evergreen trees decorate the ball in various shapes and sizes, including tabletop ones resting atop blue velvet cloths.

Snowflake lights spin along the dance floor where the lights have dimmed, and countless masked partygoers dance to a slow, soft Christmas carol. Everywhere, gowns of gold, silver, red, and green meet my eyes with matching masks. Tailored suits or tuxes for the men.

After flirting with a few tall, masked men, I make my way to the buffet tables with their feast of Christmas-themed delicacies and treats. Laughter and music sparkle in the air like flurries of winter magic and swirling spells.

Despite all this, despite the day I've had, the grandeur of all that is Christmas World, something is…missing. Not just missing. It's lost. The wonder and magic are lost on me. No matter how hard I try, I can't connect with this—any of it.

"Care for a drink with a stranger, my lady?"

I snap my gaze in the direction of the voice. And smile. A charming but elderly gentleman offers me a glass of mulled wine. Warm but wrinkled skin and a light gray beard. Something in his expression, in those friendly eyes, has me trusting him. Most impressive are those lifelike horns curling like scimitars from his head.

"Shouldn't you be at Krampus World?" I tease him but accept the glass.

"Perhaps you should be, too."

I lift my brows. That nagging chill prickling my skin returns. Before I can respond, the gentleman continues, "After all, I've never seen a beautiful woman in such a lovely gown and surrounded by such joyous festivities wear such a melancholy expression."

"Christmas World is wonderful, but I am honestly here on business," I explain while focusing on his eyes with the soft candlelight reflecting in the pupils.

"Ahhh, you are a writer," he notes while gesturing to my leather-bound notebook where I've scribbled countless observations.

"Journalist. I have a meeting late tonight with the new owner of Christmas World."

I straighten, recognizing how much I'm posturing, but I'll own it. I've worked hard to get where I am. *I'm an independent woman married to my work, and there's nothing wrong with that,* I try to convince myself. But my heart can't help but droop at the sinking knowledge of his words. Because I am alone. Every memory of Christmas World I've collected has been alone. Why does that bother me now? Alone just means people can't disappoint you. And you can't disappoint them.

"Quite the scoop for the buzzing holiday season. Would you be interested in a bigger scoop?" he offers, gesturing with an open palm. I blink, and I guess he takes it as a sign to continue when he adds, "Perhaps the scoop of why the former owner of Christmas and Krampus World sold his corporation so quickly and the nature of his holiday enigma?"

I can't deny I'm tempted. "What would it cost me?"

The gentleman smiles but not with an open mouth to display his teeth. His features seem to warm all the more. "You are a clever young woman. It will cost you your meeting tonight. It may cost you your original story. But I believe it will be worth it."

"Why?"

He smiles sheepishly, then slowly removes his mask to unveil the rest of his face. My lips part, breath hitching in my throat at the familiar corporate guru of Mr. Mephisto—the new owner of Christmas World. It's not long before the partiers in the vicinity whisper and point.

"We don't have long, Miss. Eyres," he warns me in a lower voice before sliding one of the Christmas World tourist maps toward me. "Let's just say if you'd like the real story, follow the markings I've provided on this map. Perhaps we shall see if you are naughty enough to take the risk but also nice enough to be grateful for the deal."

Deal…an icy chill sweeps up my spine, and I shiver. Why does it feel like he's toying with my future? Why does it feel like it's not the first time?

More people gather and take out their flex-phones to capture the unexpected sight of Christmas World's owner seated at a random table. And since I don't care to be the jingly belle of the ball, I take his outstretched palm, shake it once, and agree, "It's the most wonderful time of the year after all. I'll take your deal…" and see what the night before Christmas story truly has in store for me.

Mephisto simpers. A spark of electricity pricks heat in my hand, raising the hairs on the back of my neck. I waste no time. I grab the map and make a hasty retreat just before the flex-phones start flashing.

The map has led me through the maze of ice castles to a side door disguised to blend into the surroundings. If Mephisto hadn't given me this map, I wouldn't have given it a second's glance.

I don't know why I should find it so remarkable that it's unlocked. He probably arranged it this way.

After closing the door behind me, I follow the second portion of the map on the back page. One drawn this time, which extends beyond the official tourist map. I pass fog and ice machines and storage rooms with LED lights and even giant white blocks meant to mimic ice.

Finally, I arrive at another door, a simple warehouse-type door—also unlocked. This one opens to a descending stairway. No lights on either side. No light apart from the one surrounding me from the open door.

Biting the inside of my cheek, I hesitate. The darkness swallowing the second flight of stairs below me is ominous. We've all seen those movies where the girl goes down the creepy, dark stairwell. And the monster captures her in the end.

But there's something…something about the energy curling in the air, a primal and otherworldly energy that has my blood warming, adrenaline thrilling my nerve endings. I also believe Mephisto is trustworthy. And besides…maybe I want to be captured by the monster.

Chuffing a laugh, I slide my hand along the railing and take my first steps. The door swings closed behind me, reverberating into my body. I don't stop. And I ignore whatever creepy-crawly horror tries to sneak into my body to chill my bones since I still haven't reached the end of the staircase.

I lost count of the flights after ten or so. There are two reasons why I don't double back. One: I will not let all this hard work and Mephisto's bargain with me go to waste. If I showed back up at the ball like a bitch with her tail between her legs, I highly doubt he would be willing to offer me a decent story. And two: the air smells sweeter, fresher. Like gingerbread and pine.

On each side of me, the walls grow jagged and textured. From smooth cement to bumpy rock, as if the stairway has led me right into a cavern. The air grows cold, but the sweet fragrance curls into the air until I'm practically soaking in it.

Just as I turn to go down another flight of stairs, a subtle glow sheds enough light for me to find the end of the journey. At least for the stairs, which is a welcome relief, considering the sweat sheening my skin. Instead, I follow that subtle glow into a passageway.

Shadows dance along the walls, and the air thickens with a wintry chill. As the passage deepens, a rounded opening leads me into a chamber. The inside of the chamber jars me, shock freezing all speech and my limbs.

It's not the eerie sanctum.

It's the thousands upon thousands of snow globes suspended in the air, embedded in the walls, and countless shelves like libraries of these miniature crystal worlds. The shelves follow the cavern walls, spiraling upward into what seems like an eternity. Some are ornate and elaborate. Others are simple.

But the insides of those snow globes rip the breath from my lungs, bring tears to the surface, and leave me weak in the knees. Because something infinitely more precious than snow flurries dances inside those globes.

Like tiny moving storybooks, the crystal globes contain memories. Beautiful memories plucked from the lives of millions of children throughout the centuries. And every last one of them features one focal character. Krampus.

A host of warm tingles sweep across my skin, swirling most along my spine and in my fingertips. And my mind.

It's as if I've found Christmas. The real Christmas, right here in this cavern.

That déjà vu sensation sends heat to rouse my blood. It's like glitter in my mind, my body, my heart, and my very soul—impossible to shake and sparking tiny golden reminders of…something that tickles the corners of my mind.

Choking on the emotion burning my throat, I approach some snow globes, witnessing something special—Krampus building snowmen with children, having snowball fights, even baking cookies, and unwrapping gifts with them. They don't fear the monster of Christmas. They laugh. They share unfathomable joy. And these snow globes have captured the essence, the epitome, the embodiment of the Spirit of the Season.

The emotion mesmerizes me until wonder, pure wonder, trembles through me, casting those heated, glittery tingles into every iota of my being. The more I gaze into the crystalline spheres, the more I believe I have found the heart of Krampus himself.

"Velkomin, Twyla." *Welcome,* Twyla.

The feminine voice coming from behind me chills me to the bone. As if the winds of the underworld have needled their way into my flesh. It carries a winter storm on a moonless night. The mournful song of a lone wolf. And the distant echo of sacred bells chiming.

The scent of incense and decay overwhelms the notes of gingerbread and pine.

I purse my lips and slowly turn, chin low, eyes bowing because something deep inside me recognizes I am in the presence of a deity. One of the most powerful deities. And when I face her, surveying the somber garments of gray and violet robes that seem like they were formed from scraps of the first twilight to ever grace the world, I dare to lift my eyes to the goddess.

My heart staggers from her macabre beauty, her spectral power—a goddess who holds the final say in all life. One who can snuff out my existence within a mere eye blink if she chooses. She holds the most ancient of balances between life and death.

On one side of her body, she is life incarnate with silvery skin of lustrous enchantment and a deep ebony eye that holds the wisdom of the ages. Not a flaw in her sculpted cheekbone, strong jawline, and slender curve of her neck.

On the other side, her delicate bones and hollow eye socket conspire to paint a portrait of skeletal elegance. Despite the vacant socket, she still holds the ability to pierce through the mortal husk of my body and stab deep into my soul.

Upon her head rests a diadem of obsidian and bones.

With the primal forces of the universe clothing her, she approaches me as draperies of shadows drift around her like mist.

Once again, I lower my chin and eyes to the ground, wondering how I should bow to the Goddess of Death. I startle when she cups my chin and raises it firmly, brutalizing me with the icy penetration of her full eye and the hollow one.

"So, this is the young woman who captured my son's heart and then broke it."

Too aware of the chill of mortality and the iciness in my bones, I choose my words carefully. "Please forgive me for whatever was said or done. I don't know what's going on or where I am…only that I feel like this is where I'm supposed to be, where I *want* to be."

"Ja. That pernicious bishop could steal your mind but not your heart. And while I may not control the bargains he makes, I do not answer to him. Nor does he trump a mother's bond with her son." She weaves both threads of melancholy and resolve as if inviting me to ponder the pull of destiny. "I may not give you your memories back, little human. But I may show you this."

Awe paralyzes me when she closes my fingers around a new snow globe—one decorated with crystal and gold stars, snowflakes, and holly berries. But it's the vision inside the globe. Holding it firmly in one hand, holding onto it for dear life, I lift my other to cover my mouth and stem the tide of tears burning my throat.

They still come.

The visions are like something out of a fantasy, a dark fairy tale. Heat reddens my cheeks as I watch the same monster from all the other globes holding me curled up in the fetal position in his lap just after he spanked me. My heartstrings tug as if wanting to bind themselves to the visions inside the globe—of him bathing me, caring for me, and…I lurch, choking on my stuttered breath from the gazebo and how I broke down, eyes melting when I recognized he was treating me like a prized Christmas tree.

He saved me. I ran, and he pulled me from the ice. All these visions from the cabin. I swear, I can taste the treats that he snatched from my naked rump. I swear I can hear the thick old Norse accent of his voice. I swear my cheeks burn, and my womb tightens in response to all these countless memories.

Hel even shows me the second time I ran in pursuit of another, the discussion with Klaus, and all the moments leading up to the ballroom's grand and magical waltz.

"Look," she commands me, and I stare at the shifting snow that swirls to unmask what happened in the Great Hall after I shook the snow globe.

I fall to my knees as he did in those moments. A sob breaks free of my throat as I feel the weight of his pain, his loss, and the deepest wound—all because I shook that snow globe.

By the time the visions end, hot tears stream down my cheeks. My chest aches as if my heart has been slashed and is bleeding slowly, tortuously. How could I turn my back on such a fairy tale? Something I've always wanted but never believed was possible? How could I believe Klaus without speaking to Krampus more?

Once I grip my chest, wishing I could hold back the pain of the loss knifing through me, Hel lifts my chin to her eye again.

"How much will you fight for such a life, child?" She tilts her head, her one eye holding the secrets of the abyss itself. "How much will you fight for him?"

"How can I?" A gleam of hope splinters the darkness.

"The heart is not strong enough to overcome the curse forged in stolen blood and spirit. But if you forge a deeper bond with Krampus, it will break the curse upon him."

"A deeper bond?" I blink up at her through my tears, knowing she likely cannot give me a more specific answer.

"It will call to you, Twyla Eyres. His darkness will call to your light. One question remains: how much do you want it?" Her eye deepens as her voice does—ageless wisdom and the eternal playground of life and death.

"How will I find him?"

A smoky laugh, like an ethereal but discordant harmony, leaves her mouth. "So much you do not know of the dark forces of the world. Everything in this place echoes his essence, little human. And while mortals are quite stubborn and rebellious, demons are not. All you need do is call his name."

I get to my feet, hugging my elbows and doing my best to breathe through the tremors. This is my one chance to regain what was lost. Déjà vu that will haunt me at every moment if I fail. What will happen to the fates of millions of children if this curse is not lifted?

No, desperation burns away like an ember before the flame of determination. The weight of those children, of this curse, is not mine to bear. Only one being burns at the forefront of my mind until I strengthen my muscles, swallow the knot of fear, and embrace the heat stirring in my chest.

I close my eyes.

"You will not be alone..." whispers Hel as if it's the finality of her words, her time here.

A sharp, cold gust of wind billows all around me. I don't open my eyes yet, but I know she's gone, leaving the aroma of perfumed decay in the air.

With the promise of that vision like a single star on a moonless night, the north star herself, I lift my voice no more than above a whisper to say, "*Krampus*."

22

"If nothing else, I have to believe in hope…"

KRAMPUS

Klaus growls at the sudden invasion, but hope jolts through me, gifting me with a grin that curls all the way to my cock. Not even the damned priest could thwart a demon summons when it's pronounced in my very own lair. Unfortunately, since I'm bound to him—stronger tonight than any other—I have no choice but to bring him along.

As soon as the Underworld forces lock us into their primal magic and pull us through time and space to deposit me directly in the center of my lair, I see her stardust-gilded hair. My little star has found her way to my home, to my sanctum, my haven of Krampus.

The infinity of pain in my being does not exist as she captures me with those amber-brown eyes.

I recognize Mephisto's hand in this. I'll need to thank him later. But for now, my heart seizes in my chest at the sight of my kjaere. I ball my hands into fists, piercing skin with my claws as I war against the tidal wave of human emotion surging through her. Klaus has starved me like he always does this night. Left me weaker than ever.

Klaus tries to put on a calm facade, but his "jolly" cheeks redden with hints of fury. I know the bastard bishop is shaking in his perfect velvet shoes.

Twyla is all I see. And feel.

"Krampus…" she says my name in one breathless gasp—not ten paces from where I stand.

Something is wrong. Despite the tears glistening in her eyes and the longing in her body, it is not min Twyla, not min kjaere, min lille stjerne. Echoes of her exist like shards of a broken mirror.

Klaus's lilting laugh breaks up the moments of wishful wonder between us, jarring us from our stupor.

"What a surprising but pathetic turn of events. The damsel has come to save the demon in distress. The beauty wants to claim the beast."

"I think we all know who the *real* beast is," Twyla proclaims, her voice stronger as she advances toward us.

"You are too late, child. You freely accepted my gift. And Krampus's heart is already turning to ice. Soon, he will be numb and need to feed on the emotions of humanity and serve as the antithesis, the monster under the bed that all children must fear."

I love Twyla's reddened cheeks, her flaring nostrils, and fuming glare. She's torn the curtain between worlds. She is gazing upon the truth revealed through every facet beyond the curtain, the truth she has always sought.

Unfortunately, what Klaus says is also true. It takes every fiber of my strength to keep myself from launching myself at the girl I love until I've clawed out her very heart to feast upon it. The hatred and the violence brutalize my heart, turning it colder than a thousand layers of ice.

"I want him back. I want everything back. You're the real monster, Klaus. Not him. And I should have known better, should have seen, should have recognized it from the beginning. Because the real monsters of the world never admit they are monsters. They wear masks of self-righteousness mixed with self-pity to fool the weak-minded. And what is evil cannot always be seen in the light. Just as what is good can be felt in the darkness."

She swings her eyes to mine, but I still make no move toward her. If I touch her, if she touches me, it will be her undoing. All violence and monstrosity suppressed for a hundred years is surfacing.

"It hardly matters." Klaus sniffs, shoulders at ease. "Nothing less than a soul bond will break the tether by which I hold him. A tether I earned through the darkness and blood and damned souls of the Underworld."

"A tether you stole," I growl.

"So, I will find it."

We both turn to her. Bewilderment rocks my body, breaking up the brewing violence.

"That's all I need to do, isn't it?" She pins her eyes on Klaus, her lips pressed into a firm line. "I'll find his tether. It's here, isn't it? In one of the snow globes." She gestures to the surroundings, and a vein throbs in Klaus' brow, betraying the answer.

"Oh, for god's sake," Klaus groans the curse and scrubs a hand down his face before shaking off his concern with a false laugh. "You won't find it, child."

"I don't care how long it takes. I'll find it."

She grants me thc strength of will to hold back the storm inside me. The shooting star lighting up the darkness. The beacon of warmth burning in the cold depths of my heart. It's the first time I've ever hoped enough to wish…and wished enough to hope—to believe a happily ever after could exist for a monster like me.

"Even if you do find it, it won't make a damn difference. It's too late for such a bond," he tells her, burning his eyes against hers. "Don't waste the gift I gave you by chasing after a second chance that doesn't exist."

"It has to!" she cries out, heating every shard of ice that numbs my heart, stemming its frozen tide until it may beat again. "What is the point of Christmas if it can't be for second chances?"

I hold Twyla in my gaze as she scrambles for the snow globes. One by one—without ceasing, without tiring.

"If the world holds its breath for the magic of Christmas, then it means dreams must matter more tonight." Emotion chokes her voice, highlighted by the clinking of crystals as she searches for the soul tether. "Faith matters. Belief matters. Love matters. And hope, Krampus." She turns to face me, and I could almost believe her tears alone could restore my soul tether. "If nothing else, I have to believe in hope, hope for a future for us, hope for our hearts and souls. Because…you're *my* stjerne, Krampus. My kjaere."

Oh, for the love of Hel! When a blast of black frost pierces my heart, I drop to my knees, struggling against the warfare of the curse. I will her on with every pained breath I take.

"Very well, have it your way, child." Klaus reaches into his robes, which hold the same magic as my own, and produces an object caught halfway between an hourglass and a large snow globe. "You have until the last flake of snow falls. Then, he is *mine*."

We are between worlds of spirit and matter. Time does not pass the same here—just as it is not the same when Klaus does his gift-giving work in the time it takes for a fleeting Christmas Eve to pass. In and out of the course of moments and heartbeats and breaths, Twyla hunts through every snow globe she can. Ones on shelves, ones suspended in the air, others in the cavern walls.

When sweat sheens her body, and her bright eyes grow panicked, I know she's aware of Klaus's timekeeper and how the snow has reached the halfway mark.

More ice creeps into the center of my heart. The storm tears a cold, cruel path through my veins.

Riveting her gaze upon me, Twyla parts her lips with her need to say something. But no words leave her lips. Instead, she closes her eyes. And takes a deep breath.

"Twyla, what are you doing?" I ask her.

"I'm listening."

23

The naughty girl vs. the nice boy.

TWYLA

She said it would call to me. His darkness, my light.

At first, all I hear are Klaus's grunts, Krampus's heavy breaths, and the subtle drift of the falling snow that spins down the time for my second chance.

Now I lay me down to sleep…

"What?" I whisper, not daring to open my eyes yet as I follow the direction of the voice.

Not a man's voice. Not a demon's.

It's a child's.

I follow the shadows of fear haunting his whispering prayers.

I pray the Lord my soul to keep…

The words curl like tendrils of dark ice to kiss my fingertips with pain. I shiver from the fear chilling my blood and sinking into my bones. Fear I've felt. Fear of an invisible hand that would strike me down and drag my soul to hell.

A similar home to mine.

Claws of fear scrape like icicles along my spine as I follow the voice and familiar words.

And if I die before I wake

An inkling of horror prickles my nerve endings. I feel every iota of that familiar fear, the darkness closing like an invisible hand around my throat. And the irony that we were taught to fear the monsters under our beds and the spirits going bump in the night rather than a deity who held humanity by puppet strings and cut them whenever the desire sprang.

The sound of my own sobs and tears from punishments that drove the fear home echoes in my mind.

I pray the Lord my soul to take...

Because it was never the monsters under the bed. It was the ones in our homes. Generations of fear and shame and hands bearing rods ten thousand times worse than any birch branch.

Some worked their hardest to be nice.

Others became naughty…like me.

The air grows colder, darker as I listen for every breath, every whisper, every prayer.

When it all stops, I freeze.

And open my eyes.

My heart skips a beat. My breath staggers. Because there is the snow globe—right between the malevolent dark eyes of Klaus himself. Those eyes brandish a warning, marking me like blades. He stiffens. All the muscles in his neck tense as I lift my eyes to the snow globe, peer into the crystal, and behold a thousand different memories of the boy named Klaus.

Chest aching, I gaze at the swirl of visions before me. Of this boy who grew up so much like me, but he became the opposite. Pain gnaws on me as I watch the boy who was so good that he could never receive coal in his stocking. No, he was given the prettiest presents and learned to love the monsters in his circle and to hate any outside.

He learned to say his prayers, to memorize his catechisms, and to do all the right things because it was what he needed to stay white and clean of the blackness. He could never see a shade of gray, a silver lining, or…light in the darkness.

He fed on the praise. Gorged himself on it for years and lived for the power that came from the praise of doing good. Until it wasn't enough. Because giving gold to those in need was not as important as the renown that came with it. He wanted the gift that keeps on giving. The gift of immortality and an eternity of fame.

Klaus did it when he descended into the Underworld, drank the elixir of immortality, and stole the soul tether of a monster. All so he could play the white knight of the world and use Krampus as a distraction, paraded in black.

Raw fury bleeds into me, gutting me when I consider how well it works. Because we are always taught to fear what we do not know. As children, we are taught never to question. Submit, obey, and be good.

If you are naughty, no presents will come. Hell will find you. Krampus will get you.

I rake my fingers through my scalp, nails digging in and wrenching my curls free of their pretty confines. And then, I turn to my monster. He's shaking. Trembling. Growling. Clawing at the floor, Krampus battles some unseen force I cannot see or feel.

The last of the snowflakes dwindle, streaming through the hourglass globe. He's in my hands, but he's slipping through like those flakes.

His darkness. Not Krampus.

I turn to Klaus, boring my eyes into his—our willpower grinding against one another.

The naughty girl vs. the nice boy.

I seize his snow globe. He snarls and swipes for it. Misses by an inch.

And I bring it down, slamming it onto that very floor in Krampus's lair. Crack by crack, splinter by splinter, I break the crystal glass. And set the truth free.

"You are not strong enough to destroy my soul tether, you petulant, naughty girl," he growls at me as I scoop the icy cold bit of rope from the shards of crystal.

The tether is as black as sin. And lies. Even now, I feel the truth of his words from the pain of that tether biting into the fabric of my mortal skin.

"No." I shake my head. And then, I feel a grin that lights up my world like the northern lights shimmering upon Krampus's castle. "But *he* is."

I lurch for Krampus.

"NO!" Klaus screams.

24
Her heart stops beating.
KRAMPUS

It happens within seconds.

One moment, Twyla breaks into a run with her gaze set on me.

The next moment, Klaus screams. A desperate scream of his soul. Powerful enough to shatter a multitude of crystal globes. Powerful enough to birth a whirlwind of lethal crystal shards. A destructive storm of ice where every last crystal screams Twyla's ruin. They form a violent tempest between me and her—ready to cut her soft flesh to ribbons.

"Kjaere, go! Get out!" I yell at her.

A new onslaught of black ice, of starvation, of every numbing iota of the curse begins to take over. The hourglass is down to its dredges. The curse has conquered my blood, my essence, and all but the last thread of my heart that prepares to bind itself to an immortal entity who wanted the world to kneel at his feet. As I am kneeling now.

And I make out the war within her eyes. I yell at her again, growl at her to go, to save herself. Because I would kneel ten thousand times over and take this curse if it means she goes free. I would choose her above every other soul in this damned world.

Between the gaps of the deathly fragments, she gazes at me with those soft brown eyes like the purity of amber twilight and utters, "In any realm, in any world, in any life, it always comes back to hope. That's something he can't take away from us. No force in the universe could ever take that from us, Krampus."

Hundreds of crystal shards knock against one another as if taunting her, daring her to try and get through them.

Off to the side, there is Klaus with his twisted, ruthful smile and vicious indigo eyes vowing her demise.

"Come now, little human," he lilts, approaching her until his breath is a vaporous fog. One that has her shivering. And shaking her head to combat his voice. "You did not truly believe you could save him, did you? I'll give you one last chance, one final gift to leave and return to the life I gave you. Forget this demon. He will not even lift a hand to harm a naughty child, little one. He simply serves as the embodiment of punishment. And the monster all should fear."

"Twyla, fucking go!" I yell while clawing at my chest as the hunger invades every particle of my blood.

She deadpans with me in a moment of deep-seated clarity—then narrows her eyes. "Don't tell me what to do."

Min frekke drittunge. *Cheeky brat.*

Twyla turns to Klaus, screws her brows low, and retorts, "You fucked up, nice boy. *I* am the monster you should have feared all along."

My lungs shrivel. My blood turns to ice. And my heart shatters. All in the same moment that she gets a running start—eyes rooted on me—, lunges, and charges her little body through the scourge of crystal smithereens. I smell her blood before she crashes to the floor...with the tether still clutched in her hand.

My little star. Bleeding and broken before me.

Darkness and cold hunger eclipse my vision. The scent of her blood plagues me, daring me, willing me to taste her, to devour her, and the endless feast of her emotions.

Her breathing dwindles. Her arm drops. Her palm opens, and the tether winks at me as it slips from her fingers. With the sound of Klaus's thundering steps timing to the slowing beat of Twyla's blessed heart, I seize the damn tether.

And rip through every black fiber and thread—each tear triggering a blood-curdling scream from his throat—until the essence of all that is Klaus fades into nothingness.

The darkness retreats. The hunger disappears with no trace that it was ever here. The curse is broken.

It's not the only thing.

"No." One desperate plea. One resolute command. I pick up her broken body as her flesh—slashed too many times from that fatal storm—bleeds onto my arm, my fur, my chest. Everywhere, she bleeds, her essence dissolving like those hourglass snowflakes. Impossible for me to hold.

Her breath falters.

Twyla takes a deep breath, a last gasp of air.

Her eyes grow vacant, unseeing.

"Twyla, no!" I growl and clutch the back of her head where blood has soaked into her very curls.

As my little stjerne, my kjaere, my light in the darkness, my Queen, her Amorous Majesty, the Lady of the Winter Star, and Monstrous Mistress of the Solstice...Twyla Eyres softly smiles at me and closes her eyes. Her heart stops beating.

Gripping onto her with every fiber of my monstrous heart and soul, I throw my head back and unleash a roar so great, it shatters every last snow globe—tens of thousands—and rains down pinprick-sized crystal shards like a falling shower of sharp, splintered stars.

When the magic and power of my lair erupts all around us, and the edges of the world fall in on themselves, I take one deep breath and allow my heart to hope for a single beat. Because I may not have the power to hold min Twyla's soul. But my *mother* does.

25

"I need to know the truth. Does he love me?"

TWYLA

Darkness glitters all around me.

I expected to be naked as I am now, but I didn't expect death to be so…warm.

Like constellations have wrapped me in their womb and tingle every inch of my skin, scintillating in my fingertips, the follicles of my hair, and down to the tips of my toes. Visions of my life glimmer before me—as if I'm reliving them and all their emotions. Not just witnessing them like a film reel played at the end of your life.

No, here I am in warm gratitude when I first met Krampus. Here I am—in all my arousal and terror when I woke in Krampus's bed. In heat and awe when he bathed me. Here I am—melting and surrendering in the gazebo when he decorated me. Here I am—safe and warm in the haven of his arms after he saved me and brought me to the cabin. In submission and smoldering intensity when he punished me with his birch whips. In wonder and awe of Krampus Haven.

Here I am—in the depths of pain and darkness of the temple with the orgasmic highs that followed.

Here I am—in sorrow and emotion and intimacy when he danced with me. And pure terror when he proclaimed I was his Queen.

Tears stream down my cheeks, but they can't compete with the deep-seated ache in my heart. The torment of these visions, of my forsaken fairy tale…I would choose that storm of crystal shards cutting me open and bleeding me any day over this.

"Velkomin, Twyla."

I shiver. And curl into myself. It's the second time I've heard the bone-chilling, spine-tingling, soul-shaking feminine voice of the ages. Unlike last time, when the tone was resolute and insistent, the voice carries notes of approval. Not warm approval—but approval, nonetheless. Untarnished, unbiased, truthful approval.

This time, I have no qualms about falling to my knees before her, all too aware of her sovereignty here more than any other place. She could simply lift one skeletal finger to trace down my cheek and snuff out my soul instantly.

"Your soul has not yet arrived in my Underworld, child," she explains without bidding me to rise. Her dark raiment wisps across the edges of my body like cold mist until I'm trembling for more reasons than one. "You remain in the Veil that is finer than a hair strand between realms. A small pocket within the Spirit Plane. Held here by my power alone."

Thc intricate latticework of bones dethrones me with her spectral beauty. This is nothing like Krampus's lair, where his familiar essence surrounded me. His lair was still part of the visceral one where I lived. It simply existed beyond a magic veil. But here, I am nothing but a naked, shimmery soul—bound to Hel's every whim. For this moment of eternity, she has suspended my soul between life and death. On an edge sharper than a sword's point. I quake before her, hands cupping my shoulders, covering myself as best I can.

When she tips her chin to me, that hollow eye socket seems to follow my every eye blink and movement.

"You have three choices before you, mortal girl," Hel professes, offering me solace, a gift amid the darkness. "You may resume your journey into the afterlife, where you will be rewarded with a crown and position in paradise. Elysium. No sorrow. No darkness. No suffering. Joy and love and eternal bliss await you."

She dangles the promise before me, gifting me with all sorts of fantastical imaginings that would explode my mortal mind.

My heart bows in submission before her because I still wish to hear the other choices.

She makes another pass around me. One full circle with her raiment tickling my skin with the whisper of the living and the dead.

"Or you may return to your old life. One much like the last with the fulfillment of your hard work, friendship, family, respect, and love." I can't help but look up, blinking at the word—so simple but so full of meaning. It sends my pulse to thrash in my veins.

"Yes," Hel continues with her unseeing eye fixed upon me. "You will find love and happiness with a mortal partner. You will spend your life doing what you love. You will have children birthed from your womb. The family you always desired. And you will teach those children the spirit of Christmas in all its forms and traditions, including our legends and folklore. You will grow old with a blessed, mortal life.

"But you will remember nothing of your time here. Absolutely nothing. Unlike Klaus, my power will reap all these memories and magic for eternity."

She seals this assurance into the depths of my heart and soul. No judgment. No opinions. This is her guidance and wisdom, her Christmas gift of choices where none will be right or wrong.

A hushed stillness drifts across me as the haunted melody of her voice echoes in my ears. "And the third?" I break that hush with my tattered whisper.

This time, when she circles me again, she roots her other eye, the depthless ebony pool, upon me. "You will bind your soul to Krampus."

The words strike lightning into the fabric of my soul, but I don't interrupt. Not for a second.

"You will choose an immortal life, but one spent as a *human*. While you will never grow old, human blood and essence will forever run in your veins. You will always bear the weight of human emotions that will feed my son and his Yuletide monsters. It will not be an easy life, Twyla Eyres. Demons are demanding. And Krampus must learn to share your human emotions even as he feeds upon you and trains you in his way.

"You will be the embodiment of the Lady of the Winter Star. The one star that exists to shine and provide light in the darkness of Yuletide. It is a profound duty as much as it is a gift."

I ponder those words. I lower my hands from my shoulders, open my palms, and curl my fingers as if I may hold and test and weigh each choice.

As tempting as an eternity of bliss may be for a naughty girl, something deep inside me hints that it's not time. Not time for me to pass into that one-way veil into the golden arms of heaven.

A mortal life with a loving partner and the blessing of a family is what I have always wanted. A chosen career with acclaim and respect. Children of my own. It would be a life of meaning and love and reclaim from my past.

Because fairy tales aren't re—

No, that's not right. Because the truth has been revealed. All has been brought into the light. The veil between worlds pulled back to give me a glimpse beyond the curtain.

A world of inspiration and free emotions. A world of treasures and wonders. *And* monsters and shadows.

Yes, Krampus kidnapped me. But I was the one who abandoned him. It was *my* loss I felt through him in that great hall after I shook the snow globe.

I consider what an immortal life as a human will mean. The magic could be bright and new every day. I'll live inside that place of free emotions and inspiration. I'll feel everything—wonder and despair, bliss and pain, joy and sorrow, light and darkness. And hope.

What about…truth? I look up, daring to ask the Goddess of Death, inviting her to pierce my soul. "I need to know the truth. Does he love me?"

"Rise, child," she commands with ancient resonance.

I rise.

"Turn around."

I turn. And gasp.

"And ask him."

My heart leaps out of my chest, and I fall into Krampus's arms. The moment he pulls me against the fortress of his chest, just like the night he held me after that first punishment—making me feel safe and warm and wanted—I know the truth.

He became my home from the moment I said, 'Thank you'.

The missing piece I searched for my whole life. The reason we work so hard just so we can savor those tiny slivers of happiness in between the toil. Those bursts of emotions that we turn into core memories and store in our hearts to be tallied at the end of our lives.

Krampus is the fairy tale I've searched for, the fulfillment of that spirit of the season.

Cupping my face and raising it until my neck arches before him, Krampus wipes the tears from my eyes and breathes, "I love you, min Twyla. Min kjaere. Min stjerne. Min Dronning."

At first, I lift my brows, searching through the reservoir of memory and information until I strike the correct meaning: Queen.

Naked and unashamed, naked and burning brighter than ever, shining like that Winter Star, I slide my palms into his and proclaim, "I love you, Krampus. I love his Malevolent Majesty, the Lordship of Yuletide, and Guardian of the Solstice, Krampus."

With each word I say, a smoldering smile grows on his face. Here, in the Veil, between worlds with constellations tingling our bodies, I confess. I am the one who confesses, "I want to spend every single Christmas with you…and every day in between.

If you and your monsters need emotions to live, take mine." Those same emotions choke my voice and splinter my eyes with hot tears. More tears as his smile grows. "If you need a soul, take mine. Oh, please, Krampus, take mine because no other could love and protect it as you could."

Curling my fingers onto his chest, I place my hands right above his throbbing heart. Just like he pressed his hand to my heart that first night. "You're my light in the darkness. This is my vow, my truth I reveal and lay before you. You're my home. Thank you, Krampus. Thank you for everything. A million times and a million lives, I *thank you*."

Something sparks. Like electricity crackling before the space between us lights up like a thousand Christmas lights. I part my lips, gasping in awe and wonder at the two tethers feathering in the small gap between our chests. One shines like a star, like a silver winter star. I smile as my tether curls toward the other. That other is red as holly berries, glowing with firelight and everything festive because Krampus is the embodiment of all holiday traditions throughout history. The Spirit of the Solstice.

Just as my soul tether curls around the tip of his in a tender kiss, Krampus grins, showing all those teeth with that mischievous gleam in his iridescent eyes. The next moment, I feel a tug and lurch against him as his tether seizes mine. Every beat of my heart times to his as his tether coils around mine like garland, wrapping it like a gift.

"Ja, min Twyla. You are my greatest gift," he confirms as the starry substance of this veil dissolves all around us like glitter swept away by a blustery wind.

Darkness swallows us whole.

And we're left with nothing but the sounds of our heavy breaths ricocheting off one another.

When I open my eyes, I feel the smile all the way down to my warm, damp pussy. Because I'm still naked in Krampus' arms—like that first night I woke in his bed. Except, we're on the ground of his lair.

The infinity of snow globes twinkles all around us. Restored. Not one splinter. Not one crack.

With a deep sigh, I cling to his fur and slide my arms as high as they can go. And grip the boulder-like muscles of his shoulders. Then, I press my cheek to the hot brawn of his chest, breathing in the scent of his cinnamon and pine fur. And…I might be imagining the taste of eggnog.

"The work is not done yet, kjaere," he rumbles beneath my cheek, and I nearly jump at the sensation of his cock twitching beyond his pouch.

Pulling back a little, I thread my brows low in confusion. "What do you mean?"

"Our souls are tied. Not yet bound and sealed."

"How do we seal them?"

He cocks his head to one side, that tremendous tongue sneaking out in a hinting gesture, and my eyes fly wide open at the same time that he says, "I trimmed my Twyla tree. Now, I'm going to stuff her stocking. And give you a Christmas Eve present you will never forget, min dronning."

My pussy spasms, growing wetter and warmer by the second. But when I consider his bed, the gazebo, any place in the castle, and even Krampus Haven, I know in every bit of my immortal human soul where I want to go.

Blushing with fervor, I lean into Krampus, touch my hands to his chest, and whisper, "Can I choose the place?"

26

"Did you just accuse Krampus, himself, of being…vanilla?"

KRAMPUS

"This is where you desire, kjaere?" I hang upon her word, waiting to express my approval, which already has pressure increasing in my groin.

Twyla nods as the cabin's twinkle lights halo her in their glow. Snowflakes collect upon her hair, spinning silver tinsel along golden curls. With the gown she's still wearing from the ball, my Twyla is the epitome of the Lady of the Winter Star—my dream come true, my fairy tale ending I never believed was possible for a monster.

"I don't think anywhere could be more perfect," she expresses, a soft smile forming on her pretty mouth as her cheeks turn redder from the cold.

I take a mental picture of this moment as she gazes at the crystal icicles catching the moonlight and reflecting in her eyes. Without another word, I wave my hand for the arched door to open. Taking her hand, I welcome her inside to the place of our turning point.

Despite the expansiveness of the cabin, the towering Christmas tree seems to capture her within its soft, romantic candlelight like a lover's embrace. Her shivers fade once I close the door, sealing us inside the warm surroundings. I must remember min stjerne is still human. She has accepted a life that will not be easy. An immortal human is an anomaly—an extreme rarity—one gods and monsters like me would never willingly subject one to.

No, Twyla will never die or grow old. But her blood and flesh retain their humanity. She will shiver and bleed and experience sickness and pain. A life she has accepted…for me.

Without releasing her hand, I spell a steady fire in the hearth that will warm us throughout the night. Shadows and firelight dance upon her face.

"Are you hungry, min Twyla?" I ask her, double-checking on her human needs while noting her wandering eyes and trembling hands.

She shakes her head, then buries her shaking hands beneath her arms. "N-no, the ball had a banquet. But I wouldn't say no to eggnog."

I lift a brow and meet the mischief in her twinkling eyes. She presses her lips into a flirtatious smile, a heated blush spreading from her cheeks down to her breasts. Once my eyes lower to her bodice, her nipples harden. I chuckle at my lille frekke drittunge. But she quivers when I brush my knuckles across her cheek and step closer to her.

"Having second thoughts, kjaere?" I cup her chin and tilt her neck to meet her eyes.

She screws her brows low and swallows a hard knot. "W-why would you th-think that?"

"Because you are trembling, and your heartbeat is racing."

"Oh…" Twyla crooks one side of her mouth, her blush deepening. "I was just…curious and a little scared of my punishment."

"Punishment?" Whatever imaginings she may have, she still doesn't retreat from me. No dark fear, but her adorable nervousness sends more heat to throb my erection.

"For shaking the snow globe. And listening to Klaus."

"Ahhh, min Twyla, min gal liten dronning…" *My mad little queen.* I lean in, capturing the side of her face so my claws tuck into her curls. "You came back. He could not destroy the love in your heart. And you went to death to free me. You could have had any life you desired. But you chose this one. You have given me the greatest gift one could hope for. Your heart and soul—bound to mine. My kjaere," I finish and place my other hand on her chest as I once did. Except, I devilishly sneak one claw beneath her bodice to cut the topmost strings.

Her smile only grows despite her shaking her head in feigned disbelief. "You gave me light when my world was dark," she responds, tears glistening in her eyes as I slash the remaining strings one by one. "You gave me beauty and life."

My pulse quickens with her sweet submission as she arches her back, welcoming my touch while her words shake my very heart with need for her. Lust spikes heat through me, but she reminds me what is most important. Our bodies won't simply unite tonight. Our souls will, too.

"You gave me magic when I'd all but given up hope it could be real," she whimpers when I cut the final string and peel it away from her chest, sliding the chiffon down her arms until the bodice tumbles to the floor.

Fuck, her delicate shoulders and full breasts with taut pink nipples nearly send me to my knees. More since she doesn't hide or squirm in fear. She may thread her nervous yet needy fingers, but she squares her shoulders. Her skin glows in the firelight, gilded like silvery gold. Breasts growing flushed and heavy. Nipples hardening to aching points.

I lower my claws to her skirts, determined to unwrap her like my greatest Christmas present. "You gave me hope, Krampus," she says, more emotion soaking into her voice as I lower myself before her, sliding the skirts off her hips down her plump thighs until the chiffon and silk pool around her dainty feet.

My hand flexes, muscle bouncing in my hard jaw from the scent of her damp panties. The transparent fabric gifting me a view of her plump, pink labia nearly snaps all my resolve. The energy and tension between us are thicker than a hot figgy pudding.

"And hope is the greatest gift you could ever give," she finishes, gazing down at me with those teary amber eyes, her fidgety fingers suddenly still upon her hip. "I was just the naughty girl, but I'm so glad you kidnapped me."

"Ahh, min Twyla…" I don't rise. I slide the pads of my fingers along the damp lace, savoring the sound of her gasp. And how her hands scramble to grip my shoulders. "As if the lives and behaviorisms of children, of the 'least of these' can be confined to such stringent adult definitions of naughty and nice."

She giggles. "True. Especially when nice children, spoiled children, turn into self-entitled, egotistical, little pricks."

Laughter rumbles in my chest as I savor the taste of her glee, her untarnished merriment. "Such life, so bright, my stjerne. For years, my world was so dark as I hoped for a girl who could love a monster. Before you, my only brightness came when I would steal gold from the rich families whom Klaus charged for his magic gifts while he used me as an instrument of fear.

"So, if I have given you hope, you are the fulfillment of all my hopes. You are the gift that keeps giving all year long. Your love is my greatest gift. And every day is Christmas with you in my life."

"Krampus!" she squeals in need, digging her nails into my fur as I rub her through the barrier of her panties.

I'm not about to let her have what she desires yet. No matter the need tightening in me and sending more blood rushing to my starving cock. Instead, I breathe in the scent of those panties growing wetter from my teasing fingers and urge her, "So, tell me, min Twyla, my single star lighting up my night, what makes you believe you are worthy of punishment?"

"Well..." She gasps again when I snap my tongue out and lick along the glistening fabric where her juices gather. Her pussy swells, growing puffier as I torment her a little. I love how the sound of her breath fills the room more than the crackling of the fire. "I did tell you "Don't tell me what to do" which is pretty much my nicer version of "fuck off". Oh!" Her moan escapes when I slip my tongue into the heavenly hot valley of her folds, lapping up the warm fluids. She may love the taste of my cum, but I'm damn addicted to her taste.

"That you did, my kjaere. Do you still wish to tell me to "fuck off"?"

"Ugh!" She groans and tips her head back as I scissor her folds with my tongue, flicking and teasing her trickling slit. Tightening her grip, she adds in breathy pants, "Maybe. If it makes you a little less vanilla..."

I freeze. Retract my tongue. Every muscle bulges as I rise. My heart pumps like a beast off his chain. In the wake of my shadow covering her, Twyla flutters her lashes. They lower, growing heady. Ahhh, min skitten jente. The mischief grows in the glint of her eyes. Her nipples pebble. Aroused by the dangerous monster towering over her.

"Did you just accuse Krampus, himself, of being...vanilla?"

"Maybe." She smirks at me, tilting her head to the side so her curls tumble to one shoulder. "After all, it's Christmas Eve. You've spent all these weeks teasing me with your giant candy cane. You've got big daddy horns and sexy birch whips, so why are you giving me vanilla truffles when I'm expecting a chocolate feast and an extra side of *eggnog*?"

Screwing my brows low, I spread my lips into a toothy grin and lower my chin to say, "Slem jente."

"Bli min."

Oh, fuck, the possessive sweetness of her words, combined with that precious grin as big and bright as a fucking Christmas tree, snaps every thread of resolve. In the next second, she's over my shoulder, kicking and squealing the whole way to the pillar on the left side, where I set her down and position her with her hands joined, propped against the wood.

I hear her sharp intake of breath when I lean in to warn her, "So, you want to play with the monster of Christmas, min lille slem pike?"

"If it pleases his Malevolent Majesty…" she wraps every word in drippy sarcasm, defying any proper nature.

Hel, how jeg trenger henne! *Hel, how I need her!*

Snickering, I breathe in her wondrous aroma and the intoxicating fragrance of her emotions—like the Northern Lights, an ever-shifting, ever-mesmerizing tapestry of light and color to brighten my world.

"If it pleases my Monstrous Mistress…" I murmur the velvety deep words into her ear and grin at how she clenches her cheeks while every hair on her flesh prickles. "Ber om det, Twyla. *Beg for it.*"

"Mmm!" she moans and wriggles her luscious little ass. "Punish me, Daddy Krampus."

I roll my eyes and snort. As long as she doesn't overuse that particular title, which will be reserved for her lips alone…

Gooseflesh sprouts on her skin. But I'll bring more to the surface. I'll make her flush, melt, shiver, beg, and scream for me. She will sing her Christmas joy to the King of Yuletide tonight.

Without releasing her hands, I summon my first instrument of delicious torment. She gasps and hisses as I bind her to the pillar with the twinkle lights. And carefully coil the strings generating the perfect amount of heat and sensation to electrify her erogenous zones. No breakage. No surges. No burning of her tender flesh or concern for electrocution.

But her arousal is clear when I wrap the rope lights just above her breasts to settle the tiny bulbs upon the swells until her skin glows, nipples puckering and growing red. Another rope beneath her breasts to tingle their undersides. More strands around her stomach to secure her against the pillar. I kick apart her legs and coil lights around her thighs, listening to every whimper, gasp, and moan. Soon, she'll be screaming.

"What are you—" she asks after I've torn off the wet lace until she's my naked present wrapped in nothing but my twinkle lights.

Ferocious and carnal, I gaze at my perfect present, roaming my eyes across every part of her bare skin glowing in the Christmas lights. My hunger reduces me to a beast who wishes nothing more than to bury myself inside her. But it's Christmas Eve, and my Monstrous Mistress deserves a feast, as she'd said. And no one is better at providing a Christmas feast than Krampus.

I reach into my robe.

"Oh!" she shrieks when I spread apart her cheeks and insert the butt plug with its jingle bell ends. I add the nipple clamps from the gazebo along with the one for her pussy…and the balls I tuck into her gushing wet cunt. Ones that will prepare her inner muscles to take my cock.

"Hmm…" I breathe in the scent of her curls, the scent of my Christmas Queen. "I don't need to remind you to keep those balls in…and not to come, do I, min kjaere?"

"I'll do my best."

So sweet. Such balance between my challenging brat and the adorable submissive.

"Good girl."

I bring my hand down upon one lovely cheek in a single hard strike. And now, I'll light up the world of her ass until she jingles all the way home.

27

The best presents in life really are free!

TWYLA

Oh, holy holly berries!

I don't know what's more intense—Krampus spanking my ass, which just pressures the jingly plug, the clamps swelling my nipples and pussy while the balls have me dripping, or the twinkle lights making me warm and fuzzy and tingly all over. All three make a sinful, sexy, and Krampus-kinky combination. The pressure in me grows tighter, hotter until I'm clenching, squelching around those balls I struggle to hold.

The very hairs on my skin sing his praises. They chastise me for bratting out when I could have had an amazing orgasm already, probably back-to-back ones, knowing Krampus. But my body doesn't just want this smoldering punishment that I know will give me even more pleasure through the pain. My heart needs it. My soul needs it.

Yes, I saved him. Yes, it cost me my life. But he needs to know how much I will work for this, earn it. Maybe we will have those small vanilla moments now and then, but the searing intensity of our foundation should never change. He needs my emotions, every raw and real one. If I want him to give me a feast, I fully plan to give him one, too.

And regardless of how he tells me I've given him a gift, I want to show him how he's as much of a gift. One that keeps giving all year long. Because hope can never be killed.

My pulse spins faster with each hard strike from his powerful palm. I'm not prepared when the next one lands on my backside, burning and stinging fiercer. "Oh!" I shriek, throwing my head back, nearly losing the wet balls in my pussy.

"Keep them in, skitten jente," he croons low in my ear while dragging the leather along my slippery folds. "You're so fucking wet. But your perfekt rumpa is not red enough yet. I'm going to whip away all that naughtiness tonight, Twyla. But you'll always be my sweet, naughty girl, won't you?"

A fiery slap lands on my pussy, cutting off all speech. He's moved onto a flogger—one decorated with jingle bells. A cold burst of air lashes the wet folds—air I realize he is creating. A little flurry of Krampus magic. With the tingling twinkle lights electrifying my skin so close to my cunt, it makes every sensation all the more extreme. My breasts feel ready to burst, my nipples as hard as rubies.

He whacks the flogger against my ass. Hard and singing to make my muscles clench while I rise on my tiptoes…and arch to meet the crop. Because I want the pain. I want all his efforts as he works as hard as I receive his discipline. A Christmas present for me as much as I seek to give him one. Because he's making me the center of his universe—the winter star in his darkness.

I smile at the thought, almost melting into the visions and fantasies swirling in my mind. An endless cycle of giving and receiving. Christmas every day.

The burns flow into one another until it's one constant flush of smoldering delirium on my ass, on my pussy. A constant swell of pressure from the plug in my ass to the inner coiling of my womb. The jingling music forms a melody of his making, a magical symphony he plays just for me.

Somehow, my muscles remain on autopilot, tightening, but my senses, my mind floats in a trance of pure bliss. My breath feathers in my head. The twinkle lights kindle and caress my skin with their infinitesimal lightning kisses. Every last nerve ending centers on the rhythm of his strikes, to the delicious flames he's stoked into my blood, forging a path right for my heart.

My pussy gushes with need. The balls slip lower and lower. My muscles flutter.

His fingers suddenly pumping into my pussy jars me back to the present. I hiss as he disrupts my oncoming orgasm when he removes the balls. My body goes limp in relief. One that's short-lived with the first touch of something hard invading my slit.

"Monstrous mistletoe!" I gasp as he pushes the crop handle into my soaked channel, twisting and stabbing until I'm clenching all around it. And shaking. The jingle bell clamps ring a chaotic harmony—nothing melodic like his. The humiliation only makes me wetter.

"That's my good, filthy girl," he murmurs against my blistering ass, and I quiver from his tongue licking a rough, wet path along my cheeks. "Ride it like a dirty girl."

My hips roll in response until I'm thrusting and rocking, riding the handle just as he directs. With every jerking movement of my hips, he seems to stab the handle in deeper. My nipples harden, breasts aching. Spine shuddering with every flick of that tongue as he licks around my sensitive, stretched ring. He shifts that tongue, sliding it along my labia, tangles the wet, wondrous organ into my folds, and finally…the clamps drop from my pussy—as if by magic—right before he stabs his tongue at my swollen clit.

"Come, min Twyla, min dronning."

My pussy erupts. My mind shatters to the magic of his tongue circling and sucking my fat bud. I'm convinced the entire Aurora Borealis has exploded in my blood, splitting cells, charging all my nerve endings, and lighting up every synapse in my brain until I'm screaming so high and shrill, the crystals on the Christmas tree shiver, on the verge of cracking. The pressure in my cunt stabs deeper, higher, commanding my pussy to convulse. I go over the edge again, aware Krampus has shoved that crop handle in so deep, my cunt nearly swallows the leather ends. As if he's preparing my body, pushing that handle until my very womb receives it.

My muscles seize and seize until my vision whirls.

Before I pass out, Krampus twists, sliding the handle, soaked with my fluids, all the way out. If I wasn't bound to the pillar, I'd collapse into a hot, electrified puddle on the floor.

Within seconds, Krampus unties me from the pillar. Catching me in his arms, he lowers me to the velvet skirt of the Christmas tree. Presents wrapped in shimmery gold and red paper glimmer at me from one side, along with hundreds of baubles and balls, glass and crystal ornaments, and candles. So many candles flickering all over the cabin.

Not one shiny thing compares to the iridescent silver of Krampus's eyes. My Lordship of Yuletide and Guardian of the Solstice. He retrieves the plug from my ass, but he doesn't remove the Christmas lights. No, he binds more around my wrists, looping new light ropes around each ankle. Then, he yanks until I'm spread on the velvet. It's thick and soft and supports my back.

He's bound the lights at my ankles to the pillars on each side of me. And the ones around my wrists to the very base of the great Christmas tree. All those lights cast a rosy glow upon my skin. And Krampus wanders his eyes all over my body, settling them between my thighs like I'm his favorite Christmas feast.

With my skin still tingling with glittery heat, I give a breathless laugh and say, "I think twinkle lights on my skin with the clamps and the crop are at the top of the list of my favorite things!"

"Favorite things?" he chuckles darkly while lowering his muzzle to my belly. I love how his fur tickles my pelvis.

"Yeah, you know? Raindrops on roses and kitten whiskers and snowflakes on my eyelashes and girls wearing white dresses." I know I butchered the lyrics, but my mind isn't exactly clear.

"Hmm..." he licks along my belly, sliding that magnificent tongue over every trace of skin between the purring lights. "Are you saying you would like a kitten, min kjaere?"

"Well, who wouldn't want a kitten?"

"I'll give you a white dress, too, Twyla. When you are my Yuletide bride, you will wear a beautiful white dress."

"Krampus!" I gush at the idea of a Christmas wedding.

My skin hums, whether from the tingling twinkle lights or the orgasm, I can't tell.

But when he extends that tongue into a figure-8 to coil around each of my nipples, tonguing and sucking and tugging, I almost combust all over again.

His tail rears up in the air. Comes down on each side of my breasts, knocking them together, sending even more sensation into the flesh.

"Ohmymistletoekisses!" I shriek, breasts thrusting into the molten pleasure of his tongue. "Add—your—tongue—to—the—list!" I practically scream between gasps of ecstasy. His tongue is my perfect Christmas snake. Like a narrow, wet anaconda determined to take me to the highest, orgasmic heights of the holidays!

His toothy maw opens over one breast, and a deep groan leaves his throat, resonating into my chest. I almost orgasm from that alone. Until that tongue splits. My eyes fly open wider than ever as he maintains that sucking pressure on my nipples while the other extension of that tongue licks down—lower and lower to curl into my pussy folds. And deeper!

"Oh, fuck!" I yelp as he wriggles it past my slit, slithering into my soft inner flesh.

That festive snake-like tongue pumps harder, deeper, embarking far beyond my chamber. I turn into a gasping, sobbing mess of emotions as he tickles circles inside my cervix. Hips rocking and writhing, I make sounds—such savage sounds I've never heard. He's licking my very cervix and still, he pushes that snaking tongue, driving it right through until it laps at my tightening womb.

Another dark chuckle vibrates into my chest. He slides the figure-8 portion of his tongue back and forth, adding friction to the pressure on my stiff, swollen nipples. I can't tell if it's from what he's doing to my breasts, my pussy, or my womb, but shockwaves shiver little orgasms through my system until I'm arching my back, ass rising all the way off the floor.

When his eyes flicker and turn to a pulsing red, I gasp. But any of my concern vanishes as he takes one breast in his hand and squeezes it, tugging at my rock-hard buds with his tongue again. He steals all my breath when he lowers that hand to my belly. And presses.

"Holy holly horns!" I cry out because he's fucking my womb with his tongue. And pressing down so I can feel exactly where that tongue wriggles inside me.

His glowing red eyes flick to mine. They are my ultimate undoing. I scream to that sweet Yuletide tongue that is an embodiment of the Solstice fucking my womb, licking and suckling my nipples, and—oh! A narrower extension breaks off at the last second to curl around my clit, lashing it and sending my spirit spiraling and soaring.

Wave after wave of pulsing pleasure shimmer through me. Sparks shatter millions of heated tingles along my spine. Krampus growls against my chest, nearly drowning out the sound of my euphoric screams.

My mind breaks off. My spirit floats somewhere in the hot ecstasy as he somehow, some way, increases the pressure. Tongue-fucking me all over again. Bringing me to rapture again and again until my speech garbles, my bones liquefy, and my pussy gushes a hot, little sea. The second my vision dizzies, Krampus stops.

The next thing I see is him staring down at me with a smile and that magic tongue lolling out of his maw. But wait…that's impossible because my clit is still thrumming, my nipples are still tingling, and my pussy is still swelling. Ugh, no, not impossible. That's just the aftermath of Krampus. I imagine my body might feel like one giant beating heart by the end of this night.

The best presents in life really are free!

28
"Are you ready for me to stuff your stocking, kjaere?"
KRAMPUS

"Tis the season for giving, min Twyla," I chuckle and kneel between her legs to lap at her cream still gushing from her hot Christmas pudding pussy.

She's boneless, breathless, nearly limp. Soaked beyond soaked. Just how I need her to be. I let her catch her breath, content to linger here, lapping at her juices. She tastes so lovely—in more ways than one. Her emotions sparkle in the air, gifting me with samples of merriment, wonder, bliss, and sheer joy. Such pure, unadulterated joy. Pure as the first snowfall.

Her thighs shudder, her inner muscles still squeezing with every pressure from my tongue. "I didn't know your tongue could do all that!" she whispers the words, her voice a little hoarse. I will give her the eggnog she loves so much soon.

"I can do many things, min Twyla," I hint and circle her slit with my tongue.

"Like what?"

With a deep chuckle, I rise until I'm hovering over her. She tilts her head adorably before scanning me, curious as a naughty little cat.

I smile toothily, then unleash my fur. Narrow ribbons of fur from my pelvis and legs that latch onto her thighs like soft, sucking tentacles.

"Well, deck my fucking halls!" she curses so lovely, her emotions gifting me with a dirty, sexy heat. So eager…my lille stjerne ready to rise and shine for me.

"Are you ready for me to stuff your stocking, kjaere?" I tease while my pouch quivers, prepared to free my raging member. "My cock wants you, Twyla."

When I open my pouch, groaning from my dick falling out and thudding onto her belly to drip precum onto her skin, Twyla parts her lips. Gazing at it in awe.

"That's not a cock, Krampus. It's a fucking Yule log!"

I chuckle and wag my tail because she's not wrong with my heavy balls resting on her lower belly and my crown near the base of her throat. I lengthen my fur tentacles, binding them around her thighs to spread her wider, straining her limbs but stretching her as far and wide as possible. Her deep pink pussy with puffy wet folds is on full display.

"Krampus?" she squeaks, interrupting my observations.

When she lowers her chin and licks around my crown, a hungry growl leaves my throat. My tail coils around her belly, squeezing as she closes her hot, wet mouth around my crown, sucking harder. Hunger spikes inside me from her wanton emotions. Her lust spirals in the air, and I take it in tiny doses. If I gorge myself, I'll rip her apart with my cock. And I'd rather have a Yuletide glowing bride tomorrow vs. a bedridden one who must spend the next week healing. Instead, I thrust softly, pulsing into her mouth and gifting her with my flavored pre-cum.

She licks her lips before her eyes lift to mine in a sultry deadpan. "Eg vil kjenne deg inni meg." *I want to feel you inside me.*

Fuck! My horns harden to iron. "Well, jingle my balls!" I exclaim before lowering my muzzle to her blushing face.

"I know I probably butchered it. But I've been practicing, and—"

I silence her, stabbing my tongue deep into her mouth, strangling her speech, and showing her just how beautifully she spoke my native tongue. Well…not so beautifully because she did butcher it. But it's beautiful to me. My gift that keeps on giving.

Once she gags, I retrieve my tongue and ask her, "What else did you practice?"

"Um…" she bites her lower lip, cheeks reddening like the flames capturing her in their glow. "Knull meg hardt." I shake my head and chuff a laugh at her flawed but adorable accent and syntax. *Fuck me hard.*

"I will tonight, Twyla." I tease her nipples with the tip of my tail, loving how they pebble more.

Her eyes run the length of my cock. Then back to my face. "How?" She swallows a hard knot, and I scent traces of fear.

I lick at her cheek to encourage her while picking up the heavy base of my hardness. "While you cannot die, min Twyla, other damage may be done. But your little, mortal body will feel no pain, thanks to my magic. You will receive pressure and pleasure."

"Maybe just…a little pain?"

I lick her other cheek. "Very little," I bargain as I have no wish to harm her.

Then, I direct that raging erection and prime the tip at her soft, warm pussy. Claws teetering on her hips, I channel all my magic into my cock and her channel to soften and stretch her. Her muscles will respond, her very bones will shift for me.

"You're wrong, min Twyla," I tell her while lowering my hips to get in position.

"Hmm…what?" she asks, breathless while gazing down at me, then my throbbing cock.

"This will be at the very top of your favorite things!"

I grin and push the head inside her.

29

"Krampus? Are we…are we stuck?"

TWYLA

A long moan escapes my mouth as he claims me, pushing past my slit—deeper and deeper until that massive head finally pops inside my pussy.

The velvet bunches against my ass from my body forced upward from the momentum of his cock.

He moves slowly, carefully, but his words were a Christmas promise because I feel the smallest trace of pain beyond the delirious pressure of him consuming my cunt. That head alone fills all of me.

"So tight, so fucking tight!" he groans deeply before shoving in harder. Inches past my very pubic bone.

When he pulsates, swelling harder, girth thickening, then warming my insides, I gaze down and gasp. "Krampus, is your cock…glowing?" The deep red member has lit up like a Christmas tree, shimmering and shining with an otherworldly luster.

He kisses my lips with a sweet, tender tracing of his tongue. "Only for you, min Twyla. Now, skitten jente, take my fucking cock. And my monstrous soul!"

He spears his cock inside me. Overwhelming pressure fills me in the span of one second. My inner walls clamp around him, sucking him deeper, urging him harder. I soften, rolling my hips to meet him. I ache for him. Hunger for him to fill all of me. He's almost there! All over my body, the twinkle lights start blinking—like winking stars. I smile at all the magical things he does to me.

My heart seizes as he pushes inside one final time. I clench my eyes from the unbelievable pressure. He's everywhere. One great throbbing heartbeat in my body. Balls against my backside. Base of his cock nudging my clit. When he twitches, I register the feeling in my womb. And open my eyes. Look down. And gasp. Because the outline of him, of his cock, I can see the outline nudging my skin through my belly.

All the breath strips from my lungs when he eases out a few inches, then stabs back in. I cry out at the first thrust.

"Twyla, Twyla!" He summons me, lowering one claw-tipped hand to cup the side of my neck.

"I'm-I'm fine, just…please. Ikke stopp!" *Don't stop!*

It's building to something. Some extreme crescendo I can't even imagine. But he's going too fucking slow. His horns, those huge, sexy fucking horns, cast shadows across my face.

"Min flink pike."

"Not that flink." I stick my tongue out. "Fuck me, Krampus. Fuck me like a monster. Fuck me like the first monster of winter. Like the demon of Yuletide. I'm your good girl. But I'm also your naughty girl. So, please…just fuck me!"

Krampus bucks, hips knocking against mine, cock jutting in deeper, buried to the hilt. I screech, clenching all around him. He roots himself inside me, thrusting, stabbing. My whole world narrows to that cock.

"You definitely made my naughty list, Twyla."

He snaps his fingers, and I moan from the collar of golden bells around my throat, a new set of jingly clamps on my nipples, and even a red leather gag secured in my teeth. I whimper and shudder, jingling the bells on my nipples.

The second he cocks his head and grins toothily at me, tongue lolling out, I see every ounce of the mischievous devil of Christmas. His cock throbs inside my womb. "My present. My pretty, pretty present! All wrapped up. All for me!"

I clench my teeth harder around the gag as he slaps the side of my breast, knocking them together to shake the bells.

Just like he did in the gazebo. His hands come down to squeeze each one, shaking and playing my tits like a Solstice instrument.

"Unnng!" I moan when he tugs at each nipple clamp.

I'd almost forgotten about those furry tentacles until they press onto my thighs, somehow spreading me more. Preparing me.

Tongue extending and slithering, Krampus grins down at me. My eyes grow wider and wider as he wraps that tongue all the way around my pelvis, anchoring me before it slithers down to wrap around my clit. I shiver.

When his tail coils around my stomach, I nod, smiling through tears, sensing it's to protect me more. He swipes another extension of that tongue to claim my tears.

Then, Krampus fucks me. Fucks me hard. Like I asked. Fucks me boneless. His tongue rubbing its incredible pressure and festive mastery the whole time. Lightning, quick and intense, pulses through all my nerves. My belly swells from that heavy, hard cock of Christmas. Screams get lodged behind the gag in my mouth, competing with the bells ringing and shaking from my bouncing breasts.

Each thrust grows stronger, deeper, harder. Pounding me like the God of the Solstice he is. Those great horns seem to give him even more power to fuck me. His hips smack my thighs. That glorious cock glows brighter, casting a red shimmery hue all over my body. I take him, rolling my hips, spreading myself as wide as I possibly can go.

When he lowers his head toward mine, I lift my brows. He opens his maw, jaws extending until his teeth are poised all around my throat. I suck in a deep inhale. And arch, submitting to him, giving him my throat in a gift of trust. A deep, humming vibration resonates into my chest. Like a purr but so much greater. Like some monstrous drone. Like a mating call of Christmas he uses just for me.

His cock stops mid-thrust. His tongue pauses its pressure on my clit. Those iridescent eyes flick up to imprison mine. And turn from silver bells to scarlet rubies.

I open my mouth to ask why he's stopped.

Until he sinks his teeth—lightly—into my skin, barely piercing but shedding blood. Blood he tastes. One, two, three more deep thrusts. Something hard as bone forms around his cock, rubbing at the edges of my womb.

And Krampus snaps. A great whoosh of steamy breath leaves his nostrils as he spews ropes upon ropes of hot cum into me. That cock changes color, alternating its glows between red and green and even gold. Mirroring the flashing lights that bathe me in tingling warmth.

When that tongue twists and flicks upon my clit at the same time, I fall apart with him. Erupting with him.

While he's still gushing his seed into me, he removes the clamps on my nipples, heightening my orgasm. He thrusts again. Tweaks my nipples. Twirls that tongue around my clit. My nerves stand up and sing every Christmas carol imaginable. He rocks me, slams into me. And triggers a stronger orgasm to explode inside me. I spasm, clench, and convulse all around him, screaming and screeching through that gag.

The fire in the hearth vanishes. All the candles snuff. Nothing left but the warm flashing flare of the lights wrapping me and his cock's shine pulsating from where he's rooted himself deep inside me.

Together, we come and come, breaths joining, bodies fused, hearts bound. Souls sealed. Forever. Our holiday miracle of treasure and wonder in a land of monsters and shadows. And one of the greatest monsters of time, the ruling monster of the Solstice, has made me his Yuletide bride.

I love these moments after.

The shine of his cock has faded to a soft, lustrous glow. Along with my now steady lights. But I love his heavy breath against my throat, that tongue twitching, licking at the faint traces of blood from where he bit me, marked me. A mark of his Malevolent Majesty I am proud to wear. I've made the demon of the Solstice pant against my neck. I've made him sweat. A subtle sheen of sweat slicks along my skin from his chest.

That tail has loosened from my belly, its tip aimlessly wandering along my breasts to brush my hypersensitive nipples with soft, little kisses.

"You were right," I whisper in the darkness, grateful when the rope lights loosen, freeing me to lower my fingers into his fur. He shudders at my touch. And purrs. I smile and stroke my hands along his fur. When I light the tips of my fingers onto his horns, he growls.

"Ja, kjaere?"

"Your cock is my top favorite thing."

He chuckles darkly before sliding that tongue up to trace my lips in a sweet kiss. "You are my top, Twyla. The top of my tallest tree. My Solstice stjerne."

"Krampus…back in the Great Hall before I shook the snow globe, you were ready to make me your Queen. And I'd just run from you the night before. We'd only known one another for such a short time. How could you have such faith in me, such *hope* in me?"

Pressing his muzzle against my cheek, Krampus rumbles a soft, deep laugh, "Because it was more than simply you, Twyla. Perhaps it was a mad, wild belief. But it was belief in the magic of Christmas and the magic and energies that are far greater than us."

"Why?"

He reaches down for something in his fur. And when he lifts the golden card, it catches the lights around us. My heart skips a beat, and I gasp at the image. The beautiful meaning of magic, fairy tales come true, my happily ever after that was waiting for me that whole time.

"You didn't want another card, Twyla, but I did. I needed to know. And the universe answered."

He opens my palm and lays the final card of the scryer in my hand. The card of the Lovers. Tears stream down my cheeks, and I hold onto the card, clinging to it like it's the best Christmas Eve gift he could give me.

After my tears are spent, and I set the card upon the shiny-wrapped gifts nearby, I try to shift, wiggling my hips. But I find I can't. "What?" I scrunch my brows and peer down at where we are still joined. I tug my hips back, but they don't move an inch. "Krampus? Are we…are we stuck?"

He rumbles a purr against my neck and answers, "Ja."

"Is this part of the soul tie?"

"Ja." He rubs his muzzle into my hair, petting me.

Despite the soft smile I feel on my lips, I need more than his one-word answers. No matter how cute they are from this post-coital sweet affection.

"Krampus?"

He licks at the back of my neck. "Hmm?"

"How long are we stuck?"

"Mmm…until dawn of Christmas morning, min dronning."

"Oh." I ponder the notion.

The second I part my lips to ask more, Krampus circles his hips. And jerks. Pressure spikes, and heat thrashes my blood with another orgasmic wave. A hot, rolling current shimmers Christmas tingles all along my spine, splashing my face with bliss. That hardness nudges my womb again as more cum gushes inside me.

Gasping, I come down from that climax, feeling more of his labored breath on my neck. His heartbeat pounds against my chest. Somehow, I manage to hoarsely ask, "Krampus, ugh…just tell me, are we—do you have a…a knot?"

One deep inhale. He sighs out, "Ja."

"Huh. Does that mean—"

He shrugs. Licks at my neck. "I don't know, min Twyla."

A holiday warmth spreads through me at the notion. Regardless of what might happen or how any child might look from our union, I press my lips to his cheek. All that matters is this Christmas Eve. I chose this life, this soul tie with him, no matter the circumstances. If a baby were to come, it would be so grand. But even if we never have a child, Krampus and Krampus Haven will always be my family. And we have forever. Starting tonight.

My thoughts wander, growing from these roots where we are knotted to the concept of gifts. Because tomorrow, we will return to the castle. And probably end up in Krampus Haven by nightfall. He will shower me with presents again.

"Krampus…" I touch my lips to his cheek again.

"Ja, min Twyla?"

"You've given me so much, shared so much with me. But there is one thing I haven't shared with you yet. I'd like to tomorrow. Before we fall into the beautiful chaos of your, *our* castle, and Krampus Haven, will you…let me give you a gift?"

My breath catches in my chest as he turns those iridescent, silver-bell eyes upon mine, sighs a deep breath, and answers, "Whatever your heart seeks to give me, Twyla, will be the greatest present of all."

Love spreads a soft smile on my lips and a forever warmth into my soul.

Epilogue
KRAMPUS

"This…this is your gift?"

I hope she does not take my question as anything more than curiosity. Not with the tears of deep emotion streaming down her cheeks.

At dawn, when my knot faded, we spent a cherished Christmas morning, bathing together and washing one another like we did on those first nights after I stole her away. We traded banter and memories and dreams over a holiday breakfast feast at the table where I once read monster smut to her while we'd dined on treats. We took a winter walk in the frost-covered woods where she huddled into my fur.

Finally, she'd asked if we could return to Christmas World for her *gift*.

Mephisto was only happy to greet us. After all his faithful years with me, he is the perfect demon to charge with my mortal realm while I spend immortality gifting Twyla with all the magic I possibly can.

Twyla bypassed all attractions, events, and exhibits where one might find the magic of Christmas. On Christmas Day, my entertainment world is rather quiet. Especially this area where she has brought me.

A simple Christmas tree twinkles lights upon her rosy cheeks next to the display. For, it is far too reverent and devoid of commercialization to be considered an exhibit. Something where the meaning and magic of Christmas can be felt and cherished in the heart and soul beyond once a year. Something that predates my power and origins. The first, true promise of Christmas.

A whimper chokes in Twyla's throat, but she parts her lips to say in a cracked voice, "I didn't get to celebrate the

Solstice or Christmas, or anything associated with it. On Christmas Eve, our house smelled like pizza and pine air freshener every year. But there was one thing. One thing we would do, one thing we would see."

She pauses to purse her lips as emotion wells up inside her. Emotion that is both heart-breaking and soul-healing. Humbling. The very essence of peace on earth, her light in the darkness. Her Christmas star.

"It's something I never lost, Krampus. Something that made me want everything else, all the magic of Christmas. I know every tradition is rooted in your past, your beautiful origins. But…I always felt like…they would bring me back here. And I could always feel the spirit of the season…right here."

When she lowers herself to her knees before the sacred display, I kneel with her. My shadow eclipses the display. But not even I can darken the inner light of the babe with his tender, brown chubby cheeks, his fragile fingers that would later break five simple loaves and turn them into bread to feed thousands. Hands that would open mouths, heal the sick, touch the eyes of the blind to see, and raise the lame to walk again. Arms that opened wide to welcome little children—no matter how naughty or nice. A heart that never formed a list for them. A heart willing to shed its blood for the entire world over…for generations of souls. Even the naughtiest. Even the most damned and monstrous.

"Thank you for sharing with me, Twyla."

A soft smile forms on her lips. And while she fixes her eyes on the manifested child in the manger, the greatest gift and miracle of Christmas, my Lady of the Winter Star says, "Thank you for kidnapping me, Krampus."

"Thank you for saying 'thank you', Twyla."

She says nothing else. I respect the silence.

And quietly thank the forces of the universes beyond our infinite imaginings and the almighty will of the little child beyond our eternal comprehension, for the miracle and gift of our union.

Of two unlikely souls coming together. And finding their fairy tale. Their happily ever after. A promise where Christmas and the Solstice may kneel together in the spirit of love and light in the darkness.

The End

Keep reading for a sneak peek of *Her Monstrous Boys* Series

***REMEMBER:** Reviews mean the WORLD to authors. If you enjoyed, please support by rating and reviewing on Amazon. It can be one line!

Share on your Booktok, and I'd love for you to tag me @authoremilybshore!

If you're interested in seeing exclusive art, spicy bonus scenes, ARC access, please consider supporting me on Kindle Vella with your vote aka Top Fave crown. *USA only for now* Or find me on REAM. Connect with me to learn more!

Krampus and Twyla will return in a spicy novella, which will be released in December. When Twyla and Krampus are snowed in for their first-year anniversary over Christmas, how will they ever pass the time? Hint: gingerbread and eggnog will be involved! Read "Snowed In With the Krampus" - coming soon! Follow me on Amazon and social media for more updates.

Acknowledgments

To all the lovers of my monster-fudgers, thank you for coming and being so excited over all my books. It's hard to believe I started this journey with a princess saving the dragon in *Courting Death and Destruction* with minimal spice to full-on monster-fudging — tails and claws and wings, two dicks, a vibrating dick, a dick with vine tattoos that magically come to life, oh my! Yes, all those were from *The Sacrifice*.

And who knows what I have in store for more?

Special thanks to all you snobby, stuck-up bitches back in the cult who spurned me for having emergency C-sections and cared more about my fertility than my career. I cordially invite you to suck it and choke on my thriving KDP All-Star bonus-winning badge.

Special thanks to two readers who gave me sheets with naughty phrases in Norwegian.

Big thank you to all my super fans/Vellatrons for top-faving me every week and giving me TWO crowns and sometimes three for the past TWO years! It's surreal but incredible to see. And it means the world to me, truly.

Thank you, D Arte Oriel, I'm in love with the cover, and so is everyone else! And extra note of thanks to Kate Seger for the outstanding formatting when I simply do NOT have the time to do it myself. And to Painted Wings for the gorgeous decorated edges that everyone loves to holiday hoard!

Thank you to all my alpha/beta/and ARC readers! Everything you do is valuable from finding that one missed comma to a one-line review on Amazon. I write upwards of 5-7 books a year, so I have plenty to keep you busy.

As always, thank you to my ever-patient cinnamon roll husband, who can't catch up with all my books, but you're there through every tech nightmare since all I need to do is look at the computer the wrong way for the damn thing to break. Amazing that you haven't had a break*down* over all my drama. Thank you for watching horror movies with me like Krampus—the one with the demented elves and sentient gingerbread men. Sorry not sorry that I don't watch more romcoms with you, but you know all I want for Christmas is you because you'll always be my baby.

THE SACRIFICE: A Dark Dragon Fantasy Romance – Book One of Her Monstrous Boys

"Don't you know better than to play with monsters?"
Perhaps I'd rather play with the monsters than kill them. But loving them is suicide by sacrifice. Lucky, I'm not looking for a happily ever after.
I'm looking for a dark and dangerous once upon a time…

With my hands gripping the cemetery headstone so hard, my nails crack, and my skirts bunched around my waist while my sister's betrothed ruts into me from behind, I'd say I've officially hit rock bottom. Especially with the dead staggering toward us.

Darya despises the flouncy fool. Almost as much as she despises me, which she's done since I was born—unrelated to the present. After all, it's not like I planned an early morning walk around the cemetery bordering our house just so I could run into him.

Van Wetterton's hot breath that smells of bacon grease and onions curls toward my ear. He pounds harder, but I only get a vague sense of pressure as he says, "You feel this, don't you, Quinn? You'll come for me, won't you, little gray bitch?"

A bitterness burns the back of my throat. Gray bitch, gray whore, gray girl, they call me. My smoky gray hair flings down my chest, ricochets on my cheeks, and fractures my vision. One nail breaks. And bleeds. I wish I could feel the pain. Not even letting my sister's fiancé fuck me in a cemetery on Hollow Day can make me feel something. My body doesn't silence pain, but it hushes it, along with all other touch. Even the worst pain is numbed. That is the price to pay when you're half-ghost, half-blessed, half-cursed.

And numb inside.

I fake a long moan, smirking at the thought of Van bragging to his Brotherhood about how he was the first to make a ghost climax. Regardless, he and the other Brothers who've fucked me will have a good row over it. I've had them going in circles since I was sixteen and gave my "maidenhood" to Fynne Hawksburne in the woods behind my family's home. The abandoned shed was as good a place as any.

The stalkers advance toward us, their guttural rasps growing louder. Some fall over headstones and into open graves from where others have risen. It's Hollow Night. More will rise by nightfall.

"Nothing beats this rush in your blood, does it?" asks Van with a deep groan. I wouldn't know. My blood is an icy, slow river.

As he jerks one last time, the momentum propels me forward.

I hardly feel Van's cum trickling down my thighs when he pulls out and shoves his unimpressive dick back into his breeches. Guess I can mark him off the list. I've kept a ledger of names, both male and female, hoping someone in these blasted Borderlands might help me feel something.

He slams his palms together, commanding a wind to gust and push the dead back. Everyone in the god-eater's five realms has some kind of binding magic. If only I had a normal one.

"Give my best to your sister," Wetterton snickers cruelly after the stalkers have toppled into a pile of rotting corpses. "I'd say we look forward to having you at the wedding tomorrow, but everyone knows you won't be there."

"My deepest congratulations on your impending lifetime of marital bliss," I sweetly proclaim and pick up my skirts, turning to hurry away before he can see my grin.

Tonight is the Sacrifice. The monsters will come out to play.

Maybe one will oblige me with a fuck I can actually feel before it slaughters me. I laugh at the notion and sneak into the manor through the servant's entrance. They're too busy preparing for the wedding and the Sacrifice to notice me.

So, I retreat to my room for an hour's peace at best before my sisters prepare me. But as soon as the dark, clawed fingers coil around my throat, I know peace won't come.

Read more…

Author's Note

Kidnapped by the Krampus began as simple holiday monster smut. One where I blended some of my history with my husband's. We grew up in cult-like communities, both dark in their own way. This book became a testament to the place where we have come. A place where we don't need to have all the answers. We understand, we have seen, we have felt how the world is not black and white but a beautiful tapestry of color. Like the Northern Lights. Forces beyond our infinite imagination.

This book became the beauty of where our past meets our present—with hope for the future. It is an expression of the Yule log decorating our window ledge and the Nativity scene gracing our fireplace mantle. An expression of someone who prays to Jesus *and* uses tarot cards. Because if God is so beyond our comprehension, along with the energies and forces of the universe, then how can we dismiss one of the infinite ways he/she/they may speak to us?

After the darkness of my past, I've felt the healing spirit of a Mother upon my heart. And she spoke to me through the very tarot reading of the scryer in Krampus Haven. The card selection was not pre-planned or researched. I drew the cards mid-scene and listened to what the voices beyond the book would share with me. Every single card I chose showed the beauty of the plot from emotion to foreshadowing to the conflict…and yes, the happily ever after ending. The Lovers.

I cried so hard when I turned up the Lovers, feeling the beautiful and spiritual depth of this book. And the soft kiss of a Mother Goddess telling my heart that I was meant to write this book. I knew the perfect ending would be Twyla sharing her inner light with Krampus. And the reason behind her love for Christmas.

It might seem polar opposite, but I did my best to show the beauty and essence of the holiday and how our traditions overlap. And how we don't need to divide these worlds. Instead, we can bring them together…from Krampus—whose origins and true history were exactly what I researched and wrote into this book—to baby Jesus, who, like Twyla, is my light in the darkness. And the assurance of hope for the future.

I hope my dark but cozy book touched you in healing ways like it did for me. If *Kidnapped by the Krampus* brought you joy and light and love, consider it my gift to you.

And in the spirit of the season, I extend a very Merry Christmas and Happy Blessed Holidays to you and yours.

Thank you for reading…

Emily

P.S. Remember, the decorated edges make a lovely holiday collectible! All available on Amazon.

P.P.S. If you liked Krampus, you'll love *Her Monstrous Boys* Series!

About the Author

Emily used to be the good little church-going girl who snuck peeks of smutty romance books at the store. Now, she proudly writes smut into fantasy and has forsaken the religious cult of her past.

In 2020, Emily found her voice while writing dark fantasy romance. In 2021, she rebranded on Kindle Vella and has been a Vella bestseller for two years. Her writing always features enemies to lovers featuring heroines who don't need a sword to be strong, "touch her and die" monsters and villains, and trauma healing.

An abuse survivor and trained advocate, Emily has worked as an awareness speaker all over Minnesota. Identifying as bisexual and feminist, she loves to showcase sex and kink positivity, trauma-overcoming themes beyond stereotypes, and LGBTQIA+ inclusivity.

When not writing enemies to lovers, Emily is addicted to the Enneagram, rewatching Schitts Creek, cuddling with her kitty, and spending time with her online sisterhood where she can exercise her big empath heart.

Emily lives in Saint Paul with her husband and two daughters. She loves to write at her local coffee shop where all the baristas know she's an author and have memorized her order. Emily is thankful she's far-sighted and can write her spicy scenes in small print while hiding her screen.

Made in the USA
Las Vegas, NV
28 December 2024

15505924R00144